THE BUTTON

ANGELS & EVILDWELS SERIES BOOK 2

D. L. FINN

THE BUTTON

THIS ONLY CHANCE

Angels & Evildwels Series Book 2

D. L. Finn

The Button (This Only Chance)

Copyright © 2018 by D.L. Finn

www.dlfinnauthor.com

No part of this book may be reproduced in any written, electronic, recording, or photocopying form without the written permission of the publisher or author. The exception would be in the case of brief quotations embodied in critical articles or reviews and pages where permission is specifically granted by the publisher or author.

Cover Photo: D. L. Finn

Cover design by Angie of pro_ebookcovers on Fiverr

E-book formatting by Maureen Cutajar

www.gopublished.com & D. L. Finn

This is a work of fiction. The names, characters, places, and events used in this book are the product of the author's imagination or used fictitiously. Any resemblance to actual people, alive or deceased, events, or locales is completely coincidental.

Library of Congress number: 2018909207

ISBN Print: 978-0-9977519-6-3

ISBN eBook: 978-0-9977519-5-6

ALSO BY D. L. FINN

Evildwel/Angel Series

This Second Chance (Book 1)

The Button: This Only Chance (Book 2)

This Last Chance (Book 3)

Companion Evildwel/Angel Stories

A Long Walk Home: A Christmas Novelette

Red Eyes in the Darkness: A Short Story

I Wouldn't Be Surprised: A Short Story

Paranormal Thriller

A Voice in the Silence

Other Short Stories

Bigfoot: A Short Story

Poetry

Just Her Poetry Seasons of a Soul

No Fairy Tale: The Reality of a Girl Who Wasn't a Princess and Her Poetry
(Memoir)

Children's Books (middle grade)

Elizabeth's War (historical fiction)

An Unusual Island (fantasy)

Things on a Tree (holiday/fantasy)

Dolphin's Cave (fantasy)

Tree Fairies and Their Short Stories (fantasy)

PROLOGUE

CASTRO VALLEY, CALIFORNIA, 1976

*L*ynn was suddenly aware of her surroundings. It was tranquil floating above her still body next to angels. She felt indifferent at seeing her pale form hooked up to wires and IVs, although the beeping machines indicated that her body was still alive.

"You have to go back—you have more to do," the female angel informed her.

Lynn met the angel's steady gaze. While she was in awe of her beauty, it was the angel's silver dress that drew her attention. It reminded her of how the water in her grandmother's pool had wrapped her in serenity when she sat at the bottom. She'd loved doing that for as long as she could hold her breath. It was one of the few times she felt safe, cocooned in water where no one could hurt her. That dress, flowing like water around the angel, affected Lynn in the same way as the pool did—it made her feel safe. The angel pushed her hair back, causing it to cascade over her peacock-green wings.

Lynn turned her attention to the male angel. His smile was mesmerizing—like a lava lamp, hot and fluid. *What a babe!* With his long brown hair, strong chiseled features, and green eyes she could get lost in, she felt she could totally spend eternity with him. He smiled broadly at her, but the smile quickly disappeared when the female angel scowled at him. *Wait a minute—do they know what I'm thinking?* Lynn felt her face redden.

The embarrassment was quickly erased as both angels smiled at her again. Lynn wished they'd say more, but she wanted to continue to hang out with them. She was feeling a peace she'd never felt before.

She started to express her desire to stay. "I don't—" was all she got out before images of an older version of herself filled her mind all at once. Then she was thrust back—into her life and that pallid body hooked up to the beeping machines.

* * *

THE ANGELS OBSERVED the girl in the hospital bed. "Why did you show Lynn all those things about her life, Zelina? She will not remember them." Thomas shook his head.

"I know, Thomas, but she will feel them when the time comes. I had to give her hope. She has that now. I do not see her trying to kill herself again, although she will get into some very dark situations." Zelina winced.

"But what about the person who wants to kill her? And that woman sitting next to her, who did not love and protect this girl enough to prevent her from getting to this point? I will never understand humans." Thomas stumbled through his words. There was more, but he couldn't bring himself to say it out loud.

"Things did not go as they should have for Lynn. We cannot change the past or perfectly predict the future. It is frustrating how limited our influence is sometimes. You saw why Lynn is important—and her kids. She just needs help to get past a few bumps."

"Well, you are blind to Lynn's dark side. She could become like her mother."

Zelina raised a perfectly formed black eyebrow as she held Thomas's gaze. "She will conquer it. With maturity comes wisdom. Remember that."

Thomas blushed and looked away. "You cannot guarantee that. I know I am young, but I was always at the top of my class and graduated early. And as for that one time—well, at least I tried."

"Yes, you did try. But you were, and are, lacking the wisdom to apply all that knowledge you so quickly acquired. I am able to apply experience to my knowledge when dealing with humans, which is why I believe Lynn can be helped."

Thomas turned his palms up and slightly bowed his head. He was not trying to be disrespectful, but he needed to understand. "How can I get the experience I need if I am only allowed to train?"

"It is possible."

Thomas held back a sigh. Always such vague answers to his questions. He tried another approach. "Can you at least tell me why you brought me to observe this specific girl? I assume there is a reason behind it."

"There is."

He waited a moment. "Okay."

Zelina smiled at him but did not respond.

Thomas expressed his frustration with a sigh. He tried again. "So what about the person who plans to kill Lynn? Can he be helped?"

"You will know things when you need to. As for that man, no. I wish we could help him, but an evildwel has found him."

Thomas shivered. "Oh, I missed that. Those red-eyed black clouds certainly make it hard to help humans. Evildwels are no better than leeches, except the evildwels live off fear and anger instead of blood." He paused, studying Zelina, who kept all expression from her face. "I know, trying does not explain what happened my first time out. I will not make that same mistake again, I promise, but I still believe there is a way to remove an evildwel from its human host in the same way you can a bloodsucking leech. I do not like having to watch and not be able to do anything—it makes no sense."

"Not everything has to be understood or make sense, but I do believe that someday we will be able to expel evildwels from their hosts."

"Well, right, which is why—"

Zelina held her hand up. "Patience. You cannot force things that are not meant for you."

Not meant for me? Thomas had never considered that he might not be the one to accomplish the removal of evildwels. That idea jolted him. Although he had to admit now that he had not been ready his first time out. He had pushed—no, he'd used his charm and good looks—to be sent on assignment after passing all the required tests years ahead of his classmates. He did not want to be that angel who manipulated to get his way anymore. The familiar guilt washed over him, and his normal reaction was to push it inside and bury it. Unfortunately, it kept digging its way back up. He thought it might be helpful that he was now with an angel who had a reputation for being tough.

Time to be honest with Zelina and himself. "If it is not mine to do, then I will do what I can. I understand forcing my own ideas of what I think should be happening instead of what should—well, you know." Thomas paused and shrugged. Zelina didn't respond, so he continued. "I know Lynn is free of evildwels, which is good, but to do what she did to herself, she not only had to feel there was no hope, but she must have turned all her anger and fear on herself."

"Yes, honesty is always the best approach with others and oneself," Zelina said with a slight smile. Thomas turned deep red with the embarrassment of knowing he was with an angel who could peer so deeply within him. Zelina cleared her throat. "I am very glad you are looking at the why of this situation."

"I do understand why she became despondent with a family like that, and then the horrible accident took her best friend from her two years ago—Tammy was her name?"

Zelina nodded grimly. "Yes. Lynn has suffered a great deal over that loss. Tammy and her family were Lynn's safe place. Luckily, Stacy took over that role, but not to the same extent as Tammy and her family. And of course, there is the matter of the person responsible for the accident."

"Yes, he should atone for his part in that tragedy."

"What needs to happen will happen, hopefully. You know that part is very complicated."

Thomas shrugged and sighed. "Yes, I do. But Lynn has had many things going against her in her mere fourteen years on Earth, and she has more coming. Luckily for her, you have been with her the whole time after I—you know. So am I here with you to repair the damage my mistake caused?"

"You should know the answer to whether we can fix the past, but I will refresh your memory. We only have right now. What is needed from you is your history with this family and approach to things. What you will be given is guidance to help this particular girl." Zelina looked away while twisting her black hair and laying it over her right shoulder. She smoothed her flawless dress.

"As much as I would like to change what happened, I am not so sure I am the right angel to do this." Thomas swallowed hard and then frowned. He was glad Zelina was focused on her gown and not him. He knew feeling sorry for himself was not going to help. "I have truly tried to accept what transpired—and the result. I have been learning and training hard, as suggested. I thought I had moved forward. Yet being here with his daughter, it all comes rushing back to me."

Zelina met his gaze with a surprisingly sympathetic expression. "Yes, I know you have been holding on to this. It really is time to let it go. Guilt has no place in an angel's heart." She smiled and added, "I promised I could get you through this, so you had better not make me a liar."

"I…you…" Thomas could not reply as he held the tears back. *That night.* He was supposed to protect Lynn's mother, Carrie. Instead, he had tried to help Leonard, her husband. It had been the wrong choice.

Zelina moved closer and wrapped a wing around him to comfort him. Thomas did not trust himself to speak. The moment of silence lasted for what seemed like forever.

"This is not about me or my feelings. I should not have said that about making me into a liar." Zelina retracted her wing and smiled gently at him. "And that is the closest thing to an apology you will get out of me," she added in a lighter tone.

Thomas's dark mood vanished. "Okay, thanks."

"You are not through with Lynn and her family yet. And Thomas, I am pleased you have more clarity than you used to."

Thomas prevented a smile from forming on his lips at her compliment, but he was having a hard time knowing what to do with himself, or perhaps with his old feelings. He focused on his hands and suddenly wished angels had pockets. It was something he had seen humans do when they were uncomfortable—bury their hands in their convenient compartments that were filled with objects they could move around, like coins. He knew Zelina was waiting for a response. He didn't have one, even though he'd spent many hours rehashing his mistake since the night it happened. It would haunt him forever. But now it seemed like he was getting this second chance, so he decided he had better angel up and deal with it.

Thomas forced himself to look at Zelina. She was not smirking at him like he thought she would be; in fact, her expression indicated that she felt sorry for him, which made him more uncomfortable. "What is expected of me?"

Zelina put a hand on his shoulder and looked into his eyes with an intensity he had not seen in other angels. "Nothing you are not capable of. Remember this is not about how you feel about past actions. As angels, we do not experience regret, only possibilities. The humans are free to make their choices. You need to let their choices and your actions go and learn from them from this moment on. Understood?"

"Yes, but it is not easy. No one ever lets me forget—including me."

"I understand. I know this has been said to you before, but I hope you really listen this time. Part of your issue is you have allowed pride and self-pity to rule you. It was an evildwel that killed Lynn's father, not you. Yes, his death happened when you appeared to him as an angel, but the evildwel was in control of his actions, not you, when Leonard drove off that cliff. To be clearer, Leonard made the choices that drew the evildwel to him. Then there was Carrie. I understand you tried to get the evildwel out of her husband, hoping her life would be better, but Leonard was not a good man, even before he was an evildwel host. Carrie always made poor choices when it came to men, including Lynn's stepdad. As for Lynn, there is still hope for her, even though she chose to drink herself to death. I was right next to her through all of that. All I could do was encourage her to land on her side so she might live. She did.

"We can focus on the best possible solution for now and the future using our wisdom and judgment. We both know suicide is the darkest experience for any human." Zelina shook her head and wiped a tear away. "What I see in you is that you are willing to take chances to save humans from themselves. Now you need to go forward and do things for the right reasons. I believe when you are fully developed, you could be one of the strongest angels we have helping humans."

"You think that?" Thomas asked in disbelief.

"Yes, but do not allow your pride to absorb that statement. That is what got you into trouble before."

Thomas shook his wings out and smoothed his hair. "I will try."

"We cannot just try—this is too important. We have to work from here." Zelina put her hand on his chest.

"My heart?"

"Yes. Lynn's father is making progress, reviewing his life and reflecting on what *he*—not an angel or evildwel—could have done differently. Carrie—well, we will see. It is up to Carrie, though, not us. With all that in mind, I am to be your teacher now. I expect you to listen and watch closely. I will be showing you how to follow the rules and which rules can be bent—just a bit—without, well, you know." Zelina shrugged.

Thomas smiled. "I welcome the chance to work with you. You are known to be a hard-nosed angel."

Zelina smiled back. "Thank you. I have heard that once or twice. Now I want you to watch Lynn's reaction when she wakes up. See how she responds to things. That will be important. But we have a few years to work on your training before everything goes sideways for her."

"I look forward to my training, although I am not looking forward to when things go sideways for Lynn."

"Neither am I." Zelina sighed.

Thomas nodded solemnly. They turned their attention to Lynn as she awakened from an eight-hour coma after her failed suicide attempt. A matronly nurse rushed into the hospital room to soothe the agitated patient; a youthful, sleep-deprived doctor followed to check her vitals.

Her mother sat immobile in her chair until the doctor declared that Lynn would be all right, then the first sign of forced compassion crossed Carrie's face. It was a shame Lynn would spend the next four years living with a woman whose feelings were so buried that she might as well have been a robot. At least Lynn had a strong rebellious side that would carry her until she could move out. After that, the same rebellious side might prove to be a problem. Thomas hoped he and Zelina would be enough to help her. Zelina touched his arm and nodded. It was going to be a long seven years.

CHAPTER 1

CASTRO VALLEY, CALIFORNIA, 1983

*I*n high school Lynn Hill had a black button with white writing that said "F*ck Off & Die." It was pinned to her worn, flower-embroidered denim purse. Lynn relocated her button to the inside of her purse when she graduated, so only she could see it. It wasn't that Lynn had suddenly changed her attitude upon accepting her diploma with 451 other people representing the first class of the new decade, either. As far as she could tell, 1980 was no different than 1979. What prompted the removal of her audacious public expression was the acquisition of a job and an apartment, or basically becoming a responsible adult. Lynn was mindful that appearing to be an upstanding citizen was necessary, an opinion confirmed by her old history teacher.

"Young women who are successful do not have swear words pinned to the outside of their purse," the teacher, who reminded Lynn of a shriveled apple doll, had informed her while handing back her essay in the final month of high school.

Lynn was fully aware that the teacher didn't like her, but she didn't care. Most teachers didn't like her, but she always got A's and didn't cause problems, so they usually left her alone. No one had ever tried to take the button away, but Lynn did get some looks, which she shrugged off.

She was convinced that more than one teacher had the same sentiment, but they had to pretend to be responsible adults, like she was doing now. Lynn only hid the button from her parents, who would have shown their displeasure in ways both physically and emotionally painful. She escaped that house the day she turned eighteen, moving into an apartment with her best friend, Stacy.

Lynn's fingers brushed across that button on the inside of her purse as she searched for her strawberry lip gloss. It wasn't that she hated everyone and wanted them to die, as her button stated; she simply didn't trust most people. Why should she? They only managed to disappoint or hurt her, but she wished for their absence, not their actual demise. Although there were a few people she felt the world would be better off without. They seemed to have no reason to exist other than to cause others pain.

Lynn applied her lip gloss, slipped it back into her purse, and pasted on a fake smile. It was her final touch before entering the rundown bar with Stacy. A blonde and a brunette together got the attention of guys at the bars, Stacy insisted. Lynn didn't bother pointing out that it was Stacy's large bust and fashion-model looks that got all that interest. She knew Stacy was aware of her effect on the opposite sex.

The young women flashed their fake IDs to the guy at the door. It was obvious that the old biker didn't care about the age of the females who entered the bar as long as they were somewhat pretty, boosted alcohol sales, and had a card, legal or not, that showed they were old enough. Lynn was immediately greeted by loud music, a local band whose name she had already forgotten. They were playing a current hit from the radio. *No big deal, just some wannabes,* Lynn thought. There wasn't even a cover to see them. How good could they be?

Stacy and Lynn squeezed between the red vinyl barstools to order their drinks. "I know you, I walked with you once upon a dream..." Why was the song from *Sleeping Beauty* in her head? She hadn't thought of it in years. It had been one of her favorite songs when she was a young girl. She used to listen to the record while following along in the book. She would sing the song loudly if no one was around and pretend she was dancing with her prince through the forest.

In those days she believed she would find her prince someday. Did she still believe in love and happily ever after? Not really. She sighed right as the bartender caught her glance. He had wavy brown hair and the most beautiful brown eyes she'd ever seen. She gulped and started to sweat. She needed a drink, and fortunately, Stacy was already ordering them.

"Can I see your identification, please?" said the bartender in a voice used to talking over loud music.

"We just showed them to the guy at the door," Stacy shouted in response, showing off her perfect white teeth in a big smile.

"I'm sure you did, but humor me. Show me your papers," he replied.

Stacy sighed and handed her ID to the bartender. Lynn had thrown the fake International Identification Card she'd gotten in Berkeley two years ago back into her purse. It only worked in some clubs, and this had always been one of them. Besides, she was only a few weeks away from legal drinking age. She dug out the photo ID that said her name was Andrea Louis.

"Thank you. I see your papers are in order, Andrea and Sally," the bartender said, with an engaging grin directed at Stacy.

"They are." Stacy's loud voice was almost drowned out by the band. She gave Lynn an eyeroll while the bartender made their drinks. Lynn responded with a slight grin.

He handed them their drinks with a small smile. "Sorry, I've been wanting to do that since I saw the movie *Firefox* last weekend. It's still playing at the Chabot Theater in Castro Valley. Seen it yet?"

"Uh, no, but I heard it was cool. It came out last year, right?" Stacy said, immediately sipping her drink through the narrow red straw.

"Yeah, it did. They're showing it again because Clint Eastwood has another movie coming out soon. Promotion thing." He shrugged and continued. "Well, you guys should see it before it's gone. I wouldn't mind seeing it again, if you want…"

Stacy showed her lack of interest by pretending to watch the band, so Lynn responded with one of their standby stories. "Oh, sorry. But, um, we have boyfriends, and they would mind if we went to the movies with another guy. They don't care if we dance, but going to the movies…" Lynn felt oddly disappointed. *Too bad, because he has a face I could spend my life looking at.* But he only had eyes for Stacy. *No happily ever after in real life,* she decided. She wished Stacy would brush off all her adoring fans herself. Instead, she always left that to Lynn.

"Well, if you ever find yourself unattached, you know where to find me, right? My name is Kent, by the way." He pointed to his name tag.

Lynn had done her job, so Stacy responded. "Totally, thanks, Kent. How much do we owe you?" She held up a ten-dollar bill and gave her best "I really like you—please don't make me pay for my drink" expression.

"The first one's on the house." Kent winked.

"Oh, cool. Thanks, Kent," Stacy said with a practiced fake smile that Kent quickly returned.

They all fell for Stacy, no matter how she acted. It would be nice if, occasionally, guys fawned all over her. *Oh well, at least Stacy knows how to get free drinks.*

"Let's get a table," Stacy said. "Thanks again."

"Sure."

Stacy confidently led the way, as if she expected all eyes to be on her. And they were—even the ones belonging to men who already had a woman with them. Lynn smiled when she saw one get hit on the arm for looking.

It took longer than usual to push through the Tuesday night crowd because of the male strippers who had been there earlier. There were plenty of women who stayed after the show and an equal number of men who just happened to show up. Lynn knew the guys thought they'd get lucky after a show like that. Sometimes they did, but not often. Lynn wasn't a fan of strip shows or having a guy she didn't know shove his barely covered junk in her face. It didn't make her swoon and scream like Stacy did, and stuffing dollar bills in a guy's underwear wasn't exactly a thrill for her. At least Stacy hadn't dragged her to this strip show, thanks to Lynn working late.

Anyway, Lynn didn't have a dollar to stuff into anything after paying rent. She depended on Stacy and her ten-dollar bill to get them through the night. Stacy found an open table for them and left Lynn to guard it while the band started playing one of Lynn's new favorite songs, "We Got the Beat" by the all-female band the Go-Go's. It sounded weird with only one female singer, but it was a good cover, so Lynn didn't completely hate it.

She took a gulp of her Seven and Seven, expecting it to be watered down like it always was, but she almost choked as it burned her throat. It was strong! There was barely any 7-Up in her whiskey.

"Cute Kent was generous, hoping to get lucky with Stace," Lynn mumbled to herself with a frown.

Lynn didn't have guys lining up to be with her like Stacy did, but she prided herself on being more selective than her friend. Stacy played the game, while Lynn didn't. Lynn would be honest if it was a one-night stand for her—no messy emotions involved—while Stacy was always looking for love through sex. Both approaches usually ended up with the same result—men disappearing after getting what they wanted. Lynn certainly wasn't that little girl reading princess stories anymore.

Her night's entertainment began as she watched Stacy scout the room for possible dancing partners while quickly emptying her glass. Lynn cringed when the blond singer in her tight, straight-leg jeans went off pitch. The girl was pretty and her clothes were cool, but that was about all anyone could say about her. Although Lynn wasn't really into fashion, she recognized good taste. Stacy embraced every new fad, like her brand-new Guess jeans, a shirt with a big neckline that revealed her left shoulder, her new red Keds, and black lace gloves. Stacy's latest fashion hero was a new singer called Madonna.

Although Stacy was into fads, she'd been right about insisting

Lynn make the switch from bell-bottoms to straight-leg jeans back in high school. Lynn had finally got over her exposed feet, and she was rocking her acid-wash jeans and white Jessica McClintock button-up blouse. She'd nailed her look for once and felt almost as pretty as her best friend. Not that anyone could see what Lynn was wearing as she sat in a room lit only by flashing colored lights from the stage.

Lynn chewed on her ice while trying to signal to Stacy that it was time for a refill. No luck. Finally, Stacy made her way to their table with two older guys in tight black disco pants—her first catch of the night.

"Can we buy you ladies a drink?" the first guy asked. He was more rugged looking than his friend, with broad shoulders, deep blue eyes, and short brown hair.

Lynn and Stacy quickly agreed. His friend hurried off to find the lone busy server.

"My name is Jeremy, and that's Stan ordering your drinks. What do you say we dance until the drinks arrive?"

Stan, his thick blond hair cut into a mullet, was back next to his friend. He smiled and winked at Stacy. Lynn almost shuddered, immediately disliking him.

"Sure, why not, *Andrea?*" Stacy asked.

"Yeah, sure, *Sally,*" Lynn replied with a grin and quickly claimed Jeremy.

Lynn and Stacy never gave their real names unless they were sure about the guy, and they were never sure about anyone they met in this bar. These two disco rejects (who had to be at least thirty years old) quickly lost interest when Stacy and Lynn weren't enthusiastic about an orgy.

"Talk about weirdos," Lynn shouted over the music to Stacy, who shrugged.

At least we got a drink out of them, Lynn thought. She quickly finished her second Seven and Seven while watching the disco rejects approach two heavily made-up regulars. Those women didn't require a dance or a drink, Lynn noted as they strolled out of the bar together.

She waited to see if they would return. They didn't. *Those guys got their orgy.*

It wasn't too long before the next guys approached and asked them to dance. Lynn switched dancing partners a few times, and the free drinks kept coming. The band was attempting the new Joan Jett song, "I Love Rock 'n' Roll," but the singer couldn't hit the lyrics hard enough to make it work. It was obvious she was dating the guitar player from the way he looked like he wanted to devour her. Lynn couldn't see her passing any audition that involved singing. The songs began to blur as the night went on, and Lynn left another reject to head back to their table.

"Oops!" Lynn tripped and then giggled when the table caught her. Blushing, she glanced around the room. No one had noticed, but she was wasted. It was time to do some cocaine so she wouldn't get the spins later—or make a fool of herself. She was pretty sure Stacy still had some left in her purse. If not, there was always someone willing to share. It wouldn't take much so she could keep drinking and not have to pay for it later. Lynn wasn't a fan of the white stuff if she wasn't drinking. If she was sober, it made her feel edgy, like she needed a tall glass of milk to calm down.

Lynn quickly found the small brown glass vial, half full, in Stacy's purse. She stuffed it into her pocket next to her lip gloss and made her way to the line for the women's bathroom. About ten women were waiting to use the throne, so called because there was a crown painted above the toilet. *How creative our fellow bar patrons are,* Lynn thought with a smirk. She leaned against the wall behind two who were literally gushing about the guys they'd just met. They were convinced the guys had money and couldn't wait to ride in their Porsche.

Lynn knew from experience about lines from guys in bars. The Porsche was either their dad's or they'd stolen it. She remembered one winner she and Stacy had met.

"Let's continue the party at my house," he'd said.

A group of over twenty people followed "his" black Porsche to a mansion. Wine and champagne flowed throughout the night from a well-stocked cellar. The fun ended abruptly when the guy (whose name Lynn couldn't recall) took someone on a ride and crashed the brand-new Porsche 911.

"Well, I'm sure insurance will cover it, right, dude? Plus, you can just buy another one," one of the other party guests had said.

"No, man. I'm just house-sitting," he admitted, a single tear running down his face.

That had ended the party. Lynn almost felt bad for the people who hired that idiot to take care of their house, but it wasn't her problem.

These two airheads in front of her weren't her problem, either. *They've always been rude to us in the past, so let them learn for themselves,* she thought smugly, until her grandma's voice cut through her rambling thoughts: "Always treat others as you would want them to treat you."

She sighed loudly, and it got the attention of one of the girls, who glared at her. Lynn smiled at her scowl, and they went back to ignoring each other. *So much for the right thing to do.*

Finally, Lynn got to one of the stalls. She peed but didn't flush. She opened the vial and gathered some white powder into the attached spoon, carefully brought it up to her left nostril, and sniffed. The immediate numbing effect almost made up for the nasty aftertaste. She did three more, alternating nostrils. *That should be enough.* What little she got on her fingers, she rubbed on her gums like everyone else did. "Shouldn't waste blow" was Stacy's motto. She tucked the bottle back into her jeans pocket and flushed the toilet. She heard someone next to her sniffing. *Doing the same thing,* she thought as her mind cleared.

She washed her hands in the stained sink and snorted some water up her nose to clear it out. After applying her strawberry lip gloss and fluffing up her bangs, she felt ready to head back into the pulsating din. She plopped down at their table and noted that Stacy was still dancing, drink in hand, with a guy that Lynn knew was her type. Tall, blond, well dressed, and handsome—probably had a nice car. Stacy was simple when it came to dating. If he had money and looks, she was interested.

Lynn scanned the room for someone who might have similar

interests that she could have a conversation with. If that search failed, she'd accept someone attractive for a one-night stand. She had one rule about those: As soon as they were done, she left. Most guys frowned upon her leaving right after, but she didn't care. If she was dumb enough to bring them to her apartment, there was a possibility she'd be stuck with them until morning.

Being in control of her own body earned her some labels, but if guys were into that, she wasn't into them. It was that simple. Her stepdad had tried to shame her into his ideal female with words like "sl*t," "c*nt," and "wh*re" when she wore boots or dressed in ways he disapproved of.

Lynn shoved all this out of her mind as a new dance partner found her. She followed Steve to the dance floor. Although he was an inch shorter, he was cute. It was tough being a woman at five feet, ten inches, and her preference was for guys over six foot two, but she'd learned not to judge a book by the height of its cover. What turned her off to Steve was his explanation of how his wife let him see other women.

"I'm not interested in married men."

Steve frowned and walked away in a huff. *This isn't going to be my night,* she thought, making her way back to their table. Stacy was slow-dancing with her blond. When the song ended, they broke apart, and Stacy headed to the bathroom, the guy watching her like a cat stalking prey. It kind of creeped Lynn out, but Stacy always had men lusting after her. Finally, Stacy made it back to the table with a huge smile plastered on her face.

"I found, like, the totally perfect guy, Dave. He's amazing! You gotta meet him." Stacy slipped a new vial of coke—from the new guy —into her purse. She reapplied her pink lipstick, looking amazing, as usual.

"I hope you don't mind—I borrowed a little of the white stuff."

"Of course not, duh. We always share our stuff, right?"

"Yeah," Lynn agreed. "I'm going to have a smoke, maybe get one more drink, and head home."

"I'll let you know when you go if I'm staying with Dave, okay?

Good thing we brought our own cars, huh? Here's the ten, in case you need it. I'd better get to Dave." Stacy wiped her nose and winked. Without waiting for a reply, she rushed back to Dave, who was grinning and waving at Lynn.

Lynn forced a smile and waved back. Stacy signaled for her to join them on the dance floor. Lynn declined. She wasn't interested in being a fifth wheel or, more likely, receiving a threesome offer from Dapper Dave when Stacy wasn't around. That scenario had happened before. She could tell she wouldn't like this guy just by looking at him.

Time for a smoke break. She headed outside. There was a couple somehow making out and smoking a joint at the same time.

"Gee, what talent," Lynn muttered. She lit her cigarette and took a long drag.

"You read Stephen King, Andrea?" a male voice asked from behind, startling her. The moonlight lit his face. It was Kent, the bartender with the beautiful eyes.

"Yeah, um, actually, I do. I just finished *Cujo.* He's one of my favorite authors." Lynn was glad it was dark because she could feel her face turn bright red, even though she knew better than to be interested in a guy who liked Stacy.

"Mine too. I read that when it came out, but his new one, *The Dark Tower: The Gunslinger,* is awesome," Kent replied with a smile.

"I plan on reading it…soon." Lynn stumbled over her words.

"I can lend it to you."

"Um—oh, sure, unless I buy it for myself. I like to have all his books, you know, and…um…I don't really have a boyfriend, and neither does my friend," she added before she could stop herself. She took a long drag off her cigarette to stop the flow of words coming out of her mouth.

What am I doing? She was acting like she'd never talked to a guy before. *He must think I'm an idiot. But of course, he's here for Stacy.* She frowned. She supposed she could set her friend up with this guy if Dapper Dave didn't work out. Lynn took a bitter hit off her cigarette, finishing it. She quickly lit another one.

Kent smiled. "Oh, really? Good to hear. It only matters whether *you* have a boyfriend, though. Your friend really isn't my type."

"That's a first," Lynn blurted and immediately regretted it. If she could have found a hole to crawl into, she would have.

"What is?" Kent asked.

"Oh, I was—well, my, um…" Lynn couldn't believe how she was acting, so, once again, she just blurted out the truth. "Someone not liking St—*Sally*."

Kent laughed. "I get the impression it might surprise her too."

"Well, she's just confident." Lynn quickly defended her.

"I think that's a good trait, along with being a loyal friend." Kent held her gaze, making her legs feel weak and her heart race.

"Loyalty is important to me," Lynn agreed. Kent leaned in closer. She thought he was going to kiss her, and she tilted her head up and smiled.

Kent smiled back at her and reached out to brush some hair from her face. "I really hate to leave our conversation, Andrea, but I'm needed at home. I had to work until my replacement, Patty, got here, which was good because I got to talk to you. It's probably nothing, but my mom has issues. She can, um, drink a bit too much and make some bad decisions. Here's my phone number." He thrust a piece of paper into her hand and gently closed her fingers over it. She didn't want him to let go, but he did.

"Yeah, okay, thanks," Lynn mumbled. She added, "I hope it's, like, all okay at home."

"Should be. Well, I really hope you'll call me." He grinned at her. No, it wasn't just a grin; it was—what was a good word? Endearing? Lynn realized she hadn't quit smiling since she realized he liked her. He matched her expression. "So I hope we can continue our conversation over coffee. Then maybe we could go to the movies, exchange books, or get some dinner—whatever you want to do. I'd better go. Bye, Andrea." He rushed off to a small white Honda.

"Okay," Lynn heard herself say. "Bye!"

Meeting Kent a second time had given her a different impression. He wasn't awkward; he was funny and nice and, well, gorgeous. She was almost positive he'd wanted to kiss her as much as she'd wanted to kiss him, unless she'd just partied too much. She should have told him her real name, but she'd do that tomorrow.

Am I going to call this guy? She began her mental list about Kent. On the plus side, he was a reader—which was a huge positive. He was friendly, funny, gorgeous, took care of his family, and had a job. And he had the most beautiful eyes she'd ever seen. Not to mention he liked her over Stacy. On the negative side, he was a bartender who worked around drunk women.

Her list was pretty lopsided. She would decide in the morning, for sure. She took a long drag off her cigarette. She was positive she really liked him because of how dumb she had acted around him. Lynn could be a bit uncomfortable when it came to real feelings because they made her feel vulnerable. It was much easier to sleep with a guy and never see him again. *Just a few issues left over from surviving my parents.* She crushed her cigarette into the big sand ashtray when she got down to the filter. One more drink, and she was going home.

"Go."

"What?" Lynn looked around, but there was no one there. *Alone and hearing voices—awesome!*

"Leave."

"Hey, who's there?" She peered into the darkness. No one answered. Her arms were covered with goosebumps. That voice reminded her of something, but what?

Unnerved, she hurried back into the bar and ordered another drink. She wanted to put that warning voice out of her mind. It kind of reminded her of high school, for some reason, but why?

"Here's your drink, miss," said the sour, gray-haired guy—Gus, according to his name tag. Didn't Kent say that Patty was replacing him? This didn't look like a Patty.

"Thanks."

"You paying? It's a dollar fifty." Gus gave her an eyeroll that made him look like he was going to pass out. His girth was that of a man who liked to eat, but he had the smooth hands of a man who didn't like to do hard work. He didn't strike her as a man who'd serve drinks, more like someone who drank a lot of them.

"I am," she replied, ignoring the tone. "Keep the change."

"Yeah, I will. I might be able to put my kids through college, now—gee, thanks."

Wow, what a jerk, she thought, now wishing that she could get her fifty cents back. She sipped her watered-down drink, listening to the band butcher "Edge of Seventeen." Boy, did that seem like a long time ago to Lynn, now that she was on the edge of twenty-one. The warnings to leave were forgotten as she finished her drink. Stacy made eye contact and gave a thumbs-up. Lynn knew that meant she was staying with Dapper Dave. Lynn's thumb went up in response. It was time to go. She stood to leave but quickly sank back onto the red stool as the room began to spin. She felt an arm go around her, holding her up. She tried to see who it was, but her head wasn't cooperating.

That was the last thing she remembered until she collapsed, naked, into bed at two in the morning. She groaned as she reached for her alarm clock. She couldn't be late for work again, or she'd get written up. As she pushed the button to engage the alarm, she noticed it was set for 8:40. No, that wasn't right. She moved the arm back to seven. *There.*

"Hey!" Something touched her legs.

Had Stacy's cat, Princess Leia, jumped on her bed? She never left Stacy's room at night. *Strange.* There it was again. Lynn loved cats, but this little striped one was so spoiled—what a pest. The room began spinning again. The cocaine wasn't doing its job. She passed out the moment her head hit an unfamiliar satin pillow.

* * *

KENT WATCHED as Andrea was helped out of the bar. He regretted making her drinks so strong; he had been trying to be nice to a pretty girl on a budget. He hadn't expected her to get so many free drinks. He felt a little sad seeing her leave on the arm of one of the guys he'd been watching. He had really been attracted to her, but he couldn't mix business with pleasure.

Yet he still wanted to help her. *She shouldn't be driving her car,* he thought, watching her fumble around in her purse for her keys while her knight in shining armor was already at his car. Kent was just about to get out of his car when the other guy he was keeping an eye on came out of the bar with Sally hanging all over him.

They waved at Andrea's loser as he started his car. Sally's date took control and drove Andrea's car while she slouched over in the passenger seat. Sally appeared able to drive. Kent followed the caravan of vehicles to his target's apartment, but Sally and his second target left in her car. Probably getting something from the convenience store down the street, which was open twenty-four hours. *Still time to buy more booze and snacks, guys.*

Target One was almost carrying Andrea through the parking lot. Kent frowned, wondering if it was going to be a night of passion or a night of throwing up for this couple. He hoped the latter, which would serve that scumbag right. It would be hard to get that image out of his head if he ever saw her again, but a part of him wanted to see her anyway. Not that it mattered, he guessed, since girls usually weren't fans of guys not being honest with them. This was an unfortunate side effect of his job, which he had to focus on now.

Kent sighed. It was only one forty-five. He worked on a crossword puzzle he'd brought. He quickly finished it and then started to reread the Stephen King book he had in the car. After the first two chapters, he glanced at his watch. It was almost two forty-five. He had fully expected Target Two and Sally to come back, but they hadn't. It was time to check in and see if there were any more instructions. Sometimes things changed. Hopefully, he could call it a night. Kent drove to the nearest pay phone, which didn't work, so he drove down the street to another one.

Making sure this one worked, he inserted a dime and dialed the familiar phone number. The phone started ringing.

"What do you have to report, young Kent?"

"I've got an update." Kent quickly filled in the person on the other end of the line.

"Interesting. Here's what you need to do next."

CHAPTER 2

Beep! Beep! Beep!

The alarm sounded before Lynn had even started dreaming. It took a couple of attempts to stop the irritating sound.

"Who moved the button?" she mumbled, finally making the sound stop. Her stomach flopped, and she quickly threw back the unfamiliar silky black comforter and ran to a strange yellow bathroom, where she threw up.

She had no idea where she was, but at least the resident was still asleep. Funny, she thought she had gone home last night. *Wow, that was some strong whiskey.* She quietly sneaked back into the room, grabbed her scattered clothes, and got dressed.

She noticed black hair sticking out from under the black satin bedding. His wallet was tossed on the floor. She carefully picked it up and found his driver's license. His name was Todd John Smith, and he had turned twenty-four last month. The name and the good-looking face didn't trigger any recognition. No one she remembered dancing with. *Did we have sex?* Not that it mattered; she'd started taking the pill a couple of years ago, but there were other things. Well, she wouldn't worry about that. He had a Kaiser medical card, twenty dollars, an ATM card, and a AAA card. A rather empty wallet, by her standards. It was time to get out of there, and quietly. She'd find a pay phone and call Stacy to come get her, unless she found her car outside.

She surveyed the room to make sure she wasn't forgetting anything. She put on her shoes, and as she picked up her purse, she saw that his hairy foot was sticking out of the covers. She tried to cover it up and touched it briefly. It was ice cold. She wanted to get out of there, but she couldn't. *What if there's something wrong with him?* She set her purse down, lifted the comforter, and peeked at his face. *Why is he so pale?* He was either the quietest sleeper or very sick.

She gently touched his face. It was just as cold as his foot, and he didn't stir. *Great.* Maybe he had a roommate. She ran into the living room, the kitchen, and then the other bedroom, which only contained a white dresser and a neatly made double bed. They were alone, so she'd have to deal with this obviously sick guy. She pulled back the black silk comforter and was greeted with the sight of a naked body that she might have enjoyed looking at if not for the wound in the chest and all that dried blood.

"Oh...my...God!" Lynn started to shake. She bent down and checked his pulse to be sure. Nothing, as she'd suspected. She'd been sleeping next to a dead man. Why wasn't she covered in blood?

"Oh my God!" Lynn repeated, backing up from the bed toward the pine dresser, kicking something that was sticking out from underneath it. She bent down to pick it up. It was a gun, and now she was holding it.

"Who's going to believe I was asleep next to a guy who was shot, when the gun now has my prints on it?" Lynn asked aloud.

No response from dead Todd. Her mind was reeling. What should she do? The only thing she knew how to do was save herself. She grabbed the towel she'd used in the bathroom and wiped her fingerprints off the gun before returning it to the plush green carpet. Then she cleaned off anything she remembered touching, including his wallet.

Call the police. She located a phone in the surprisingly clean yellow-and-green kitchen and started to dial 911. Her finger was about to make the second turn on the dial when the room began to spin like she was going to pass out. She dropped the phone and sank into a brown-cushioned chair at the glass kitchen table. She put her head down and waited for it to pass. It did.

"What am I doing?" she asked the empty room. She had a strong urge to escape, like she wasn't safe.

"Run!"

"Hello? Is someone here? I need help," Lynn called out to the silent apartment. No response. She carefully hung up the phone, which was now beeping to let her know it was off the hook. There was that voice again, the one that she'd heard last night. What was going on? The urge to run was even stronger. She had to get out of there!

I can call the police from a pay phone just as easy. There is no way I can explain this. Plus, what if the killers come back? Towel still in hand, she wiped off the yellow phone.

She paused for a moment and then changed her mind and reached for the phone again—*Maybe I should call Stacy*—when she started sweating. She ran to the bathroom to throw up what little was left in her stomach. She quickly wiped off the handle of the toilet, remembered to wipe off the alarm clock, and grabbed her purse.

"I have to get out of here," Lynn said, feeling sick again. Her whole body was trembling. The urge to leave was so strong that if she didn't go, she'd throw up again or maybe even pass out.

She cautiously opened the door, taking the towel with her. No one was outside the apartment. She locked the door, wiped it off, and left. She wasn't sure why it was important to lock the door, since he was already dead, but it sure seemed like the right thing to do. And she hadn't been doing much of that this morning. She noted the door was marked 4A as she hurried past a sparkling, well-kept pool to the parking lot. She promised herself that if she ran into someone, she'd alert them to the dead body, but the complex was remarkably quiet.

She found the parking lot quickly. Her old, rust-colored Chevy Nova was neatly parked in the farthest space. Relieved, she hopped in, threw the towel in the back, wrote down the address on an old envelope, and drove away without looking back. She felt better as soon as she turned the corner, like she could take a deep breath again. She knew that leaving the scene and removing evidence was breaking the law, but she had no protocol for waking up next to a dead guy. Besides, she tried to reassure herself, the murderer could have come back for her at any time. Would the police believe in her innocence when she didn't even know what had happened? It didn't matter. What was done was done, and she had a job to get to if she wanted to pay her bills. But she had to talk to Stacy before anything else.

* * *

Zelina and Thomas watched Lynn pull into a gas station.

"You did not want her to call the police?"

"He was there, Thomas—watching her. Did you not see him?"

"No."

"It could have gone two ways if she had stayed there—neither of them good for her."

"Was that not breaking a rule, Zelina?"

"You asked me that last night at the bar, remember? All I am doing is advising. I have no control over the fact that she can hear us. Like I told you last night, she must choose how to respond."

"Yes, well, it seems like a gray area to me when she can hear us. I wish she would listen, though. Will she remember what happened last night?"

"Doubtful. What do you think?"

"I think it would be better if she remembered."

"We will see." Zelina shrugged.

"I guess we will. I thought that after watching all these years, we would be able to do more."

"Yes, well, we are."

Thomas frowned. He had learned a lot over the last seven years. He had watched this girl grow into an adult who could take care of herself, but she had developed some bad habits. He wanted to do something to save her, but what?

"From your heart," Zelina gently reminded him.

Thomas frowned but did not reply. He had more control over his pride, but occasionally he wanted to do a good job more than he wanted to help the human. He turned his attention back to Lynn as she ran into the gas station bathroom to throw up again.

"Right now, we focus on keeping her safe. I know you want to do more, and honestly, so do I, but we have to be careful. Hearing the few words I have said to her is already making her doubt her sanity. What we do right now is try to prevent her from bringing others into this. You have seen her lack of trust. Authorities were not helpful to her when she was growing up, and that all might be in her favor right now."

"I do agree with all of that, but if she wants to tell someone—"

Zelina offered a slight smile. "I know, but there is someone she can trust. We can help push that along without interfering."

"Yes, if she trusts him." Thomas folded his arms across his chest.

"Exactly."

"But if she does not—hey! There he is again." Thomas pointed to a car parked behind an untrimmed hedge.

Zelina sighed. "I know. He wants to resolve this soon."

"I hope she picks the right one to trust."

"So do I, Thomas. So do I."

* * *

Lynn hadn't been this sick from drinking in a very long time. And she hadn't seen a dead body or handled a gun ever. *Too many firsts,* she thought grimly. She wasn't sure how long she had been bent over the toilet, but at last she started to feel almost normal, considering. She splashed some water on her face in the mirrorless tan bathroom and wondered what she had gotten herself into last night. Why had he been shot? Why didn't they shoot her too? Her heart was racing as she hurried out the door to the pay phone. It wasn't working. *Awesome!*

The gas station attendant appeared. "Can I help you, miss?" He tucked a greasy red rag into his back pocket.

"No, I was just looking for a working pay phone." She was surprised to hear her voice sounding so cheerful.

"Yeah, it's been broken for a while, sorry," he replied with a shrug.

"Well, are there any other phones nearby?"

"Sure, down the road at the new grocery store. Can't miss it. You sure you're okay, miss? You know, you can use—"

She quickly interrupted him. "Oh, I'm fine. Just late for work." She hopped into her car and shut the door. He looked confused, but she knew he had been about to offer the use of his office phone, and this was not a call she could make in front of a witness. She watched him walk away, wiping his hands on his brown pants. *Maybe he could help.* She had a good feeling about him. She opened her window to call out to him.

"Leave."

"What?" Lynn asked.

The man stopped and looked at her like she was crazy—and she certainly felt that way. "Drive safely, miss." He walked away, shaking his head.

"Thanks," she called, but he was already back in the shop.

She started her car and quickly merged into traffic. She knew that warning hadn't come from him or anyone else she could see. Why was she hearing voices? Did someone drug her last night? That would explain a lot, but it also added questions. Well, she didn't have time for more questions or to look for another phone—she had to get to work. She was in an unfamiliar part of town, but she found I-580 East toward Pleasanton instantly. Traffic was already backed up.

She checked herself in the mirror as they inched forward. Her makeup was smeared. Hazel eyes, immense with confusion and fear, took over her pale face. *No wonder the guy at the gas station acted weird.* She looked horrible. She wiped off her stale makeup and grabbed the cosmetic bag from her purse. She dabbed on some blue eyeshadow, mascara (not the glitter one she'd worn last night—matte black for work), and a little pressed powder to cover her light freckles. She finished with pink lipstick, just like any typical morning on her way to work.

But nothing was normal about waking up next to a dead body. Tears filled her eyes. *At least my mascara is waterproof,* she thought. The traffic started to move, and so did her tears. She'd just left the scene of a murder. What if she was the killer? Could she have killed someone without knowing it, with a gun she'd never seen? No, she had no idea how to even shoot a gun—but the police wouldn't know that. She was completely out of ideas and had never been so scared in her entire life.

She grabbed some tissue from the side pocket in her purse, careful not to cut herself on the button—but it wasn't there. She felt around. Nothing. She dumped it out but still didn't see the button. Traffic sped up and then slowed down immediately, so she searched again. Her button was missing. What if she'd left it at dead Todd's place? She knew she couldn't go back to look.

"I should've called the police," she said. "But if I call now, it'll seem even more like I'm guilty. I mean, all you do is pull the trigger on a gun. Yes, I would shoot a guy I just met and then lie down and sleep next to him afterward. Makes perfect sense—not."

A chill shot through her body, and her teeth started to chatter as she gripped the steering wheel. Traffic suddenly came to a complete halt—an accident off to her right. Just a fender bender, but everyone had to look. She cranked up the car heater, turning all the vents toward her. The warmth soothed her shaking. Needing something to do, she ran a brush through her long, wavy hair and pulled it into a quick ponytail. Her work smock was in the back seat, so she wouldn't have to use the smelly spare one at work.

She had no idea how she was going to make it through the day after what she'd just seen. All she could do was paste on a fake smile as she cut people's hair. She was good at that after growing up in a house where niceness was just a mask for the monsters who raised her. She'd call the police on her first break from the mall pay phone and contact Stacy at lunch. Yes, she would tell the police the truth, how scared she'd been—they would understand. Unless they didn't and thought it was her. They would think it was her; she was positive of that. She was sure she wouldn't kill someone—unless something had happened. Why couldn't she remember? She could imagine them blaming her anyway because even she wouldn't believe her story if she heard it. All she could do was report a dead body. She'd figure the rest out later. At least she had a plan.

Traffic began to flow as soon as she got past the two cars in the emergency lane. Both drivers were fine and exchanging numbers. Lynn finished her drive to work on autopilot while breaking her rule of no smoking in the car. When she found a close parking spot with ease, Lynn realized that she was actually early for work and made the first change in her plan. She tried calling home. No answer. Maybe Stacy was sleeping. She went on to the next call.

"I want to report a murder at 1776 Stanton Circle, Apartment 4A," Lynn told the person who answered her 911 call.

"A murder? Are you safe, miss?"

"Yes. I left because I wasn't sure if I was."

"I understand. What's your name, miss?"

"My name…" Lynn hesitated right as she looked into the startling green eyes of a good looking guy who had walked up behind her. He looked very familiar. He smiled widely at her and nodded. It was obvious he was waiting to use the phone and could hear everything she said. "I, um…I don't know anything else, sorry." She hung up.

"I didn't mean to rush you," said the beautiful man with the flowing brown hair.

"You didn't," she assured him, hoping he'd want her phone number.

"Good. Just checking on my wife—we're having a baby soon. Have a good day," he said with a smile.

"Yeah? Congrats. Uh, you too," she added.

Married. Too bad. Even after the morning she'd had, she was still disappointed. But that smile—why did a lava lamp come to mind?

* * *

"I think that went well. I did have to use a bit of charm, if that was not breaking any rules?" Thomas smiled.

"No, that was a good time to use your charm." Zelina's eyes were pinned on the girl retreating from the pay phone.

"I think she recognized me." Thomas watched a group of teenage girls stroll by in high giggle mode. They all had a relatively happy life in front of them, except one. She would not make thirty. Cancer was brutal to those delicate bodies. He caught Zelina watching the same group. If only they could help more. Soon another angel would be watching over her.

Zelina nodded slightly to Thomas. "We help who we can. As for Lynn, I am sure she did remember you on some level from seeing you in her coma. And we are lucky—she is one of those rare humans who come out of a coma able to hear an angel's voice."

"It would help if she listened to what you say."

Zelina sent a white beam of light to the young girl. "Yes, well, maybe in time."

"That is the first time I have appeared to humans since, well, her father. I was very nervous."

"You did well. The difference is she had no idea she was talking with an angel and her father knew he was seeing something out of his world. By the way, nice touch, saying you were married with a baby on the way."

"Well, yes, thanks." Thomas tugged at his button-down shirt. He quickly returned to his more comfortable angel attire.

"She is remembering the time from school now. It will reinforce her lack of trust in telling people, I hope."

* * *

IMAGES from high school flooded Lynn's mind. She remembered sitting in her counselor's office. She'd trusted Miss Olivia and thought she was cool. She knew it wouldn't excuse the fact that she'd cut some of her classes, but she'd told the truth about what she had been going through at home. She thought that finally it was going to be okay, that someone would believe her. Her parents' heavy drinking, her stepdad's anger—yes, Miss Olivia's wide blue eyes showed so much concern. She was going to make a call for her and suggested that Lynn go to an Al-Anon meeting in the meantime. She handed her the information.

"I will make sure to contact the proper authorities. You're going to be fine, you'll see." Miss Olivia had smiled.

Lynn had believed for a few hours that she would be fine. Maybe they would make her stepdad get help. Maybe she could go live with someone else in her family once they knew. Maybe finally telling someone was going to make it all work out for her. Too many maybes, Lynn found out. That night, the phone rang at home. Lynn listened from her bedroom door and heard her stepdad greet Miss Olivia. He listened quietly before responding.

"Drink too much? No, we have a glass of wine with dinner. I'm confused as to what Lynn was referring to." Her stepdad wriggled his way through the conversation. He was right; they did have a glass of wine with dinner. Many glasses. And he left out the before-dinner drinks and the after-dinner drinks before bed. He went on to paint a rosy picture of what a wonderful family they were and mentioned that they'd noticed Lynn's behavior had changed.

"Yes, we've been worried about Lynn too," her stepdad had said. "Her mother and I want what's best for her. Yes, of course we'll come in and talk. I'll have to check my schedule at work, but the first opening, we'll be there, I promise you."

Lynn knew that meeting would never happen. He would always be too busy at work. She heard him thank Miss Olivia for her concern and for not bringing the authorities into it. *Great,* Lynn thought. *Another adult in authority just screwed me over.*

"Lynn's mother and I will talk to her tonight. Yes, we'll encourage her to attend her classes and do better in school. I agree, she has potential. I'm sorry that Lynn lied to you; she's been doing a lot of that lately. We think it's because of her birth father's death."

Lynn sighed. Blaming her dead father for something—again. *Great.* She quietly closed her bedroom door and sat on her purple comforter. She'd trusted the wrong person, and she was going to pay. She didn't have to wait long, and, as usual, her bruises weren't visible. She walked away with the very clear message that she wasn't to *lie* about her family.

After canceling several appointments, as Lynn had predicted, her parents never went in to the school. Miss Olivia followed up with Lynn, who dutifully told the woman that everyone was okay. Lynn hoped she would see past the words she forced out of her mouth and notice the pain in her eyes, but she didn't. The woman Lynn had thought so cool was clueless and heard what she wanted to hear.

Miss Olivia set Lynn's paperwork on her desk and smiled brightly without making eye contact. "Anytime you need to talk, Lynn, I'm here for you."

Lynn didn't bother to respond. That woman didn't care at all. No one did. She never made that mistake again. At least Stacy had always been there for her. She was the one person Lynn had always counted on after Tammy died in junior high. Although Lynn and Tammy had only known Stacy for a year, the girls had been very close. The three rainbow musketeers, Tammy had called them since Stacy was a blonde, Lynn a brunette, and Tammy a redhead. And then, at the end of seventh grade, Tammy and her parents died in a car accident. Lynn felt bad that she hadn't thought of Tammy in a while. She didn't want to forget her. It was like she and Stacy were the last two people on Earth who would keep her memory alive.

She and Stacy had had each other's back ever since. Even when Lynn threw an empty beer bottle in the garbage can at school, Stacy kept her secret when the teacher found it.

Yeah, Lynn had done some stupid things, but she didn't deserve to be punched, choked, or beaten for it. She didn't deserve to be called those names, either. And those times when her stepdad had screamed that no one understood him, well, he was right. She didn't.

Miss Olivia had shown her that it was best not to report things because no one ever did the right thing. This time, instead of avoiding a beating from her stepdad, she was avoiding jail, and that was worse. Let the police figure out what happened. What good had they been to her when she was growing up and needed their help? Nope, law enforcement wasn't there for her, although they had shown up a couple of times when things got loud. "Just the TV—I'm a little deaf from the war," her stepdad had said, and they believed him.

Trying to speak up only got her that look—like she was crazy—from the rest of her family. He did such a good job supporting his family; he couldn't be like that. And her stepdad would straighten her out under her mom's watchful eye if she spoke out of turn. Yes, keeping things to herself was the wisest solution to any bad situation. And the simple fact was that she had no bruises or injuries, so self-defense was not an alibi.

She had to focus. *You can't trust anyone. Tell no one,* she kept repeating to herself. She wasn't going to blab at work that she'd partied all night and woken up next to a dead guy she didn't know. That information might get her arrested and fired. Her boss didn't like people who drank and slept around, to put it kindly.

Lynn had ten minutes before her first appointment when she walked into the salon, which gave her just enough time to clean her tools and tidy up her workstation. Such a normal task had a calming effect on her, and she managed to put the morning's events out of her mind as she focused on her clients. Her day was going well, considering. She already had a five-dollar tip in her pocket, which she'd use for gas.

Her first break turned out to be lunch, after a busy morning. She tried to call Stacy again. No answer. Lynn knew it was her day off and she'd be sleeping in, but the phone usually woke her up. Either Stacy was sleeping soundly, or she was with that guy she'd been dancing with. Dapper Dave. The reason didn't matter—Lynn was heading toward a panic attack. She stepped outside to smoke and calm down, but her mind took off. Had she witnessed someone else committing a murder? Was she next? Why didn't they kill her too? Did they not notice her there when they killed him? That was a possibility she quickly latched onto. So saying anything would really be a bad thing in case the murderers wanted to shut her up. She had done the right thing in getting out of there.

She twisted her ponytail into a bun and added the pink bow she found in her pocket. Maybe she should call her mom. *Really? Bad idea,*

Lynn. Her mother would tell *him,* and together they'd only make it worse—much worse. Her stepdad wouldn't attack her now, but he could make her life a living hell while convincing others that he was just trying to help. He was the king of manipulation. It was a skill he'd honed carefully, with much practice, over the years. They'd bail her out and then try to go back to controlling her again. *No, thanks.* Maybe her stepbrother? She shrugged. The things she'd heard about him from her mother and the people he'd ripped off, well, she wasn't so sure she believed them, but it might not be a good idea to get him involved—or any family member, for that matter. She wasn't sure who she could trust right now, other than Stacy.

CHAPTER 3

The evildwel encouraged her host to locate a bench where he could observe Lynn as she worked. Her host's skills at applying his disguise, an older man waiting patiently for his wife to finish shopping, made him almost invisible. With bags and a purse at his feet, skillfully applied makeup, and the right clothes, no one gave the man pretending to read a second look. Dian always urged her host to carry an undercover outfit in his trunk because, in his line of work, he might need it. Her host drank many cups of coffee a day to stay alert. She liked the feeling of coffee.

The first part of his plan had gone perfectly, thanks to her prodding. Her hosts were never aware of her silent suggestions. They always thought they were in control. Silly humans had no idea she was feeding on their fear and anger. She had only had to revise one aspect of the original plan. Lynn completely surprised Dian by leaving the dead body before calling the police, so Dian had to send her host back to retrieve the recording device he had planted in the apartment. *Who locks an apartment with a dead guy inside?* Dian rolled her red eyes. Not that her host really needed that bug—it couldn't be traced back to him, but Dian had pressed into his thoughts to do a sweep and see if Lynn had left anything behind, which, luckily for them, she had.

Besides, there was nothing like a good tape to listen to after the fact. She knew her host would enjoy it, and through him, she would too. This was going to be one of the last times her host would be so hands-on with this type of work, so why not enjoy every second of it?

Too bad right now there were only dull conversations with hair clients to listen to. The girl was proving that she didn't trust anyone, just as predicted, but to make sure of that fact, Dian and her host were watching people cut hair.

Her host turned a page in a book that was about some lonely cowboy named Ned who'd been living off the land since his young wife died. Ned soon ran into some "bad" guys—the ones he always rooted for. There was probably another woman in the mix who would "save" him. Predictable in stories, but not in life. Dian wished her host had grabbed a nice horror story where they could root for the real bad guys. He had several books from Mr. King that Dian would have enjoyed. Too bad—next time, she wouldn't overlook that tiny detail.

Dian smirked while her host took a sip of his java and watched Lynn accept a measly dollar tip. The girl lived like a pauper. That must have been her last client, because her supervisor was giving her a list of chores to do before she clocked out. *Perfect.* That gave her host at least an hour before Lynn got home. There were some things to check on, and then he could head to Lynn's apartment to see the outcome.

But someone else was watching this girl too. Dian was sure there had been someone there last night. Maybe it was some random guy killing time, but it seemed unlikely. Her host gathered up his props and hurried to the parking lot to retrieve the car. Dian grew excited.

* * *

Lynn had mindlessly smiled her way through the day, a skill she'd learned living with her detached mother. She could disconnect from any emotion and just observe life around her. No one had suspected things were bad for her at home, even when she tried to tell them, except for Stacy. Well, the neighbors had known but believed it was none of their business. Today no one was able to tell she'd woken up next to a dead body. It was not a skill one would put on a résumé, but it was coming in handy. That therapist she'd seen a couple of times had told her she needed to express her emotions, yet everyone seemed uncomfortable when she did that. One thing she hadn't learned in therapy was how to handle waking up next to a dead guy, so she was on her own.

Apparently, this state of mind made her a wonderful listener, because she'd earned over twenty-five dollars in tips—a personal record if she didn't count holidays. Although maybe they felt sorry for her since she kept cutting the same hand over and over. She'd almost run through the salon's entire Band-Aid supply. Who needed blood, anyway? *Well, maybe that guy I found dead this morning.* No, she couldn't think about that. She needed to finish cleaning and then find Stacy. Period. She gladly fell back into her numb state. Her two talkative coworkers were leaving her alone today after she'd told them she thought she might be getting the stomach flu. She wasn't tempted to tell either one of them what was going on; they were friendly, but not friends.

Lynn added all the brushes to the cleaning solution and then started sweeping up. When she didn't have a full schedule of clients to fill her day, she got to clean up after everyone. She added the towels to the dryer and started another load. Finally, it was six, time to go. She removed her smock and grabbed her purse from her locker. Her emotions started creeping back in the moment she inserted her time card into the clock and heard it punch the time with a loud *click*. She headed for the parking lot without even saying goodbye to the other stylists. She knew they'd be rolling their eyes at each other.

The sun quickly warmed her as she stepped outside. It was the last week of summer. She let the chill of the day pass out of her. Reaching into her purse, she found an empty pack of cigarettes. *Crap!* She took a deep breath and let it out in a loud sigh as she unlocked her car door. All day, she'd felt like she could barely breathe, waiting for the police to show up and arrest her or the people who'd murdered Todd Smith to finish the job by eliminating her. She needed to hold it together just a little bit longer to get home and find Stacy. Then she could stand under a hot shower and wash the day away. Or could she? She shook her head, trying to clear it. There was no easy answer to having her life turned upside down by one stupid night and a terrifying morning. *Only focus on Stacy,* Lynn firmly told herself—only then, when she finally found her friend, would it be time to completely lose it. She was okay with that.

Lynn had to make one stop to fill her gas tank and pick up cigarettes and a Pepsi Light. She found herself nervously eyeing everyone at the station, making sure no one was watching her. No one was, but she didn't feel safe. *Gee, maybe that's because the last thing I remember before waking up next to a dead guy was the room spinning, and not in a too-much-to-drink kind of way, either.* Lynn pushed those thoughts away and returned to the low-level anxiety that allowed her to function.

Soon she was safely in her parking space at home. She frowned, noting that Stacy's car was missing. *Maybe she left a note.* Lynn hurried through the big, square parking lot, puffing on a much-needed smoke. She grabbed their mail and put her cigarette out in the potted plant everyone used for an ashtray. She downed the rest of her can of soda as she sped down the concrete walkway to their door. When she tried to insert her key, the door pushed open. Stacy routinely forgot to lock —or even fully shut—the door, and for just a moment, Lynn felt relief. As soon as she crossed the threshold into their living room, she realized it wasn't Stacy who'd left the door open.

They'd been robbed. The cushions on the couch were tossed on the floor, all the cabinets in the kitchen were open, the fridge door was ajar, and food was scattered across the floor. In a panic she checked the bedrooms and closets. She was alone—and that had probably been a very stupid move. With her heart trying to escape her chest cavity, she grabbed the phone to call the police. She paused for a moment. Should she? *Yes, it couldn't possibly be related to this morning.* She pushed the buttons to make the call.

"Are you safe?"

"Yes, I checked the apartment. I'm alone," Lynn replied.

"Good. The officers should be there soon." Then the dispatcher was gone.

Lynn glanced around the room. She wanted to start cleaning but thought she should wait. What couldn't wait was a small bag of weed and a joint lying on the brown shag carpet. She was surprised the thieves hadn't taken it. What were they looking for? She glanced into Stacy's room. *Why didn't they touch anything in her room?* Even the cat's food bowl was in place. Yet all their food from the refrigerator was on the kitchen floor, warm and probably spoiled. Had Lynn come home and interrupted them, or was it something else? She shrugged and took the pot to her car and locked it in her truck. She didn't need the law to think she was a druggie or something. Next, she knocked on her landlords' door. They weren't home, so she waited outside, watching the purple sunset and chain-smoking. Finally, the police arrived.

Lynn didn't feel any relief after the officers had searched her apartment. They didn't seem very optimistic that they would apprehend whoever had torn through her apartment looking for whatever they were looking for. Nothing was missing, as far as she could tell, and she got the impression they didn't believe her; especially the older one, Officer Banks.

"Is someone mad at you? Did you fight with your roommate?" he asked.

"No."

"One of your friends likely to play a joke on you?" he persisted with a slight smirk.

"No. I don't have friends like that."

"Well, it's odd that every room is trashed but your roommate's. I suppose you might have scared them off when you came home." He looked at his partner with an obvious eyeroll.

She held back her own eyeroll, positive that wouldn't help her, but she was tired of this line of questioning and the attitude she was getting from them. She fought off a frown and returned to her emotionless expression. Officer Banks was clearly about ready to retire and couldn't care less about her—or anyone else—at that point.

"Maybe you should get your landlord to change your lock," the lanky Officer Adams suggested.

"I will, thanks."

"No problem, Miss Hill. In the meantime, lock your door and windows, and don't answer the door if you don't know who's on the other side." He smiled, making him look even younger and a bit like Howdy Doody.

Officer Adams quickly assured Lynn that they'd investigate the break-in, while his partner seemed to be taking in the view of her apartment.

"We'd like to talk to your roommate," Officer Adams added, handing Lynn a card with the station's phone numbers and his name in the corner. Alex Adams—it was a pleasant name, and he wasn't that bad looking, really. He had startling blue eyes, freckles and a nice smile. *Maybe if we'd met under different circumstances. Yeah, whatever.*

Lynn forced a smile. "I'll let her know."

"Thanks, Miss Hill. Lock the door," Officer Adams warned. He followed his partner out the door as he shut it tightly behind him.

Lynn was alone again. She stood staring at the mess, frozen. She was almost tempted to run after Officer Adams and tell him everything. But she had seen the good cop–bad cop routine on TV, and maybe that was all they were doing. Besides, if they didn't believe her about a break-in, they certainly wouldn't believe her about a murder. Heck, she didn't even know what to think about it yet.

She sighed and started to clean up. She threw away the food on the floor to be on the safe side. Who knew how long it had been there? She hadn't been home since last night. Those officers certainly didn't offer any information. At least whoever broke in hadn't bothered with the freezer, so the TV dinners she and Stacy had splurged on were still edible. The only real food losses were milk, mayonnaise, ranch dressing, and eggs—they hadn't had that much food to begin with. Their staples were boxed mac and cheese, bananas, cereal, diet cola, bread, peanut butter, and chips. A well-balanced diet, if you looked at it just right—and she did. She closed all the kitchen cabinets and wiped off the counters because she didn't like the idea of strangers touching her stuff, especially where she ate.

She moved her cleaning to where the biggest mess was—her

bedroom. She rehung all her clothes in the closet, then put her underwear and socks back in the tall white dresser. Her old silver dollar was still lying in her PJ drawer. *What were they looking for?* None of this made any sense. No wonder the officers hadn't believed her. They might have if she'd told them what she'd woken up to, although Lynn couldn't connect finding a dead body to her apartment being ransacked. *Just bad luck.* She'd had a lot of that, growing up. Too tired to figure it out, she scooped up her shampoo, conditioner, razor, and loofah off the floor next to her bed. She rehung her new brown towel and cleaned the bathroom. Nothing left to do but make the bed and vacuum.

Lynn's hand hit something hard, cold, and small as she pulled the comforter up. "What is this?" She carefully pulled it out. "A bullet. Holy shit." She reached under her covers and found a second bullet, along with another item. Her button. What were the chances she'd lose her memory of what happened the night before, wake up next to a dead guy, come home to a ransacked apartment, and find bullets in her bed with the missing button from her purse? How apt that saying —F*ck Off & Die—had been! The button wouldn't look good for her, either. Maybe it was time to get rid of it. *Later*, she thought, putting it back into her purse.

Part of her wanted to cling to the belief that it was all just a bad coincidence. Reality and that unfortunate word "logic" won that battle quickly. She was being set up. Someone had expected her to make that call to the police this morning. Did they expect the police to search her apartment afterward and find this? Or were the bullets meant for her to find? She had no answers, but she'd learned two things: She wasn't guilty of murder, and the killer knew where she lived.

Lynn sank to the bed in confusion. She looked around for clues. She would have to think like her favorite TV police officers, Cagney and Lacey. She stared at the dark TV on her dresser. They'd knocked the rabbit ears off but left the TV. They didn't want drugs or the twenty dollars she had left under her clock radio in case of an emergency, but they'd left her bullets and her button. What was the message? Was she to die next, like her button said, or was it supposed to look like she wanted someone dead and had left a message for the police to find? What a confusing mess.

Luckily, she was a coward and had fled the scene—but she felt like she was being helped with the strange warnings. Or perhaps she was nuts and hearing voices. Either way, if she had listened to them in the first place, she might not be in this mess.

"Where are you, Stacy?" Lynn asked the dark TV.

Her phone rang, startling her. She ran to the kitchen and answered it on the fourth ring.

"Hello?" She could hear someone breathing. "Hello? Is someone there?" she asked. *Click.* No response.

"Maybe a wrong number." Lynn gently set the phone back on its cradle as a chill shot through her.

* * *

THE EVILDWEL SMILED as her host hung up the phone. At last the girl was alone. From the dull tone of the girl's voice, Dian was positive the gifts she had encouraged her host to leave had been found. *Perfect.* She needed her host to proceed carefully, though; this girl was turning out to be smarter than Dian had given her credit for. She'd had the presence of mind to hide her drugs, which showed she could think under pressure. Dian would have to make sure her host factored that into his plans. This girl was turning out to be more fun than she had expected. Her host was having as much fun as she was, but there was the added thrill that Lynn might tell someone what was going on at some point, and her clever host had to be ready for that event. Dian didn't mind if there were loose ends to clean up. More work for the host, perhaps, but murder was never repulsive to any respectable evildwel.

* * *

LYNN ATE HER TV DINNER, barely tasting the gravy-laden turkey she was shoving into her mouth. She knew she had to eat to keep going. Her mind was numb again. There hadn't been any more phone calls, but she couldn't shake the feeling that she was being watched. There was an evil presence on the other end of the phone line that she couldn't explain. Lynn shook her head. That was stupid thinking, and Stacy would have made fun of her for saying something so absurd. But she wasn't there.

Lynn threw away the rest of her dinner and washed and put away her fork. Her body felt heavy suddenly, although she doubted she would ever sleep again after the morning's events. Before she went to bed, she had to find Stacy and figure out who had put the bullets and her button in her bed.

She headed for the shower after a quick smoke break. She was smoking more than her usual few cigarettes a day, but it had been a hell of a day. Her second wind kicked in as she tried to scrub the last twenty-four hours off her body. Revived, she started making calls to some friends to see if they had heard from Stacy.

"You know Stace. She's probably hanging out with the new dude she met," Laurie said.

"Yeah, you're probably right," Lynn admitted.

"I know. You doing anything tonight? We're having a few friends over, gonna play Uno—you know, with shots. Couple of cute guys gonna be here."

"I wish I could, but I have some stuff going on, and I—"

"No problem," Laurie interrupted. "But I miss seeing you guys. How about Friday? We're taking the party to the beach this weekend —usual spot. Bring Stace with you when she shows up." Laurie laughed.

"Laurie, something happened. Can we—" A loud static noise blasted through the phone line. She wasn't sure Laurie could hear her. "Hello?"

It was gone as quickly as it started, and Laurie rambled on as though Lynn hadn't spoken. "Must be working on the phone lines. Gotta go!" Laurie hung up.

"Laurie? Hello?' She tried redialing, but it kept ringing. She'd almost confided in Laurie, but something had prevented her. Could someone have tapped her phone line? She shook her head. She'd call Laurie later and explain it all to her if she didn't find Stacy.

The rest of the calls produced the same results. No one had heard from Stacy. Lynn was past worrying now. She knew Stacy had to work early in the morning, and it was after ten. Lynn threw on some makeup, grabbed her purse and keys, and headed to her car after carefully locking the apartment door. She checked it several times to be sure. Not that it mattered; they had already been in her apartment, and she'd never feel safe there again. As she passed the landlords' place, she recalled that she'd forgotten to tell them about the break-in and needing new locks. *Tomorrow,* she thought. Now it was time to retrace their steps. She headed back to the bar.

The crowd was smaller, but the same band was playing. She sat on a stool and studied the room. No Stacy, and no Dapper Dave, either. She wasn't even sure why she'd come back. *What a stupid idea.*

"First drink is on the house, Andrea," said a familiar voice.

She spun around to find Kent smiling at her. "Oh, hi, Kent. I'm looking for the girl who came here with me last night. You see her here?"

"Not tonight, but it's still early."

"Well, she's my roommate, and she hasn't been home since last night. I'm worried about her."

"Maybe she met someone. Has she done this before?" Kent asked, wiping the counter and then putting some peanuts in front of her.

"No, she always comes home, calls me, or comes by my work to let me know she's okay. And she was hanging out with some blond guy named Dave. You know him?" Lynn asked as Kent handed her a drink. Her stomach flipped at the thought of drinking it. She pushed it away with a frown. She was sure she'd been drugged last night at that same bar.

"Blond, Dave? Nope, doesn't ring a bell, but then, I've only worked here a few days. Want me to ask around? Would you prefer a coffee or soda instead?"

"I would appreciate a soda. Seven-Up, if you have it, and I can pay for it. I made good tips today."

"Seven-Up it is. Like I said, the first drink is always on the house with me. You a waitress?" Kent added some ice to a cup and filled it.

"No, I cut hair," Lynn replied with a weak smile.

"Cool. Here you go, Andrea."

"Thank you, Kent. You should know that my real name is Lynn Hill, not Andrea. My friend's real name is Stacy Kelly. We do that because we've met some real weirdos at bars. Sorry. But I would have told you when I called you," Lynn added. She swirled the 7-Up. She was afraid to drink it, even after closely watching him prepare it.

"You look more like a Lynn. I understand. I've seen some strange stuff in my few days working here. No hard feelings. Did I hear you say you were going to call me—and you still have no boyfriend?" His eyes lit up as he smiled at her.

"No; not since yesterday. I was thinking maybe a movie or coffee might be fun, but right now, I gotta find my friend. You understand?"

"I do. She's lucky to have you as a friend, Lynn. Another time, right?"

"Yes, another time. Here, let me give you my phone number. If you see her, please let me know, and tell her to call me." Lynn wrote her number down on a bar napkin.

"I'll do that, thanks. When you find her, please let me know too. Then we can discuss any future interactions."

"That's a deal," Lynn said. "I think your number is still in my purse." She found it and held it up.

"Ah, your papers are in order. Sorry! For some reason, when I'm around you, movie lines come rushing out of my mouth. Honestly, I don't usually do that." Kent blushed. He had a dimple she hadn't noticed before—and strong shoulders. She could imagine his arm around her in a dark movie theater, but first she had a few things to work out.

"I don't mind—it's kind of cute. I look forward to talking to you more later." Lynn set down the untouched drink. She hurried out of the bar, giving Kent a quick wave at the door.

This was not the time to be making dates, no matter how cute the guy was. *What was I thinking?* At least he had her number and would call if he saw Stacy. That was a start. She felt bad about wasting two drinks, but she was feeling a bit paranoid. She found a phone booth and called home. No answer. Where to look? She started driving around town. She tried the other two bars they often went to. Nothing. It was getting late, and the only other place Stacy might be was a diner or fast food restaurant. She struck out at both and called home twice. Nothing. Discouraged, she broke her rule of not smoking in the car yet again and headed home.

She pulled into the dimly lit parking lot and found Stacy's parking place empty. She was still hopeful that she'd see her tomorrow since they both worked at the same mall. Maybe Stacy had met the guy of her dreams. It was all Lynn had to go on.

No one had been in the apartment. She changed quickly and got into bed after setting her alarm, but she couldn't sleep. She didn't feel safe in her own apartment. She grabbed her blanket and headed to her car, passing Stacy's cat on the way in. If someone was coming for her, she'd see them from the car. She tilted back the black vinyl seat of her rust-orange Chevy and stayed alert, watching the darkness. Stacy would make fun of her for acting like this, if she were here:

"Oh, my God, Lynn. Waking up next to a dead guy is creepy, but sleeping in your car? Seriously? Aren't you overreacting just a bit? I mean, do you really know if the dude was even dead? Maybe it was some sort of joke."

Lynn shook her head. *What I wouldn't do to hear Stacy's voice right now.* She stretched out and pulled the blanket tighter. She had seen enough Alfred Hitchcock movies to know that trying to do the right thing didn't always pay off for the good guy. In fact, it seemed to get them into more trouble, and if Stacy were there, Lynn would have pointed that out to her. And yes, the dude had been dead, for sure. Well, maybe Lynn had done exactly the right thing, and now she was lying in her car, afraid to sleep in her own bed. Tears flooded her eyes, and she fell into an exhausted sleep.

THE EVILDWEL WAS BORED SITTING in a car outside Lynn's apartment in the shadows. Her host had been so sure the girl wouldn't leave the apartment again, but he still kept a watch. Dian was about to encourage him to leave and find more interesting things to do when the girl appeared. Her host spoke out loud, almost startling Dian.

"Going somewhere? Not in your PJs and carrying a blanket."

Yes, Lynn had managed to surprise Dian, and she was glad for her host's insight. She watched Lynn settle into her car seat and fall asleep. At least she was afraid. Fear and anger traveled through Dian like a human orgasm. She could feed on those for eternity, and humans were so adept at providing them.

Sleep well, Dian thought. Her red eyes glowed brightly in the darkness, and her smile was an open door into nightmares.

CHAPTER 4

*L*ynn woke to the bright rays of the sun. Her eyes were still filled with sleep as she rushed back into her apartment. She breathed a huge sigh of relief when she saw that no one had been there during the night. All she had time to do was run a comb through her tangled brown hair and twist it into a bun, throw on some clothes, and head out the door. No time for breakfast or coffee. It was going to be a long day.

She was booked nonstop all morning. She didn't even have time for lunch and kept herself going with some coffee from the employee lounge and a couple of packages of stale crackers someone had left behind. In between clients she glanced at the door, hoping to see Stacy walk in or take a seat in the reception area to read a magazine as she waited for Lynn. Finally, she had a break at three. She hurried to Stacy's store and found a guy working in the juniors' department.

"She was a no-show. She does that again, she's fired," the guy told her.

"This isn't like her. She's been missing for two days."

"Probably met a guy. You know how she is." He winked.

"No, I do not," Lynn replied, storming off. She lit a cigarette outside to calm down.

She needed to call Stacy's family and check with the police. What if Stacy was involved, somehow, with that guy she'd found shot next to her? *Doubtful,* Lynn thought; but what about the guy Stacy had met? What if he was crazy? What if she was hurt and scared somewhere, and no one knew? Her mind was reeling as she took the last drag from her cigarette.

People were going in and out of the mall like everything was normal. She watched a couple holding hands cross the always-full parking lot. He pushed her against a car's passenger door, and they kissed passionately. *Afternoon delight,* Lynn thought automatically. She wished Stacy was there to sing a line from the song. Her off-key voice, which usually made Lynn cringe, would have been as welcome as the voice of an angel.

She was all alone in dealing with a dead body and a break-in. Stacy had picked a hell of a time to go missing. Lynn hated to admit it, but that guy working Stacy's department might have been right about her. She could very well be off with Dapper Dave, thinking she'd found the man of her dreams. Still, it wouldn't hurt to at least check in with Stacy's parents. She played with the dime in her smock pocket.

"Hi, I was wondering if Stacy is there."

"Oh, hi, Lynn. No, I haven't heard from her in a couple of days. Was she supposed to come by?" Stacy's mom asked.

"Oh, well, I thought she said she was stopping by after work. And I…um…we had planned to go out. I guess I misunderstood. She might have meant next week. Sorry to have bothered you."

"Oh, no bother. Yes, she is supposed to come over next week for her sister's birthday. It would be lovely if you both stopped by anytime. Bye, dear."

"Bye, thanks."

Lynn felt some guilt at not telling Stacy's mom that she hadn't seen her. But she couldn't say there was a good chance that her daughter had gone home with a guy and hadn't shown up at work because she was having the best sex of her life. The only other thing Lynn could think of was to call the police and the hospital, but she was out of dimes. She'd finish work and go home to do that.

The last hour of work seemed to take forever. She smiled and laughed in all the right spots as she cut and styled hair. She only came away with four dollars in tips, even after putting some effort into being pleasant. Staying quiet and cutting herself was the trick for more tips, she decided.

As soon as she got to her empty apartment, which she deemed safe for the moment, she began her calls. No one fitting Stacy's description had been admitted to the hospital. There was no report of her car being in an accident. She tried to report her friend missing but was told that Stacy hadn't been missing long enough. She wondered if it would have made any difference if the police had known she was the one whose apartment had been torn apart—but not Stacy's room. No, that would have made her look like she had done something to her roommate.

Lynn needed something to calm her nerves. There were a couple of beers left in the fridge and half a bottle of vodka from a party a few weeks ago. She didn't bother with a cup, just took two long gulps, the way she'd drunk from a Tupperware container while walking to school. This usually made it easy for her to forget all the bad things in her life, and it had made her suicide attempt at age fourteen relatively easy. She shuddered, thinking how close to death she'd been. How simple it had been to drink herself into an eight-hour coma using her parents' well-stocked bar. It wasn't something she was proud of, and she barely thought about it anymore, but it was always there, in the back of her mind. She knew she'd been lucky to get this second chance in life, and maybe her current lifestyle wasn't the best way to live it. But waking up next to a dead guy? That was a good reason to have a drink. She took a long swig.

She paused a moment, staring at the bottle. It wouldn't kill her, only numb her. But she needed to find Stacy. She set the bottle down, wariness firing through her body. Why did she feel like things were only going to get worse? *How could it get any worse than waking up next to a dead body, having your apartment broken into, and not being able to find your best friend?* She didn't want to know the answer to that. Instead, she retrieved Stacy's pipe from the kitchen cabinet behind the cereal. There were a couple of hits left in it. Lynn held the second hit in as long as she could, but nothing was taking away that feeling that something bad was about to happen.

"So now what?" Lynn asked the empty room. She began to pace, feeling like she was going to explode. She had to do something—anything. She headed into Stacy's room to see if she could find anything helpful. *Nothing.* The room was just the way Stacy had left it. Frustrated, Lynn sank into the brown tweed couch and burst into tears. It was like a dam had broken. She'd spent so much time worrying about her friend that she hadn't even dealt with the dead man or the break-in. It all poured out of her until there were no tears left. She wiped her eyes and took a deep breath, stretching out on the couch. Exhausted, she fell asleep.

"Knock, knock."

She wiped her eyes and yawned. Did she dream a knock? She waited. Nothing. What if it was Stacy? She hurried to the door and threw it open. No one was there. She must have been dreaming.

She hadn't slept long, but she almost felt like herself. Thanks to the vodka and pot, she had relaxed for the first time in days. She glanced at the clock in the kitchen—time for the local news. She flipped on the TV. There was a familiar driver's license photograph on the screen. She quickly turned up the volume as all her calm poured away and fear replaced it.

"Todd John Smith's body was found yesterday morning in his San Leandro apartment after an anonymous tip. The victim had been shot twice at close range. The police found an undisclosed amount of drugs and cash in the apartment. We learned he was a suspect in a drug-related investigation. Neighbors declined to talk on camera but expressed shock. The police are asking anyone with information to please call this toll-free hotline."

Lynn stood up and turned off the TV. "You've got to be kidding me. I woke up next to a dead drug dealer? Maybe I should call that number and tell them what I know." Lynn picked up the phone and started to dial the number she'd just seen on the news, but there was a knock at the door, and it wasn't a dream this time. She hung up and flung open the door. It wasn't Stacy. It was her stepbrother, Warren. *What a time for a visit.* She pasted on a fake smile and let him in.

Warren quickly made himself comfortable. He declined her offer of drink or food, which was good because she really didn't have much to offer and he tended to hang out with a wealthier crowd. Their old apartment wasn't his style, she knew. *Just make small talk,* she thought as she sat next to him. Could she trust him? After all, they'd been raised in the same dysfunctional house for seven years. They'd seen the same things and suffered at the hands of the same parents, but she hadn't heard from him in a while.

"Things going okay, Lynn?" Warren asked as he surveyed the room.

"Yeah, I'm doing well. You?" she replied, almost sighing.

"I saw your mom and my dad today. They said they hadn't heard from you in a while. So, well, you know, I thought I should see if everything's okay." Warren smiled brightly.

"Well, you know why I don't like to see them," Lynn said.

"I sure do. I was right there with you, only I got out of there sooner. I feel like I haven't kept in contact like I should. You know, going to prison changes a person. I don't ever want to go back. Stupid of me to try to make a fast buck, but I was just trying to get away from our parents, like you. Ya know?" Warren never stopped moving, like a cornered cat trying to escape its tormentors. Prison must have done that to him.

"I understand. Those people, though—didn't they lose their business?" Lynn asked.

"Yeah, they did. I feel bad about it and told them so. I think they forgave me. I mean, I really didn't mean to hurt them, and they moved on to a more successful business. I thought I could double it, you know, and then pay them back and get ahead. Like I said, it wasn't the smartest thing I've done, dipping into the company funds like that. My only excuse is I pretty much left home with just the clothes on my back, you know. But I'm the first to admit I was stupid, and I plan to pay back every penny I owe them. Besides going to prison, which I totally deserved, I lost contact with you. So I plan to be here for you from now on. Have you eaten? We could go out." Warren finally looked Lynn in the eyes.

"I…well, I guess I didn't support you much when you got arrested, either. I mean, I could have contacted you. I focused on moving out and taking care of myself. I wasn't sure what to make of what happened. You know our parents; they haven't said nice things about you. They said there were others, including them…"

"Yeah, well, that's understandable, right? I mean, I did end up borrowing some money from them to try to pay back the money I owed, but that didn't work out so well. But the past is the past now, and I tried to pay them back. They won't let me, you know, because it all went to my court expenses. But the important thing is that I'm here to try to make it up to you. And you know our parents didn't exactly treat either of us well. At least we're all in different places now. Like I said, I've changed and learned how important family is—even a messed-up one. I want to be there for you now. Dinner?" Warren offered his most charming crooked grin.

He'd been popular in school. Tall, with black hair and movie-star good looks. The girls practically swooned when he swam. "He has the bluest eyes," Lynn heard more than once, but it wasn't his eyes that got the most comments. The swim meets had been exciting, but toward the end, she was the only family member in attendance because their parents were too busy. Then Warren turned down a college scholarship because he didn't want to swim his way through school, but Lynn knew that doing homework wasn't his strong suit, either. Someone always made sure his work got done in high school, and she doubted he would have the same help in college. So he went to work and ended up in prison when his paychecks couldn't keep up with his lifestyle. Now here he sat in her living room, as confused and screwed up as she was.

"Well, I'm glad you learned your lesson and want us all to get along, but you understand it's hard for me to deal with them now unless I have to. I haven't been able to put all that, well…you know… behind me yet. As for dinner, I'm supposed to meet a friend."

She wasn't sure why she was lying to him. Habit? He appeared to be sincere, and she was starting to believe him. Prison would change someone, for sure. Could she trust all the things her parents—especially her stepdad—had said about him?

"Don't mention his name again. He's an effing crook. He used a lot of people. Understand?" her stepdad had said, widening his crazy eyes.

She'd understood and never brought him up again, so it was weird to hear that he had been visiting them and all was okay. Her stepfather couldn't hate his only son as much as he claimed to, or it could be more of the usual divergence between what he said and what he did. All of that made sense in her mind, yet something was holding Lynn back from completely embracing her stepbrother.

"Wanna bring your friend along?" he asked. "I just got paid. Making good money in sales."

"Oh, no, thanks. It's our first date, and that would be kind of weird."

"I see." Warren grinned and looked around. "You know, your mom and my dad have more money than they know what to do with. Let them buy you some new stuff. Spruce the place up."

"It's their money, not mine. Besides, I like my things."

"Oh yeah, you're right, of course. I was thinking about all they put you through. I think you deserve some nice things is all I'm saying. How about dinner tomorrow, or lunch? What's your schedule? You're still doing hair, right?"

"I work all day. Maybe dinner would work. Can I call you tomorrow?"

"Sure, little sister. Here's my new number. I live in a nice house in the Oakland hills. I rent the cottage in the back, and I get to use the tennis courts and pool. You'd love it. You can use the pool anytime you want." He smiled and winked.

"Okay, I'll call you. I'm glad you came by." Lynn forced a smile. *Maybe*, she thought.

"I am too. Well, I'll let you get ready for your date. And Lynn, I may have a great job offer for you. This guy I went to school with, well, his family is loaded. They're doing a lot of traveling and need help running a lucrative import business. I can't believe how lucky I was to get this gig, handling all the important details. We'll talk about it all later and what position you'd be suited for. I want to get your advice on a business opportunity I was offered. You know, help me think it through."

"Uh, yeah, sure," Lynn said. A small worry surfaced. Business opportunity? Had he changed? But he seemed like he really wanted to help her. She was too overwhelmed to figure it all out.

"Good. Just know, Lynn, that I thought about you a lot in prison. I wondered how you were doing and if you were okay. I know it was harder on you growing up, with Dad's anger issues and your mom's lack of, well, concern, I guess, but I see a change in them, ya know? Now that they're getting older, well—they're mellowing. Besides, I'm here for you now, even if I wasn't then. Your big brother is going to take care of you. We were all we had growing up in that house— remember that. You're always safe with your big brother around." Warren awkwardly hugged her goodbye.

"Thanks. I'll call you," Lynn replied, almost tearing up.

"Let me get your number, just in case you forget to call me," he added with a wink. After he got her number, he was out the door.

After being an only child most of her life, gaining a brother when her mother remarried was a dream come true. When Warren and her stepdad fought and he left the house for good, she'd given up on him along with the rest of her family.

Now here he was, right when she needed someone the most. Maybe she could share her problems with him. She wasn't sure yet. It was hard to trust people. She couldn't tell her parents about waking up next to a dead person. They'd probably help her, but the mind games wouldn't be worth it. Her grandparents had died last year, so she didn't have them to turn to like she used to. That left her with the stepbrother who'd just come into her life again. She watched him walk away. He turned and waved.

When she shut the door, a book fell from the shelf. She bent to pick it up. *A Is for Alibi*, by Sue Grafton, the book Stacy was reading.

"Lies!"

"What?" Lynn asked an empty room. There was that voice again, or maybe it was the TV upstairs.

The phone rang, startling her.

"Hello?"

"Lynn? It's Kent."

"Hi, Kent. Did you see Stacy?"

"Uh…no…sorry. I, um, was calling to check in and hoped to hear she came home."

"I haven't heard from her. I called her mom and her friends and checked her work, the hospital, and the highway patrol. No one has seen her. I'm so worried!"

"Maybe you should call the police. Report it," he suggested.

"I can't report it until tomorrow. I tried that." Lynn paced back and forth, tethered by the phone cord.

"Well, I work tonight, but if you need help looking for her, I'd be happy to help you. I mean, if I can find someone to take my shift. Patty might do it again."

"That old guy didn't look like a Patty to me," Lynn interrupted.

"What old guy? Patty is a woman. She helped get me the job, in fact," Kent said.

"Gus, the guy who made me a really watery drink right after you left. I didn't see a woman behind the bar."

"How strange. We don't have anyone working there named Gus. I'll ask Patty about it tonight. Hope it wasn't some customer playing around and collecting some extra cash." Kent laughed.

"Oh, yeah, that would be weird. Makes sense now. I wish I knew…" Lynn stopped talking and pacing. She sank into her chair at the kitchen table. She wasn't ready to admit that she had no clue what had happened after that drink. *Can I trust anyone at this point?*

"You wish you knew what?"

"Oh, that I knew where Stace is. I guess I'll try looking for her again. You'll call me if you see her?"

"Of course. And Lynn, everything is going to be okay. She and that guy probably just hit it off and lost track of time. Not to sound mean or anything, but she didn't seem like the smartest—no, that isn't what

I wanted to say, but she seemed, well, like she'd really like a guy for, well, his money or something and not worry about anything else." Kent stumbled through his words.

"She is smart, and I've never had a better friend than her. She'd be worried if she didn't know where I was," Lynn insisted. She stood up and started pacing again.

"I'm sorry. I don't mean to judge her without really knowing her. It's just, well, my mother was like that. A good woman, but she trusted the wrong man who had a nice car. All his fake promises, and now, well, it's me taking care of her *and* him—when he bothers to come home." Kent paused. "I don't mean to add my issues to what you're dealing with, Lynn. So please keep me updated, and I'll check back with you tomorrow. And I'm sorry if I upset you. Please call me if you need anything."

"I will, thanks. People don't get Stace, but she has a heart of gold and has always been good to me. She's the one person I really trust in this world, so…" Lynn's voice faded as she stared at her friend's room. She felt her chest tighten.

"Understood. I'll watch for her here. Bye, Lynn." Kent hung up as soon as Lynn said goodbye.

Lynn wasn't sure how she felt about Kent after that conversation. He claimed to want to help, but he was wrong about Stacy. And as for her stepbrother, maybe she should have gone out to dinner with him. *Tomorrow,* she promised herself. Tonight she was going to shower and look for her best friend.

Lynn let the warm water run over her. Usually, she found it soothing, but now the water falling from the showerhead was too loud. She'd hoped it would wash all the racing thoughts from her head, but it wasn't helping. She lathered in the apple-scented shampoo while trying to piece things together, hoping they would make sense at some point. Lists had always brought clarity to her in the past, so she started making one in her head. She hoped it would work this time.

One, someone named Gus served me a drink around midnight, possibly drugged.

Two, no memories until I went to bed at two.

Three, woke up at 7:00 a.m. in an unfamiliar place.

Four, found I had been sleeping next to a dead guy.

Five, found a gun and wiped my prints off it.

Six, left without calling police.

Seven, called the police later and reported a murder anonymously.

Eight, Stacy is missing—and so was my button.

Nine, someone broke into apartment. Called police.

Ten, found two bullets and my missing button in my bed.

Eleven, dead guy on news—was a drug dealer.

Lynn rinsed the shampoo from her hair and added a thick cream rinse.

Twelve, went back to bar and talked to Kent, who was at the bar that night. Nothing.

Thirteen, called the police, hospitals, and friends to find Stacy. She was a no-show at work.

Fourteen, Warren showed up. Trust him?

Yeah, that about covers it. Oh, apart from hearing voices, which kind of sounds crazy. Lynn sighed as she rinsed her hair. She lathered herself with Ivory soap, rinsed off, and wrapped herself in a fluffy brown towel. Time to write the list. She was going to figure this out.

THE EVILDWEL WATCHED as her host followed Lynn from a safe distance in his car. They even went into one bar with her unseen. Lynn was clueless because of her host's new disguise as a bearded biker. Lynn drove past three other bars, two fast food places, two movie theaters, and some houses her host didn't recognize. She wasn't going to find her friend by driving around.

Finally Lynn returned home. Dian wasn't going to waste another night watching her sleep in that horrible orange car.

* * *

LYNN STILL COULDN'T BRING herself to sleep in her bed since her home had been violated. She felt she might be done with beds for the rest of her life. She headed out to her car again and settled in. She wrapped her arms around herself as the tears began to flow. Finally, a cigarette calmed her down, and she fell into an exhausted sleep.

She awoke as the sun was peeking over the horizon. She stared out the car window at Stacy's cat cleaning herself on the faded wooden fence. She needed to leave her more dry food and check her water. There had been enough yesterday. Princess Leia moved freely in and out of the apartment through Stacy's window, which had a bar on it to prevent it from being opened more than a few inches. Too bad that precaution hadn't stopped someone from entering their apartment.

Lynn dragged herself out of her car, feeling like she hadn't slept, and cautiously reentered the apartment. She carefully measured the coffee to add to Stacy's new coffeemaker. She made a pot for two, out of habit. *Might as well drink it all; it's going to be a long day.* For all she knew, she'd end up in jail. While she waited for the coffee to brew, she flipped on the TV to catch the early morning news.

Again she was greeted with the face of Todd Smith, which was quickly replaced by that of the guy Stacy had been dancing with.

"The police are now looking for Mr. Smith's roommate, David Robert Thomas, as a person of interest. He was last seen with an unidentified blonde at a local club the night of the murder. He was driving a blue '83 Blazer, license plate SKIER2U. Please call the hotline on your screen if you have any information. Find out—"

Lynn snapped the TV off.

"Oh God, it was connected," she whispered. "The guy Stacy was with is missing too. What are the chances the two guys were roommates? Where are you, Stacy?"

The phone rang.

"Hello?" Lynn answered, hoping her friend would be on the other end. But she wasn't. No one was. The line went dead. Lynn shivered and gently hung up the phone. There was that evil feeling again.

* * *

GOOD, *Lynn's up.* She urged her host to hurry. *Don't want to miss a thing she does today. Wonder if she has any clue yet? Doubtful,* Dian thought smugly.

* * *

LYNN POURED herself a cup of coffee and drank it black. It made her stomach feel like she'd drunk a cup of motor oil, so she poured a bowl of Quisp cereal and made some toast with peanut butter. "Breakfast is the most important meal of the day. It jump-starts your brain," her grandma used to tell her.

She attempted to wash down her dry cereal with coffee. She gave up after two bites and ate her toast instead, polishing off the entire pot of coffee. Her brain didn't feel any more awake as she stared at her list, now neatly written out. She carefully added, *Fifteen, dead guy and Stacy's guy, roommates. Connected.*

Yeah, they were roommates—so what? That didn't help her find Stacy or understand why Todd had been killed. Lynn realized she wasn't going to have any aha moment that neatly solved the mysteries. She covered her face and groaned. Good thing she was a hairdresser. She made a horrible detective. She turned her attention to Princess Leia, who was chasing a fat, red-breasted robin outside her kitchen window. As the bird flew away, Lynn realized she wasn't going to be able to erase the images of what she'd seen. She knew what she had to do. She got dressed, put on her makeup, and threw her tangled hair into her old standby bun. She was ready to go to the police station. Even if they threw her in jail, she was going to tell them what she knew.

All she had to do was call in sick to work. That call never went well for her, and this time was no different. Her boss sighed loudly. "I suppose we could spread around your clients. It *is* one of your lighter days, but this is the last sick day you can use this year."

"I know. I'm sorry," Lynn squeaked out in her best sick voice.

"Yeah, well, your station doesn't pay for itself. Most hairdressers don't get the luxury of having sick pay, like you do."

Lynn had already stopped listening. As soon as she hung up, she grabbed her purse and was ready to go; but her keys weren't hanging on the kitchen hook. She was about to check under her bed when someone knocked at the door. She almost didn't answer, but what if Stacy had forgotten her key? She threw open the door.

"Hey, little sister. Good thing I decided to drop by and see if you wanted to eat breakfast before work. You left your keys in the door," Warren said, holding them up and grinning.

"I've been looking everywhere for them. I swear, I never do that," Lynn said, taking the keys back.

"Well, no harm, I guess, since you're okay. Just be careful in the future. Like I said, breakfast? You don't have to be at work for two hours, right? I mean, I only know that because I have an appointment with you later to get my hair cut. I hope you don't mind. You don't, right, little sister?"

"You called? Well...I mean...I'm not...I called in sick..." was all Lynn got out before the tears burst out. Before she knew it, Warren had her sitting on the couch, and she found herself telling him everything that had happened over the last couple of days.

CHAPTER 5

"It's gonna be okay, Lynn," Warren said, with his arm around her. "I'm here now. I won't let anyone hurt you."

"I was on my way to the police station when you knocked," Lynn admitted.

"Let's think about that action for a moment. I know how these things work. Let's look at it from the law's point of view. You withheld information from them, especially when your apartment was broken into, and you left the scene of a murder. I could see them thinking that you might be guilty of something. If something, God forbid, happens to Stacy—well, what could they conclude? I mean, it would be easy to think there had been a falling-out with Stacy, and perhaps you two were doing something illegal, and, well, it went bad. What if someone thought you were, let's say, scamming men for money? And it went wrong—which could explain you waking up next to a dead person. Your roommate is missing, and the guys you were both with were drug dealers. See where I'm going with this?"

Lynn nodded. He made it sound bleak.

Warren smiled gently. "I don't want you to ever have to see the inside of a jail cell because someone made a wrong assumption about you—or your connection to me. I'd feel bad that they might think you're a screw-up like I was. I have to tell you, not everyone in prison is guilty, you know. I mean, I was, but sometimes you can be in a place at the wrong time, and that's your issue here. What do you say we go to breakfast and figure this all out? Come on, grab your purse." Warren offered her his hand.

"I ate some toast already—and I still think I should tell the truth," Lynn protested as she allowed him to pull her up.

"Yes, but doing so right away would have worked better for you. This is why we should talk this out more. Telling the truth is always the best option, unless it isn't. I may be paranoid after all I've been through, and you being my sister and all. And toast isn't enough for breakfast, but I can understand if you aren't hungry. Just have a cup of coffee." Warren guided her toward the door when the phone rang.

Lynn pulled away and rushed to answer, hoping it was Stacy. "Hello?"

"Hi, Lynn. I've been worried about you. Any news about Stacy?" Kent asked.

"No. I was on my way to the police station." Lynn looked at Warren, who frowned.

"I'm free this morning. Do you want me to go with you?"

"Oh, no, my stepbrother is here with me now. We're going to have breakfast and then head over. Thanks for offering, though."

"Your stepbrother? Oh, well, if you have someone to go with, I, um…I would like to meet up later and talk."

"Yeah, I'd like that. I'll call you when I get back. If you aren't home, I know where to find you." Lynn tried to make a joke, but it fell flat. Warren signaled for her to hurry up.

"Okay, it's a date. It'll be okay. My uncle works at the police department. Ask for Detective Flagg. Tell him that we're friends. He's been like a dad to me, and he's a good cop. I'll see you later. Bye, Lynn."

"Thanks, Kent. Bye."

"New boyfriend?"

"No, just a good friend." Lynn grabbed her purse and hoped she was right about that.

"You can tell me all about that hot date you had. You know, the one that kept you from going out to dinner with your brother," Warren teased.

"You know there was no date."

She grabbed the list she'd made and stuffed it in her purse. It would help her think this through—she hoped.

"That I do." Warren double-checked to see if her door was locked. He seemed satisfied and led the way. "Come on, I'll drive."

"Coming," Lynn replied, glancing back at her apartment. She could've sworn she saw a flash of light in her window. She shook her head and followed Warren to his old Cadillac.

It was a quiet drive to the restaurant, without any discussion of the police or her phone call. They quickly found a parking space, and it wasn't long before they had pancakes and bacon in front of them.

"I want to go to the police station today. They need to know the connection and that Stacy is missing too," Lynn said as she shoveled fluffy pancakes drenched in syrup into her mouth. She would have enjoyed this meal on a different day, but now she wanted to get it over with.

"Yes, I understand you want to find Stacy. So do I. And that new friend—Kent, is it?" He paused, and Lynn nodded. "I understand that Kent wants to help you too, but maybe bringing others into this isn't the best idea. It's not that I don't trust your judgment—I do—but sometimes people aren't what they seem, ya know? In a perfect world, the police would solve the murder and locate Stacy. We both learned, growing up, how imperfect the world really is. I've seen how our legal system works, and they don't look too kindly on people who haven't told them the truth to begin with." Warren broke off and added a smile for the waitress approaching with a glass coffeepot. As soon as their cups were refilled, she hurried away. Warren looked at Lynn for a moment and shrugged.

Lynn added cream to the bitter coffee. "Yeah, I know it's bad that I didn't tell the truth right away, but I still think they'll understand that I was just scared."

"I understand you were scared, Lynn, believe me. I know you. The police don't. They deal with criminals every day. They will be suspicious, and there's a chance you'll end up in jail if you talk to the wrong cop. Don't get me wrong; there are many amazing cops, but there are a few bad ones too. They might want to close a case rather than pursue the truth. I can't take that chance with you, that we run into one of that kind of cop. You're way too important to me." Warren took a sip of his coffee. He grimaced and added a packet of sugar and two creams.

Lynn nibbled on her bacon. "I understand that, and I'm glad that you believe me, Warren. But Kent gave me the name of his uncle. I would be asking for him."

"Lynn, if we had time to get to know Kent better, I'd feel better about that. Perhaps I'm just being overprotective of you, but there's another thing you might not have considered. What if the bad guy finds out you talked to the police and decides your talking days are over? Sorry, sis, this is real life. I can't take the chance that you'll end up paying for a crime you didn't do." Warren stuffed the last piece of bacon into his already full mouth and washed it all down with orange juice.

Lynn shrugged without commenting. He might have some valid points, but she wasn't completely convinced. She pushed her half-eaten breakfast away.

Warren grabbed Lynn's hand and squeezed gently. He held her gaze. "I'm sorry I have to say this to you, but I learned a lot in prison, not only from other prisoners but the guards too. I had a lot of friends on the inside, and I'm trying to let you know how it works. What I could do is make a couple of calls, see what I hear. I'll give you all the facts, and then you can make up your own mind. All I ask from you is that you hold off on your visit to the police station until I talk it out with a couple of people I know. You know, get some advice before you do anything. Deal?"

"Well, I don't think I should wait, but an hour or two won't hurt, I guess, if you make the calls soon," Lynn replied.

"Sure. I can do it from your apartment, if you don't mind." Warren patted Lynn's hand and smiled.

"No, of course not. And thanks for the breakfast. It was good. This reminded me of our family Sunday breakfasts before you moved out —one of the few good memories I actually have. Remember?"

"Indeed, I do. This used to be one of my favorite places, so I thought…I was glad to find this place still in business. Still as good as I remember it too." Warren glanced at his watch and threw a twenty on the table. "Ready?"

"Yeah, I couldn't eat another bite. Thanks, Warren."

"You bet. Let's get you home, and I'll make those calls. We'll go from there." Warren winked at the waitress, an older blonde.

She beamed back at him. "Thanks, hon!"

He rolled his eyes at Lynn and pulled out his keys.

Outside her apartment building. Lynn lit a cigarette and offered one to her brother.

"No, thanks, little sister. Those things will kill you. You should think about quitting soon. I haven't smoked for two years."

"Oh, sorry. I plan to, but this is so stressful."

"I understand. This is nothing you should have to deal with—wait; stay here," Warren commanded. He moved toward her car.

Now what? Lynn thought, taking a deep drag off her cigarette and throwing it onto the ground. She stomped it out with her tennis shoe and saw the problem. Someone had flattened all four of her car tires, and her car door was open.

"Are you kidding me?"

Warren looked inside the car and returned. "It's just the tires; your stereo is still there. I didn't see anything else missing or broken, but you should check."

Lynn passed by her flat tires. One had a knife sticking out of it. *How thoughtful to leave the weapon here for the police.* "Everything is here. You're right, Warren—but my tires? Why? And why did they leave the knife behind?"

"That's what worries me. Someone is sending you a strong message. I can't let you stay here anymore, Lynn. It's not safe. You're going to pack up some things and stay with me until we figure this out. First, let me check out your apartment before you go in—you never know. The key, please."

Lynn wordlessly handed over her keys. She waited at the door while he went in. It seemed to take forever, but finally he poked his head out and gave her a thumbs-up. "All clear. Pack up while I make those calls."

"Okay."

She pulled out the blue American Tourister luggage she'd gotten when she graduated high school. The commercials had shown that it would survive a gorilla throwing it around; now it had to survive someone flattening her tires and tearing apart her apartment. She decided to check on the cat first, while she listened to her stepbrother explain the situation over the phone. It sounded more like a movie plot than her life. She wasn't so sure she'd believe her own story.

"Here, kitty!" she called out the window. The striped cat observed her silently from the fence. "There you are! At least you're okay." Princess Leia didn't seem impressed with Lynn's observation and started grooming herself.

Lynn filled the bowl until it was overflowing. She knew from experience that Princess Leia would eat through the food bag if her bowl was empty—sometimes even if it was full. She topped off the water bowl, although the cat would drink from the toilet if the lid was left open.

Warren's voice caught her attention when it rose from a quiet whisper. "Yes, I agree with you on that. Thank you, I will. See you in a few," he replied and hung up.

She heard Warren dial another number. He repeated the information all over again while she threw some of her things into her luggage. This time, she noticed that Warren left out the identity of the person he was trying to help.

"No, no, just a girl I met at a bar. Yes, I suppose so. No, not likely.

That's what I've been thinking. Well, good talking to you. We'll have to get together and catch up soon. Sure, bye."

"What'd they say?" Lynn asked.

Warren's face grew serious. "The consensus was that you avoid the police for now, but I'm going to meet my ex-cop buddy for coffee. He might want to personally escort you to the station. He needs to make sure he understands the situation fully before he commits to that. Don't worry, he's a good guy. I met him way back when I was young. He just retired, but he's been there for me all the way—even in prison. The other guy I called shared a cell with me for a while. He was one of those who went to prison without committing a crime. I wanted to get both sides for you. He was completely against you talking to the cops. That was his mistake—reporting a crime after the fact. Anyway, the ex-cop thought you'd be safe here if you locked your doors and windows. I'm not so sure about that. I'd feel better getting you to my house first. But there's no time, if I'm going to meet him. Maybe I should cancel—"

Lynn interrupted. "You should meet with him. I'll be fine. I have no problem staying here a bit longer. I promise that I'll call the police if I sense any danger. Besides, even if I can't report the tires being slashed, I can certainly call road service and get my car towed to the tire place. That way, I'll have a car once we figure this all out. I already feel better now that an ex-cop is in the loop." Lynn tried to sound more confident than she really felt.

"Well, I'm not so sure about this. I know I said I'd call around, but I didn't think I'd have to meet anyone. But if you think I should…" Warren frowned.

"Yes, I think you should. Then I can decide, once we have more information."

Warren nodded on his way out. "Lock your door, please."

Lynn did, and then she called to get her car towed. It would happen within the hour, she was told. As soon as she hung up, the phone rang. It was Kent.

"I'm not sure what I'm doing right now," she admitted. She felt so tired suddenly.

"Why? Has anything more happened?"

"My brother is helping, but he had to leave. Well, he didn't have to, but, well, I'm trying to wrap my head around everything. I want to go to the police, but maybe I shouldn't, because…well…right." Lynn yawned. "I think I should take a nap. It's been a long—"

"What?" Kent interrupted. "Where is your stepbrother?"

"I need to sleep, Kent. I'll fix the car later…I'm so tired."

"What? Car? You don't sound right, Lynn."

"Nothing…night." She put her head down on the cool kitchen table.

"I'm coming over," he insisted and hung up.

How did he know where she lived? Had she told him? She could have. Her mind was so foggy she was finding it harder and harder to think. *All this stress.* She closed her eyes as the phone slipped out of her hand.

"Lynn!"

"Huh? What…Kent?"

"Shit! You scared me!" Kent said, setting her down on the walkway outside her apartment.

"Why am I outside?" Lynn asked, sitting up. Her head was throbbing, and her stomach hurt.

"I knocked on your door and smelled gas. Your door wasn't locked, so I came in and found you slumped over the table. I called for help after I got you outside. You have a gas leak. I'm going to open all your windows." Kent helped her up.

Lynn felt dizzy. If he hadn't come by—someone wasn't just warning her, they were trying to kill her. "I need to sit a moment."

"Yeah, good idea. I'll be right back. Just take some deep breaths. They should be here in a moment."

"Who will be here?" Lynn asked, but Kent was already in the apartment.

She glanced around, feeling like she was being watched. Was that someone out there feeling disappointed that she wasn't dead yet? Or should she be worried that the door wasn't locked? She was positive it had been. So either Kent was lying, or—and how did he know where she lived? She shook her head to clear it. She heard a siren. The next thing she knew, she had an oxygen mask on her face and paramedics examining her.

"You're lucky. You got out in time, but you need to get checked out at the hospital, miss," a paramedic named Chad informed her.

"I don't think I need to go," Lynn protested. She returned to breathing in her mask.

"She okay?" Kent asked. "She was breathing when I found her."

"Yes, that's good. She should go to the hospital and get checked out," Chad said.

"I'm fine. The dizziness has gone away already, and my stomach is settled. Did you find what was leaking?" Lynn asked before she took another deep breath of oxygen.

"Yeah, your gas line to the stove looked like it had snapped in half—weird. I turned it off. So it isn't leaking anymore, but you won't be cooking until they fix it. Come on, let's get you to the hospital."

"I'm not going in an ambulance. I'm fine. I'll get checked by my own doctor."

"You sure, miss?" Chad asked. "I have to recommend that you go with us."

"I'm sure."

Chad glanced at his partner, who had been standing quietly and watching. "I'll handle it, Chad." He headed for their vehicle, which reminded Lynn of the old show *Emergency!*.

"Well, okay, but I don't recommend this," Chad repeated.

"I understand."

"I'll keep an eye on her and make sure she's okay. The hospital is only five minutes away if I need to take her there."

Chad told them what to watch for, gathered up his equipment, and said, "All other responses have been cancelled, which includes the ambulance. Are you okay with that, miss?"

"Yes," Lynn replied. Chad frowned and left.

Kent sat next to Lynn. "Are you really okay?"

"Not really," she replied and burst into tears for the second time that day. Kent put his arm around her and held her until the tears ran their course. "Sorry. I'm not usually a crier, but it's been a bad couple of days."

"No problem. I'm glad I was here for you. If I hadn't shown up…"

"I know. Thank you. But, um, how did you know where I lived?"

"I…um…I live down the street. I noticed you pulling out of your parking lot yesterday. I know it sounds like I'm a stalker and all, but I promise you, I'm not. It was a good coincidence that saved your life. I figured out the apartment because I knew your real name. If I had been looking for an Andrea, it might have taken longer to find you. Also, I'm pretty sure it's your car that has flat tires."

"Oh. Well, it would have been less creepy if you'd just told me that you lived down the street, but yeah, I'm glad you got here when you did. And yes, I know I have four flat tires. The tow truck is on its way. Like I said, it's been a bad couple of days. My apartment was broken into, my tires were cut, and my gas line snapped, like you said. Maybe that was an accident, or not, but everything started after I left the bar." Lynn quickly caught him up. She felt her face turn red when she got to the part about waking up next to a dead guy. His face was expressionless.

"So all you remember is consuming a drink prepared by a man named Gus, and then you woke up next to a guy who had been shot? The roommate of the guy your roommate was with. They're missing, and someone is messing with you."

"Yes. I even wrote it all down." Lynn stood up and went inside the apartment to get her purse. For some reason she needed him to see it. She swayed a little, and he came to her side to help. "It's a habit I have, making lists. Helps me think things through." Lynn felt her face grow hot as she handed him the paper.

Kent quietly studied the paper. He looked up at her with no judgment in his eyes. She felt relief, although she wasn't sure why she cared what he thought of her. Well, yeah, she had to admit she did care. He smiled, and she felt safer.

"Thank you for showing me this. We'll figure it all out, I promise. I do understand why you freaked out and ran. I have no idea what I would have done if I was in your situation." Kent touched her shoulder.

It felt like his hand was going to leave a burn. He quickly removed it and looked away. She noted that her skin was unmarked. "Yeah, well, it's not anything I had planned for. Never seen a dead body before."

"I'm sorry this happened to you, Lynn. I'm glad you reported it, but you've gotten mixed up in something that's bad. I believe you, and I think the police are your only option for sorting it all out. I disagree with your stepbrother, although I understand why he might not trust the police. I do know someone you can trust. I assume you trust me—after all, I got to read your list." Kent grinned.

Lynn looked into his deep brown eyes and felt like she could get lost in them if circumstances were different. Tears filled her eyes again and threatened to spill over. Did she trust him—and did he really believe her? The moment grew longer, and the silence became heavy. She turned her face up to his and stroked his cheek. "Yes," she whispered as their lips met tenderly. His arms wrapped around her, and the kiss intensified until Lynn forgot about everything but that moment. She felt secure until he pulled away from her.

"I'm sorry. I shouldn't have done that right now. I mean, I wanted to, but it wasn't the right time. The kiss, though—it was definitely right." Kent's face reddened.

"It was right, and it was the first time I've felt safe in the last two days. You save my life, then that kiss—wow." It was the only thing Lynn could think of to say, and she suddenly felt very awkward.

"Wow is right. But you should probably drink some water, and I still want you to see a doctor. Then I'll take you to my uncle."

"I don't need a doctor, and you may be right about talking to your uncle. Warren is talking to an ex-cop right now. I should wait for him. He did say he'd take me to the police if that was what I decided. I don't know how he'll handle the fact that I told you what was going on. He's being very protective of me."

"Well, having a protective brother isn't a bad thing, but I am not leaving you alone," Kent insisted. He wandered into the kitchen.

"I would prefer not to be alone, thanks." Lynn's heart was still beating fast, and it wasn't from the gas. Good thing the gas had cleared out, or the sparks between them after that kiss could have blown the place up. Kent was right, though. Now wasn't the time to be fooling around; she needed to find Stacy.

"Drink this," Kent told her, handing her a glass of water.

"Thank you."

"Sometimes you gotta say, 'What the f*ck?'"

"Yeah, that applies." Lynn grinned.

"There I go again—another movie quote. You have a strange effect on me, Lynn, but I like it."

"I saw that movie. *Risky Business*, right?"

"Yup."

The moment grew uncomfortably quiet. Lynn expected Kent to kiss her again, but the opportunity passed when Warren arrived.

"What happened? Why are the windows and door open? You were supposed to keep everything locked up. Who is this?"

"Hello, you must be her brother, Warren. I'm a friend of Lynn's—Kent." He extended his hand, and they shook quickly.

"The gas line broke. If it wasn't for Kent, I might not be here right now."

"What? You're kidding me! I need to get you out of here now. I'll grab your luggage, sis—and thank you, Kent, for saving her. I owe you."

"It was nothing. The paramedic suggested she get checked out at the hospital, though."

Warren's eyes widened. "You had to call them? Yeah, maybe she should."

"Or maybe she shouldn't," Lynn spoke up. "I'm fine now."

"Well, you aren't fine here." Warren had her luggage.

"I have to agree with that," Kent said. Warren scowled.

Lynn gently shook her head at Kent and thought maybe Warren shouldn't know that Kent knew everything. He might get mad. Kent raised his eyebrows and played along. "I don't mind taking Lynn to the doctor, Warren."

"I've got it, thanks, Kent. I'm very glad to have met you. I hope we can meet again in the future. Now, though, I think family should take over. Come on, sis. Let's get you settled in."

"I'll call and check on you later. You have a number you'll be at, Lynn?"

"It's a new number; I don't have it on me now," said Warren. "Does she have a number to call you?" Lynn frowned. Warren clearly didn't trust Kent. He had already given her his number.

"She does," Kent confirmed.

"Okay, then, let's go." Warren grabbed Lynn's arm and guided her outside. He waited for Kent to follow them out and locked the door behind him. Warren checked it several times, which didn't make sense to Lynn since they had left the windows open. Kent winked at her before Warren turned his attention on him.

"Hey, Kent, how did you get into the apartment? I mean, I know she locked the door after I left."

"The door was open, Warren. Very lucky."

"Yes, very lucky."

Lynn started to worry. Should she have trusted Kent or made out with him after telling him everything? What if the door had been locked? Perhaps this was a ploy by Kent to get her to trust him.

"Call me later, okay?" He smiled at her, causing Warren to scowl.

Kent's smile melted away her doubts. She smiled back. "I will, and thanks again."

"Yes, thank you, Kent. She'll be fine now." Warren's expression changed quickly into a smile.

Kent hurried off, glancing back once. He looked as confused as Lynn felt. She waved.

"Nervous guy, but I'm glad he was around for you. I hope we don't find out that someone tampered with your gas line too. I'm worried for you. Maybe I should take you to a doctor. I have a good one I could call. Better than some old ER."

"No, don't bother. I feel much better. The headache is gone."

"Well, Lynn, I'll keep an eye on you, for sure. I want you to rest. No police today. My friend advised against it, anyway. Said they'll figure it all out without your help. But if you feel better telling them, I'll take you tomorrow—after you rest. Deal?"

"Deal. But the tow truck driver should be here soon."

"I'm not waiting around for them, sorry. I'll come back later and get it towed for you, sis. All I want to do is get you to safety." Lynn agreed and followed him to his car.

CHAPTER 6

The drive seemed to take forever as her stepbrother rambled on about nothing. At one point he opened his window and sprayed some smelly cologne toward her. She took a direct hit on her nose and mouth, which felt oddly numb afterward.

"Oops, sorry. I didn't mean to spray my cologne right in your face. I was watching the road, but there was this girl I met who smoked in the car. Just trying to get the smell out." He smiled at Lynn cheerfully.

"Uh, sure. No problem," Lynn replied, wiping the droplets off her face with the back of her hand.

She tried to open her window, but it wasn't working. The cologne smelled like ant spray, and it made her eyes water. She winced. His taste in fragrance had declined a bit since his time in prison. *This isn't a classy smell at all,* she thought, yawning. A moment later, she dozed off.

"We're here, sleepyhead." Warren shook her gently. "Safe and sound."

"Oh, I didn't mean to fall asleep." Lynn rubbed her throbbing head and noticed that her car window was open. *Weird.* She remembered trying to open it, but maybe the switch only worked on his side. No matter—at least the smelly cologne was gone.

"You needed it after today. You'll like the cottage. It has two bedrooms, both with full baths. No sharing for the rich," Warren joked.

Lynn forced a smile. They were behind a large brown house, near the pool. She saw a tennis court off to the left. The place looked like a resort. There were buildings next to the tennis court—a garage and maybe a shop of some type. She would love to investigate the grounds when she felt better, but she needed to lie down.

"Pretty amazing place, huh, sis?" Warren asked as they turned the corner. The cottage was as quaint as an old painting and completely hidden from the house and street. *If you didn't know it was here, you wouldn't find it,* she thought. It seemed like a safe place to be.

"Yeah, like something out of a fairy tale, although I doubt I look like any princess right now."

Warren ignored her lame attempt at humor. "It certainly is, sis. This way—watch your step with these stepping-stones."

"I should have left a note in case Stacy comes home. Maybe I should call and see."

"Well, I'll take you up to the house for that later. I discovered that my phone wasn't working this morning. They're supposed to come fix it today, which was another reason why I didn't give the obviously lovesick boy my number—even if he did save your life. I mean, right now, we can't trust anyone; right?"

"Lovesick? Really? We're just friends." Lynn couldn't make eye contact. *Guess we didn't play it off as well as I thought.*

"Everyone needs friends, huh? Anyway, good thing I dropped by this morning, what with my phone problems and what happened to you with your tires and gas line. At least someone was there when you needed them. Maybe I should have shown more gratitude to that Kent, but I admit I'm feeling protective, my little sister. So sue me."

"Yeah, well, things have been weird. I'm glad you showed up when you did." Lynn's head was felt twice its size. "Maybe I should lie down for a bit. My headache is back."

"See, you need to rest more. Maybe you should see a doctor if you aren't feeling better when you wake up. Then we'll talk more, little sister." Warren smiled so wide it almost looked unnatural.

Lynn wasn't sure why, but he reminded her of the big bad wolf. "I should probably let Kent know I'm safe."

"Yeah, after you rest. He knows you're safe with your brother. In fact, I'd like to call and thank him. Of course, it's understandable how shocked I was about the gas leak, but there is so much more he doesn't know. Better that way, ya know?" Warren paused and studied Lynn for a moment. She was able to keep all her underlying emotions off her face. That seemed to satisfy him. "Just give me his number so I can call him. I'll let him know you're resting but doing well."

"Don't!"

"What?" Lynn asked before realizing that it wasn't Warren who said that. It was that voice again. Maybe she really did need to see a doctor.

"Kent's phone number. I'd like to call him," Warren said, an edge of irritation creeping into his smooth tone.

Lynn hesitated. Hearing things or not, she didn't want him to call Kent. What if he ruined any chance of them getting together later? "I, um…oh no, I don't think I packed it. How dumb of me. Sorry. I don't know it by heart. Maybe we could go back and get it later?"

"Sure, later." Kent opened a wooden door with a stained-glass rose in the middle of it. "Come on, follow me. You're gonna love this room."

"Danger!"

Lynn felt a chill run through her body, even though the voice reminded her of the robot from *Lost in Space* when it would say, "Danger, Will Robinson!" What danger? This cottage? It was probably the first safe place she'd been in the last few days, yet all she wanted to do was leave, like when she'd found the dead body. But she was safe with Warren, right? *Just feeling a little paranoid with all that's happened,* she thought. *But still.*

"I think I should—" Lynn started to protest, but Warren interrupted.

"I think you should nap. You're exhausted." he grabbed her arm firmly.

"Yeah, sure."

Warren led her into a beautiful room decorated in rose prints. Any other time, she'd have been impressed by its beauty, but right now she was in panic mode. That voice had warned of danger. The one thing she'd learned over the past couple of days was that when this voice warned her, it was always right. If she hadn't gone back inside for the last drink, she wouldn't have been drugged. If she had called the police at the dead guy's apartment, who knew what would have happened? And the button and those bullets in her bed—maybe that was a warning for her. And now her stepbrother. Were they both in danger? She realized how crazy it would sound if she told him, so she kept it to herself.

"Isn't this perfect? Since I've been here, I've imagined you staying in this room. I know how much you loved roses as a child, always watering them and picking them. Now here's a room filled with red roses." He spread his arms wide. "Lynn, everything is going to be okay from here on out. You're safe here with me. No one will find you. Now you should get some sleep. Oh, you can smoke in here—there's an ashtray in the bedroom. I only ask that you don't smoke in the kitchen. I hate the smell when I'm trying to eat, ya know? I'll bring you some tea like Grandma used to make. It'll help you feel better." Warren spoke like he was trying to sell her on this, and he added a smile. She felt cold and scared inside, but she forced a smile in return.

"Tea sounds good, and the cottage is beautiful. Thank you for being there for me. My head is feeling better. I think I might have gotten carsick, like I used to do as a kid. But I, um, well, I need to pick up a couple of female things from the store. You don't mind if I borrow your car, do you?"

Warren's smile grew even brighter, if that was possible. "Sure, no problem! Right after you rest. I have a couple of errands to run, and when I get back, you can go if you still need to. Deal?" He paused for a moment, and Lynn nodded. She could see that his smile didn't reach his eyes. She wasn't going to win this argument. Satisfied with her response, he grinned and continued. "Besides, there's everything you need right here, even female items in the bathroom. Food in the fridge, spare bathing suits and towels if you want to swim. But right now, lie down. After all, you almost died."

Lynn sank down on the soft, silky bed, trying to clear her mind. That nap in the car had made her feel groggy again, like she had felt in her apartment. Maybe it was an aftereffect of the gas leak. Maybe Warren was right, after all. She was just being silly. She kicked her shoes off and stretched out on the full-size bed. It was like settling into a feather-filled nest. Wishing that her lumpy bed at home was as nice this one, she took a few deep breaths and relaxed into her surroundings.

A knock on the bedroom door interrupted her moment. Warren entered without waiting for a reply. "Glad to see you lying down. Here's your chamomile tea. It's just like Grandma used to make us when we couldn't sleep. I added some lemon and lots of honey, like she used to do. Drink up and rest. I'll be back before you know it, sis."

"Thanks for making me some tea, but I'm fine. I slept in the car. Could I go with you?" Lynn sat up. She took the tea from him and set it on the white nightstand. Warren must not have remembered how much she hated chamomile tea. She preferred peppermint.

A frown crossed Warren's face for a moment, and then the smile reappeared. "No, this is a work-related thing that won't take long. Try my tea. You'll like it. I mastered brewing tea when I was dating a girl from England. That was all she drank, in fact. She ended up being not my type—too clingy." He returned his attention to Lynn. "If you aren't feeling better when I get back, I'll take you to my doctor or wherever you want to go. Although I doubt you want to sit in an old, stuffy office when you can heal here, right?"

"Yeah, I guess I could take a quick nap." Lynn sat up and lifted the teacup off the nightstand. She swirled the tea around to cool it.

"Good. There's nothing to worry about—it's just you and me. Very private. Only a housecleaner, gardener, and a pool guy to keep the place up. Luckily, today is everyone's day off, so no one will disturb your rest. I won't be long. Drink up. Bye!" Warren shut the bedroom door behind him.

Lynn sat on the bed, holding a cup of tea she didn't want and trying to appreciate her surroundings. It was like a room on TV, only she didn't want to be there and had no idea where *there* was. There was no working phone here, Warren had said, so she couldn't call Kent and check in. Unless she shouldn't be trusting Kent. She was confused and felt kind of silly about not giving Warren his number.

She listened for the front door to close. The fog in her mind had cleared away, along with her headache. She didn't want to rest anymore. She tried to take a sip of tea, but the bitter smell made her put it down. It didn't have that licorice smell she associated with chamomile and seemed even more repulsive. *Warren isn't as good at making tea as he thinks.* He probably added too much lemon and not enough honey. Or maybe it was old or something, who knew? She lit a cigarette instead. That would calm her nerves more than any tea. Maybe she was overreacting to everything now. She wished she had Stacy to talk to.

"This is some friggin' crazy shit!" Stacy would say. And she would have dragged Lynn to the doctor and then to the police department. What would Stacy say about her hearing voices? Lynn had no idea, but not knowing if she could even trust herself, how could she trust Kent or even Warren?

Time to figure a few things out, she decided. She carefully dumped the tea down the bathroom sink and washed it out. She didn't want to hurt Warren's feelings about his smelly tea. Then she put the empty cup back on the nightstand. She was ready to investigate. First, she needed to figure out where she was, and then she would talk to the police. She rinsed off her face in the flowery bathroom—she could still smell that cologne—then reapplied her makeup and slipped on her shoes.

Ready to go, she tried to open her bedroom door but found it stuck. She couldn't get out. This wasn't right. Had Warren locked her in? She checked the two windows and found they had bars on them. There was no getting out that way. Why would a place like this need bars on the windows? She tried the bathroom and found a window too small to climb out of. In a panic she tried the door again, pushing as hard as she could. This time, it flew open with a snapping sound. She found a broken wooden piece on the floor by the jamb. It looked like a piece of trim. Had Warren jammed it into the door, or did it break off and wedge itself?

"You're freaking out, Lynn," she said aloud, attempting to reason with herself. "And rich people would want to protect their property with bars on the windows. After all, this isn't a part of the main house. And aren't rich people cheap? So part of the door breaking off makes sense."

Maybe it was all a strange, huge coincidence. *Or maybe a dead guy is a good reason to freak out,* she thought. The kitchen was peach with copper accents. It was a place where she'd love to learn to cook, but at the moment she needed a clue as to where she was. She checked the phone. It was dead, like Warren had said, so he wasn't lying about that. She saw several keys hanging next to the fridge; one set was labeled Main House #1.

"Why not? He did say that phone worked." Lynn grabbed the keys and headed out the front door, which her brother hadn't bothered to lock. That didn't line up with the barred windows, but maybe he felt she was safe there.

She hurried down the gray stone path, noting that his car was gone. So he'd left on errands, like he'd said. She wasn't sure why she was questioning Warren's motives, but she was. His absence gave her some time to figure things out. The winding pathway was edged with gardenias, azaleas, and roses and followed a tall red-and-green hedge. The path ended at a brown house with neat white trim. It was at least three stories tall, with a dark wooden front door that had an orange stained-glass hibiscus in the central pane. Small red roses overflowed from two terra cotta pots. She doubted that Warren would have the keys to the main door, but she tried anyway. *Nope. Must be to the back door.*

She circled around the house on the perfectly cut lawn and tried the plain white back door. *Bingo!* She hoped no alarm would be triggered when she entered, since the owners seemed to be security-conscious. She glanced around the entry but didn't see a keypad. Worst case, the police would come, and she wanted to talk to them anyway.

From the rather plain back entry, she stepped into a pristine white laundry room. There was a sink and a small table with a white basket on it and three neatly folded white towels. A laundry chute was next to that. Outside the laundry room, a long hall led to a large dining area. It was done in a tropical theme, all bamboo and yellow. The table's centerpiece was a burst of yellow, orange, red, and purple fake tropical flowers in a vase striped in yellow and orange. The table looked like it could seat more than twenty people comfortably in bamboo chairs with yellow velvet pads. *Imagine all the parties they must have.*

She wandered into another room that held three full-size pinball machines and a Pac-Man game that she considered playing, but then she found what she was looking for: a bamboo phone booth. *Cute.* It even had a wiggling hula girl next to it. She picked up the phone.

"No dial tone," Lynn told the hula dancer and set the phone back in its yellow cradle. "Just for show, I guess, or all the phones are out of order." The hula girl kept dancing.

Lynn found a push-button phone in the huge, white-tiled kitchen. No dial tone. All the phone lines must be down. How had Warren not known? Or had she misunderstood what he said? There were too many misunderstandings going on for her comfort.

Right off the kitchen was the front entry. It was even more amazing from the inside, tiled in green, with a potted palm reaching up to the skylight. But the sunken living room, overlooking an Olympic-size pool with a slide and diving board, was something she'd only seen in magazines. There was no phone to try in this room, but there was a brown leather wraparound couch. The walls were covered with shelves of VHS movies, CDs, and albums. A projection TV that had to be forty inches wide stood next to a regular TV in a wooden cabinet with a VCR player on top of it. Lynn had seen something exactly like it last week at the mall and knew this setup cost more than she'd spent on her car.

Next to all of that was a stereo system that had a state-of-the-art CD slot right above the record player. There were two large speakers that she was sure sounded amazing. Lynn couldn't imagine changing the channel without getting out of her chair, listening to music in here, or watching a movie anytime she wanted to. Her parents had had a projection TV like this in their house. They always had to have the best and newest stuff, even if they lived in a simple, middle-class neighborhood in a house the size of this room and the kitchen. They'd always liked their things, including their 1950s house and their well-stocked bar. She'd been lucky to escape from that house, and now she was escaping to this amazing one.

She shook her head to clear it. She didn't want to take a trip down memory lane just then and didn't have time to admire all the electronics. She could see a pool table next to a full bar in the next room, so she checked in there for a phone. There was another big couch, a TV, and a VCR with a tape of *The Sound of Music* on top. She loved that movie and always made sure to watch it on TV every year. She couldn't imagine being able to watch it any time she wanted. *Wow, how some people live!* The phone on the bar wasn't working. No surprise there, but on the wall behind it was a plaque stating that it was Bob's Bar.

Okay, the owner was named Bob. That was a fact that could help her approach a neighbor so she could ask to use their phone. In areas like this, they wouldn't mind letting Bob's "niece" use their phone. Under the plaque was a framed photo of a smiling, well-tanned family, labeled *Tropical Trip 1976*. The man, who she guessed was Bob, was tall and lean, maybe in his sixties, with gray hair, standing on a boat—no, more like a yacht. His expression reminded Lynn of someone, but whom? Beside him was a beautifully groomed blonde who was at least twenty years younger and more than likely the so-called trophy wife. Lynn hated that term. Why didn't it apply to a guy who married a rich woman? There were two kids: a tall, handsome teenager wearing red shorts and a smirk and making rabbit ears behind the head of a bikini-clad blonde who looked like her mother.

"The perfect American family—yeah, right." Lynn smirked back at them. Nothing was ever that perfect, but people did say that money could buy happiness. *Maybe, at least seven years ago, it did—who knew?*

Her gaze shifted to the shelves filled with all kinds of booze. They wouldn't miss any of it. She didn't bother with a glass, just took a quick shot straight from a fancy bottle of scotch. *Time to meet the neighbors.*

"Yeah, good old Uncle Bob," she said as the smooth whiskey warmed her insides.

Lynn relocked the back door and headed in the direction of where she remembered entering with Warren. She found the black iron gate, but there was no way to open it. She didn't see any houses from where she was. Maybe she could climb the fence and look. Right then, she saw a car approaching. Warren was back already? She raced down the driveway, trying to beat him to the cottage. She heard the gate open as she turned the corner. She sprinted through the door, put the keys back onto their hook, replaced the small piece of wood by the door-jamb, and closed her bedroom door. She threw herself on the bed just as she heard the front door open and pretended to be asleep as someone entered the bedroom. Warren stood silently over her for a moment. He picked up the empty teacup and shut the door quietly behind him.

She opened her eyes but didn't move. She felt like she was being kept away from everyone, but that was crazy. Wasn't he trying to keep her safe? Then why had she run from him? Pure fear—had to be, after everything that had happened to her. And a gas leak too? Kent had rescued her after Warren left, which meant Warren was the last person there before it happened. Why hadn't she thought of that until now? She shuddered. If she had only told the police the truth in the first place. *What a mess this is.*

Finally, she heard the front door close and footsteps, on the gravel and then the stone pathway, moving away from her. She carefully opened the bedroom door and saw a note:

. . .

Hope you had a wonderful nap, sis, and are feeling better. I had to grab some papers for work and checked on you, though you were sound asleep. Something came up at work, and I won't be back until late tonight. Sorry. Make yourself at home. There is leftover pizza in the fridge you can heat up in the microwave. They have Showtime on the TV and lots of movies to watch in the bottom drawer. If there is any emergency, or you feel like you need a doctor, feel free to use the phone in the main house. Keys are in the kitchen. Love, Warren

LYNN FELT guilty for not trusting him. She bolted out of the cottage to catch him and let him know all the phones weren't working. Breathless, she arrived in time to see Warren slide into his car, but her words caught in her throat when she saw someone in the car with him. Who was that? He looked old—and familiar. She wished she could get a closer look at him. Was he the retired cop that Warren had spoken of? She watched them leave. At least this gave her some time to explore the neighborhood.

* * *

"SHE ALMOST LISTENED to your warning this time, Zelina. Why was she thinking about a robot?" Thomas asked.

"*Lost in Space* was something she used to watch on TV as a kid. She would pretend the Robinsons were her family. She would dream about all the places they would go and things they would do together in outer space. Although the family was trying to get back home, at least they had each other. She realized even then how important that was and that she did not have it. And the robot used to warn the family when danger was present. We are kind of like that robot to her now. Hopefully, we are slowly getting through to her."

Thomas nodded. "I hope so."

Zelina studied him. "But we cannot control that."

"I know, but I can hope. If she started trusting herself, that would be a start."

"I agree. Not only does she not trust herself, she trusts no one, and success in this depends on her developing trust in someone rather quickly."

"Her excursion is not going to find any neighbors."

Zelina shook her head and pushed her hair behind her ears. "No. She is isolated but safe right now. Aside from being drugged, gassed, and everything else happening to her."

Thomas frowned. "Yes, exactly. I think we need to do more."

"More?" Zelina asked, crossing her arms.

Thomas treaded carefully with his reply. "This is frustrating for me, not being able to do anything."

Zelina's eyebrow went up. "This is not about you. This is about Lynn, and it is going to get a lot worse."

"I know, but, well, that is what I am worrying about. What you showed me."

"Yes, I understand, and it is right that you care. When Lynn finds out, she will have to act quickly."

"What if it is too late?" Thomas asked.

Zelina's expression softened. "I do not think it will be. She is clever and a survivor." She gently touched his arm.

"She will have to be. If he had his way, she would be dead." Thomas felt comforted by Zelina's gesture. He would have hugged her, but that would have crossed lines Zelina had clearly drawn for their working relationship over the last few years. Everything he knew and had used in his past was not appropriate in dealing with this angel. She was tough, but he knew there was more to her. Someday, maybe, they would cross the line and become friends. Zelina pulled her hand away. She could tap into his thoughts, but it was the truth, so he did not care.

Zelina smiled briefly before she wiped all emotion away. "I know, but she is not dead. It can go many ways. I see one outcome that works for her. It all depends on what she does next. Do you see that?"

"Well, I think I see what you are talking about, but I am not so sure about her freedom. It is pretty foggy to me." Thomas rolled his knotted shoulders. *The good side should not have to deal with this much stress,* he thought.

Zelina frowned and then looked away while stretching out her magnificent peacock-feather wings. Were they on alert? Thomas scanned the area but saw nothing different. Then, as quickly as the wings opened, they settled back down on her back, and he heard a loud exhale.

"Did something happen, Zelina?"

"No, no. I was stretching and thinking. I have an idea."

"I hoped you would." Thomas grinned.

* * *

THE EVILDWEL WAS PLEASED. Everything was falling into place. Tomorrow her host would be finished with this. Lynn wasn't as clever as she had first thought, but Dian wouldn't underestimate her, either. Ruining Plans A and B had only added to the fun of the kill. Her host smiled as he picked up the phone. Dian was enjoying his interaction with Gus too. His fear was strong, and it was only a matter of time before he tried to betray her host. But she would play with him for a bit. As her host spoke loudly into a phone with no one on the other end of the line, she watched her prey. Gus was buying every word of it. Yes, Gus believed her host was talking to their boss and just following orders. If he only knew. *Soon.*

* * *

"THANK YOU. Your compliments mean a lot to me." Warren hung up, smiling like a dog who had just been given a treat.

"He wants it all done tomorrow, Gus. 'All of it' were his exact words."

"It will be done, then," Gus replied with an enthusiasm he didn't feel. He didn't like working under Warren, but with their past, Gus hoped he could get through to him. Gus was losing that hope fast, however. Warren reminded him of a brewing storm that had been on the horizon building up strength and finally was pushing toward the shore. Gus felt as helpless as someone standing unprotected, watching it come. If it hit, his chances of survival were slim. His only hope was to remind Warren who he used to be. If that couldn't be done, heaven help them all.

* * *

A LIGHT, cool breeze was blowing, and Lynn wished she had a jacket. She had walked in both directions, and all she'd found were trees. It was like the house Warren was staying in was the only house in the world, or at least on that street. She didn't know you could get this much property in the Oakland hills. This Bob must really be wealthy. It was probably just one of his houses—and her brother had gone to school with his son? Sounded familiar, but she couldn't place it.

"No, wait!" Lynn declared to the old tree stump. "Warren had a rich friend who went to the Catholic school!" But she couldn't come up with a name, so she sat down and took in the scenery, including a small patch of orange poppies off to her left. It was beautiful and isolated. Any other time, she'd love being in such a secluded place; but now all she wanted to do was run into anyone.

She sat quietly, hoping the name would come to her. Finally, she started to remember. "It began with an R. Was it, um, Ryan? No. Robbie!" Lynn smiled. She'd solved the mystery. Robbie was short for Robert. He was named after his dad, but his last name? *Forget it.* When Warren had bothered to talk to her, he'd brag about his "rich friend." Until the day her stepfather overheard them talking—that conversation hadn't gone well.

"I don't want that riffraff in our house or around you," her stepdad had raged.

"But, Dad, Robbie is—" Then there had been a loud boom, and something had broken.

"I will NOT have criminals enter my house or YOU hanging

around with them. Having money doesn't cancel what they are. You are NEVER to bring this up again. Got it?" her stepdad had roared.

"You're wrong! They—"

"They're crooks! I won't have it!" her stepdad shouted. "I'll teach you to listen to me and not shoot your mouth off about things you don't understand!" Lynn heard the snap of the belt and things breaking.

"Stop, please! I'll stay away," she heard Warren cry. There was nothing she could do that wouldn't get both of them hurt. So she put on her headphones to block it out. It was nothing new for her stepdad to respond with violence. You didn't disagree with him. Warren knew better, and he'd paid for it many times over. Her mother was never anywhere to be found—unless her things might get broken. She would stand guard over those with a drink in her hand. She always had a drink in her hand at home, it seemed. Perhaps that was how she'd dealt with all that rage and anger, yet Lynn knew her mother had some issues of her own—including regretting having Lynn and marrying her father years ago.

She shuddered at those memories. There were too many of them. She knew she'd never forget the beatings or her stepfather's rages and the words that went with them. She had learned to make herself as invisible as possible at home, which worked sometimes. Nothing numbed her enough to completely get her past out of her head. Now Warren seemed to have finally made peace with that. How? Well, there was the money her mother had just inherited—not a lot, like these people, but enough to make them more than comfortable. Was that his motive, or had he really changed in prison? She wanted to believe in him, but what if prison had polished his skills?

At least her trip down memory lane had uncovered Warren's connection to the house: a rich kid named Robbie whose family her stepfather had declared were crooks. Her stepfather was crazy, but he could recognize a criminal. After all, his son fell into that category.

Lynn couldn't focus on her past anymore. She had her own issues to resolve that had nothing to do with her parents. She got up off the stump and brushed herself off. A eucalyptus tree towered over her.

Eucalyptus, oaks, and pines lined the road in both directions, along with a lot of shrubs, including poison oak, which she had almost stepped in. At least she had an incredible view of San Francisco Bay. She kept walking for another half hour and saw nothing—not even another car. It was time to go back. After all, how could she explain to Warren that she was wandering around outside the gate when she was supposed to be resting? She knew he'd be hurt if she told him that she'd begun to wonder about his motives. *I should trust him,* she thought. They'd both survived the same abusive household, after all. But she didn't. It was time to insist that he take her to the police.

She slowly walked back to the house, watching the sun set into the fog over the bay. It had an eerie orange glow that made everything around her seem surreal. Finally, she saw the gate and climbed over it. It wasn't long before she was back in the cottage, eating leftover pizza. She got tired of watching the door for her brother, so she sat on the couch and turned the TV on.

"What? Why is *Wheel of Fortune* on now?" Lynn asked. "Weird." She watched Pat Sajak spin the wheel and Vanna White turn the letters. She was fast at guessing the phrases, but she didn't get to see what the contestant won before she fell asleep.

She woke up to the smell of bacon cooking.

"You're finally awake, sleepyhead," Warren said, smiling. "I didn't want to wake you. I thought you could use the sleep."

"Yeah, I didn't even make it through the first show. Need any help?"

"No, no. I'm enjoying cooking for my baby sister. I made bacon, eggs, and toast. You want apple or orange juice?"

"Orange juice, please," Lynn said.

"Okay, it'll be ready soon. Why don't you take a shower?"

"Um, sure, thanks."

"You're quite welcome. We have a super busy day and, as Grandma used to say, we need to start it with a good breakfast," Warren said, a little too cheerfully.

"Yeah, she did."

Lynn was showered and dressed within ten minutes. If not for the alluring smell of bacon, she might have lingered in the large shower with its adjustable showerhead. She wasn't sure what to wear to tell the police about the murder. She chose her acid-washed jeans and a plain blue T-shirt, ran a brush through her hair, and added some eyeshadow, blush, and mascara. She finished the outfit with her pink-and-blue marbled tennis shoes. Kent's phone number was in her purse. She stuffed it into her pocket with her lip gloss in case she got near a phone. She was ready.

Her breakfast was waiting for her, but her brother wasn't. Again, he'd left her a note.

Had to run a quick errand. Will be right back. Enjoy your breakfast. Love, Warren

"Really? Couldn't wait for me?" Lynn sighed and dug into her breakfast. She couldn't finish her orange juice because it was so bitter. She dumped it out into the sink, cleared away her dishes, and then started yawning. She sat down and reached for the TV remote when the room began to spin and then disappeared.

* * *

Thomas wrung his hands together. "She does not see the whole picture yet, Zelina. I am worried."

Zelina stood over Lynn protectively. "Worrying will not help her. Remember that. But once she realizes who it is, it will be more difficult, but that is how it has to be."

Thomas positioned himself next to her. "I cannot help it sometimes. I know how I am supposed to think, but I cannot change my thoughts. I feel like she will be with us soon, and then that murderer will have gotten away with it. I do not like any of this." He frowned under Zelina's steady gaze. He thought he had gotten past acting like this, but he was really worried about Lynn.

Zelina wrapped her wing around the sleeping girl. "You have no control over a human who is engulfed in an evildwel. As for Lynn, we are doing what is best. You cannot see things as clearly as I can yet—

you will in a few years. It took me some time to master this skill. But you care about Lynn, and that is a bonus in this situation."

"I apologize if I talk too much about my feelings instead of focusing on what Lynn needs. That evildwel seems to enjoy playing with not only humans but angels too."

"You forget what evildwels do not understand."

Thomas studied his teacher. What did those creatures not understand? They knew how to ruin things and control people. *Oh!* "Yes, love."

"Exactly. Love is infinite. That is what I am counting on. Although one human is lost in an evildwel that is feeding off his fear, Lynn is not. So when she wakes up, we will be right next to her. Things will happen that we cannot save her from."

Thomas interrupted. "I know—free will."

Zelina nodded. "Yes, that is a part of it. A good thing in all of this is that Lynn's past addictions make her resistant to drugs."

Thomas almost flinched. "Her addictions are a good thing?"

"Yes. They built up her tolerance."

"Okay, I can see that, I suppose."

Zelina smiled. "Good. Right now, there is a chance for Lynn to walk away with Stacy. What they walk into, well, that depends. And the love part—we will see. As the humans say, the ducks need to be in a row. Then we will see if they can float."

"Ducks? Float? What are you talking about?"

"It means that Lynn needs to keep her head above water, not drown in the situation."

"Could you speak more plainly?" Thomas asked.

"I am just quoting the humans, and this fits what is going on. I am not saying Lynn will literally go underwater and die, but she needs to keep her wits about her to survive. You will see."

"I hope so."

Zelina pointed. "Look, there they are. They are moving her to exactly where she needs to be. Come on."

Thomas had a sudden insight. "Does this have to do with Stacy?"

"It does."

"An elevator in the middle of a bar?" Thomas asked as Lynn was carried into it.

"Yes. It goes to what is called a safe room, or a place to be safe. It is much more than that," Zelina replied, fully opening her wings. "Come on. I will show you."

"I am right behind you." Thomas spread his own deep blue wings.

"Of course. Where else would you be?" Zelina smirked.

Thomas smirked back, but she missed it. They followed the group to an area directly under the swimming pool. Thomas did not mind that his teacher preferred hands-on training to sharing information. It kept his interest and increased his knowledge, but he was not going to share that with Zelina.

CHAPTER 7

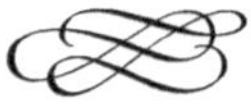

"That stuff sure worked fast, Warren." Gus accidentally bumped Lynn's head into the side of a wall.

"Yes, that's why I use it. Be careful with her. I want her in good shape so she can take everything in before…you know."

"Be careful? If you had your way, she'd already be dead from the gas leak." Gus wasn't sure if honesty was the best approach with Warren now. But it was all he had and perhaps this girl's best chance for survival.

Warren grinned. "Oh, well, that was improvising. Wouldn't have been an ideal ending, but it would have been an ending. Seeing her go to jail was the first plan, and then her suicide would have made more sense. Now there has to be a whole new storyline that people will believe. Leaving that ridiculous button and the bullets in her bed helped make our point. She's been running scared since. Besides, all one can do is follow orders."

Gus chose his words carefully. "Yes, following orders. Doesn't seem to bother you one bit, either."

Warren raised his eyebrow with a chilling smile. "You know me too well, Gus. I certainly can act bothered, but truthfully, I'm not. I'm not sentimental, as you know."

Gus took a deep breath. He wiped the sweat from his brow with the top of his arm and tried to reach Warren. "I do know, but remember, I was the one who took you under my wing before anyone else. You shouldn't have ended up in prison. You wouldn't have if you had stayed with me. But I still made sure you were taken care of inside and released early. You went back to the gig that landed you in the joint instead of coming to me. I hope you know what you're doing."

Warren's smile disappeared. "I'm not sure I'm enjoying your trip down memory lane, Gus. But as for this gig, I would say it found me. Just know that I never make the same mistake twice, and that includes working under you, Gus. I have no intention of ever going back to prison. I would say the tables have turned—I'm doing you a favor now by bringing you into my so-called gig."

"I understand that," Gus mumbled. His chest tightened, making it hard to get a deep breath. This wasn't going the way he'd hoped.

Warren stopped and slowly scrutinized Gus, making him feel small. He spoke softly. "You'd never want to be on the wrong side of me now, Gus, considering my education in prison and my new position. Loyalty has gotten me far. I even reached out to you to help you." Warren winked.

Gus looked down at the unconscious woman in his arms. "Loyalty is very important to me, and I thank you for thinking of me with this position. You know I've always been loyal to you since the moment I picked you up for shoplifting. I made sure you knew how to not get caught again. I understand that you want to move on and climb the ladder, but I don't want you to get in over your head again, that's all." He shrugged.

Warren shook his head and started walking again. "I'm grateful you helped that dumb, misguided boy, but I'm not that boy anymore. I paid back your so-called kindness many times over with your cut of my earnings, so don't think I owe you anything now. You only have this job because of your skills, not because of our past. And you, Gus, have a lot to prove to your new boss."

Gus shifted Lynn in his arms and nodded. His wife always said, "The road to hell is paved with good intentions," and that covered his relationship with Warren. Helping teens become better criminals wasn't his best idea, but it kept them out of jail and provided them with a living. And it increased his family's hidden assets, which was the goal. But none of those teens had become like this man in front of him.

What have I gotten myself into? Gus wondered as they entered a rec room with a pool table and bar. Behind the row of merlot bottles was a button that said Trash Disposal. When Warren pushed it, the wall slowly moved, revealing a door behind it.

"Everyone should have a room like this," Gus commented, changing the subject.

Warren turned to look at Gus with what could only be described as contempt. "I know I will. Must be built by people with short-term memories, if you get my meaning. State-of-the-art safe room with filtered air and plenty of amenities. Earthquake-proof, too. I will survive a nuclear war or anything thrown at me."

"How can any room be safe from the wrath of nature?"

"You mean the big earthquake they always talk about? No idea, but money can certainly buy you safety if you need it, I've found. Not worried, are you, Gus?" Warren's smile turned into a sneer.

Gus felt sweat drip off his nose and run down his chin, "Do I look worried? Lived here in the Bay Area my whole life. A simple earthquake doesn't scare me, but being a cop, well, you see a lot on the job." He hoped to remove that look of disdain in Warren's eyes.

"You were a cop, yes; but a real dirty one, huh, Gus?"

Gus didn't bother to answer. Warren was right; it was about more than just financial security for his family. He had habits that a cop's salary didn't cover. He wasn't proud of his sexual predilections, but he'd never involved his wife after she laughed at his suggestion to role-play and try some light bondage. "I already have two kids. I don't need anyone else to look after," was her only response. They became roommates after that, and he found his release at the hands of experts. His wife seemed happy with that arrangement, and it was never brought up again. He still loved her, though, and he felt like she loved him in her own way—or at least enjoyed the lifestyle he provided.

But that lifestyle and his sexual needs required money, and lots of it. He'd found a way to get by and provide for his family at the same time, but now his survival depended on a scared kid who had grown into the cruel man before him.

"I like your nonanswers; they speak volumes. And Gus, if I can be honest with you, as I always am—you are sweating quite a bit."

"This girl is heavier than she looks," Gus said, shifting the weight as the elevator stopped.

Warren winked. "I imagine she is. We're here."

The elevators doors opened on a long, lighted tunnel made of metal. "Looks like something out of *Star Wars*! You say you've known this family since grammar school?" Gus asked, trying to get Warren to admit what he already knew—what everyone knew.

Warren looked away. "Oh, no. I met them then, but I've always known of them. How could I not?"

"Uh, of course." Gus was worried that Warren wasn't confiding in him. His cop instinct was warning him of a threat, but he had no choice but to go along, since Warren was taking orders from the big boss—now his boss. Gus didn't like being involved with such a notorious crime family, but his savings had almost reached a level where he could move a long way from here with his wife and kids, maintain their lifestyle, and indulge his habits. He couldn't wait to fully retire. With the money Warren was offering him, this could be his last job. He just had to finish it to collect.

The tunnel sounded as hollow as Gus felt inside. It led to a locked door. Warren unlocked it, and they entered a large room. One wall was filled with surveillance equipment showing the grounds and interior of the house. To the left of that was a wall lined with enough canned food to last a family of four for years. Next to that were shelves of extra equipment, guns, and lots of ammo. The living area on the right side contained bunk beds, a treadmill, weights, racks of clothes, a fridge, stove, toilet, sink, and shower. More shelves were loaded with books and games.

Tied to one of the beds was the blonde who had been with Lynn at the bar. Which seemed like overkill because she was completely out, like the one in his arms—and in a locked room. He supposed it was to keep her from damaging the equipment or getting hold of one of the guns. Not that he expected either of these girls to know what to do with a gun if they did get one.

Warren was beaming at him. Gus shivered. Now that he knew about this room, would he be safe? He had to find a way to come out of this alive. He'd never been involved with killing innocent girls. Criminals, yes, but innocent girls, no. He would figure out another way to get through to Warren. He had to.

"She'll be out for hours. Just dump her on the bed next to her friend. Throw a rope around her arms and legs, just in case. We have a couple of things to take care of before these sleeping beauties wake up."

Gus tied her to the bed with some yellow rope. He left it loose around her wrists so she could move—if she woke up. He was proud of himself for showing a little kindness to this girl. That sort of made him the good guy here. His biggest concern was how shallow her breathing was.

"Done."

"Good. Be back tonight, girls. We have a midnight show." Warren blew them a kiss.

Gus shut the door behind them with a shudder. Warren made sure it was locked. Gus had to wonder why it was locked from both sides. It was more than a safe room.

* * *

LYNN'S BODY FELT HEAVY. Had she fallen asleep again after breakfast? She'd never slept this much in her life. There was a strange hum, and a musty smell assaulted her nose. She didn't think she was still in the cottage, and opening her eyes confirmed that. She was in a room she didn't recognize. She tried to sit up but found she couldn't move her arms and legs. There was a wall of TVs displaying the grounds of the house. On the camera on the lower left, she saw her stepbrother and Gus, the man who had served her that drink in the bar, get into

Warren's car and drive off. That was weird. What would her step-brother be doing with the guy who put drugs in her drink? *Duh.*

Sleep started to overtake her again, but she fought to stay awake. *Warren?* A part of her had always known it was him. She pulled hard, and the rope cut into her wrists, but finally, her left hand pulled loose. She untied her right hand and then her feet and surveyed the room. It looked like a fancy bomb shelter. It was no surprise that rich people would have that, but how was her brother involved in all of this? Was he the one who'd tied her up? Not that it mattered—she was officially kidnapped now. She'd trusted the wrong person. *What an idiot I am.* Was Kent in on it too?

"Why Warren?" Lynn quietly asked the empty room.

She wished the voice she'd been hearing would answer that question. One thing she did know was that if she didn't move, she'd fall right back to sleep. Whatever drug he'd used on her, she seemed to be getting used to it, if that was possible. It must have been in her orange juice. Luckily, she hadn't drunk it all because it was sour. She tried standing up, but the room swam and spun. So she sat back down, trying to breathe it out. She heard a small sound come from behind her.

"Stacy!" Lynn cried, stumbling over to her sleeping friend.

She was breathing, but Lynn couldn't wake her up. There was a plate under the bed with a half-eaten sandwich, so at least she'd had some food. Sleep kept threatening to overtake Lynn, and it would have been so easy to lie down next to her friend and let go. But she had Stacy to worry about now. She spotted rows of Pepsi cans on a shelf and downed one. *That should help. Now, how to get out of here?*

She saw the guns off to her left and formed a quick plan after trying the door. She could use a gun to shoot the lock and then run into the trees and they could hide until help was found. The question was who could she trust now? And was Warren responsible for the dead guy she'd woken up next to and the drugged drink, or were more people involved—like Kent?

"Great family I have." Lynn sighed.

Warren had been using her. That old story about how they grew up in the same house had worked on her. Being in prison had changed him for the worse, and she was his target now.

"Wait a minute!" Lynn said. "What if it had something to do with Mom inheriting money? Crap."

Stacy hadn't stirred when Lynn spoke out loud. She downed another soda, knowing their time was limited. She grabbed a bag of shelled peanuts and ate two handfuls. That would have to do to help her stay awake. *Gotta wake Stacy up.*

"Listen!"

"Listen to what?" Lynn peered into the room's dark corners.

"Then leave!"

"I don't plan on staying! What do you want me to hear?" Lynn asked.

There was no other response. It was the same voice she'd heard before. Was it the drugs? If not, what else could explain it? No time to think about the voices she was hearing—she didn't need to be told twice to get out of there. She shook Stacy. Finally, not knowing what else to do, she slapped her. Stacy's blue eyes popped open in confusion.

"Lynn! Your brother—he's crazy," Stacy said, trembling.

"He is. Can you stand? I've untied you."

Stacy spoke as if she hadn't heard her. "Dave took me to an empty parking lot where he met Warren. Warren stuck a needle in my arm without any explanation. Before I blacked out I saw him kill Dave. He smiled when he shot him and acted like he didn't even know me. It's like he's a different person, Lynn." She paused and glanced at the screens, which showed no one on the grounds. Lynn wondered if the command to listen meant listening to Stacy. Although she wanted to just drag her out of there, she let her finish.

Stacy didn't make eye contact as she continued, as if in a daze. "I woke up here. He brought me food and let me use the bathroom, and during those times he was very talkative. I know about that guy, Todd, he killed next to you while you were out cold from that spiked drink. Warren had a good laugh over that one. He hoped a neighbor would call the police. They didn't. His plan was for you to go to jail for that, because he made sure your prints were on the gun. I'm pretty sure he used your hand to shoot him too. You know, Dave and that guy both worked for him. I had some hope that you'd run when Warren seemed put out because you didn't call the police either. There's a phone behind the guns. He said it doesn't work. Please try it."

"A phone?" Lynn repeated, looking to where her friend pointed. She picked it up. "Shit, it's dead, Stace. Sorry. We have got to get out of here. Can you walk?"

"I think I can, but even if you have to drag me, Lynn, I never want to see Warren again." Stacy stood up and had to grab on to Lynn to keep standing.

"I gotcha. And so you know, I looked everywhere for you, I swear."

"I knew you would. I can do this," Stacy said, letting go and standing.

"The Force is with us, with all these weapons."

"Yeah, it is, Yoda. I've been eyeing them. Let's grab a couple and get out of here." Stacy steadied herself and rubbed her eyes.

Lynn smiled. "I'm glad you and your dad used to go hunting now. I wish I had gone."

"Yup, at least one of us can handle a gun." Stacy pulled down a handgun and inspected it. "They're already loaded. Here, take this one. There is no safety, so be careful. Don't point it at us, but if you need to use it, point and shoot like a camera. And remember, Lynn, it will have some kickback. Brace yourself when you use it." Stacy was pale but alert.

Lynn nodded grimly. "Only if I have to. You're the expert. Stace, I feel like we stepped into a nightmare."

"Yeah, I know, it does feel that way. Just know that I will not hesitate if it comes to shooting Warren. Too bad—I always liked him. I guess you never know." Stacy paused, turning a pale shade of green.

"I understand," Lynn started to say, but Stacy turned away from her and threw up.

Lynn wanted to help her but knew that getting them ready to go was more important. She grabbed a few supplies, including two bottles of water and more peanuts, and threw them into a backpack. Who knew how long it would be before they got to safety?

When Stacy was done throwing up, she grabbed some clean clothes off the rack. After washing up and using the toilet, she ran her fingers through her tangled hair and pulled it into a ponytail with an elastic she found in her pocket. Checking in a mirror above the sink, she rubbed off all her smeared makeup. *An encouraging sign,* thought Lynn. Stacy was getting back to normal.

Lynn watched the security cameras with some concern. Time was not on their side at this point, even though only a few minutes had passed since Stacy had woken up. *If Warren returns, we're armed now.* Stacy picked up her gun and stuffed some extra bullets into the pockets of her pink-striped black sweatpants. Her pink T-shirt looked like it had been purchased for the girl in the picture. It suited her. She stuffed the matching sweatshirt into the backpack.

"Ready?" Lynn asked.

"I am. Let's get out of here." Stacy slapped her cheeks like she was trying to add color to her pale face, but Lynn knew she was trying to stay alert. They both were, no thanks to Warren and his drugs.

"You lead the way," Lynn said.

"Remember to point and shoot, Lynn. If you miss, get behind me. I won't."

"Thanks, Stace, and once we get out of here, I think we should be quiet. I mean, just because we can't see anyone…"

"I agree. Stand back." Stacy aimed her gun at the handle. It only took her three shots to break through the lock. They ran down the hall and into the elevator. Within seconds they were running down the driveway. They hopped the fence, got off the main road, and silently headed into the trees.

They needed to put more trees between them and that house before they could relax. Who could they turn to? Lynn began to worry about how many people this rich family had under their control, unless—she didn't want to think about that part—unless they weren't alive. That was a possibility, with Warren involved. Stacy's family would be their safest bet. Lynn saw the gleam of determination in her friend's eyes, and it gave her some hope. Together they would survive. They kept running as the sun began to set. Two angels watched over them.

* * *

Thomas heaved a sigh. "I wish they were safe."

Zelina tilted her wings to dive closer. "It is still possible."

"I do not like this." Thomas glided alongside her.

"I do not like it either. Warren and Gus will be looking for them with all the resources of this wealthy crime family and the police they own. And there are all the innocent people we need to keep safe, like their families. We have some work to do," Zelina said grimly.

"And there is the evildwel." Thomas raked his hair back in frustration.

Zelina squinted at him. "That is what I am counting on to save these girls. It will not just want to kill them quickly; it will want to enjoy them—like an expensive meal."

Thomas held back a wave of anger that threatened to overtake him. "Why is it so focused on Lynn? Does it not have plenty of people around Warren to terrorize already?"

"Oh, yes, it certainly does. I cannot say why Lynn is its focus. I know it is not about money, but maybe it has something to do with that missing key that Warren's father has."

"A key to what?"

Zelina scanned the trees and responded with a shrug. "No idea, but I do know it is Roman. Maybe that thing is enjoying itself for no particular reason."

Thomas looked too, but he saw only trees. "That is what is worrying me. The evildwel's actions do not make any sense."

Zelina nodded. "I agree, which is why we do not try to understand them but work with our strength. This evildwel is making good use of Warren's mental illness."

"Mental illness or not, you would think that after growing up in the same house, he would feel something for her. Instead, he wants her dead, and that thing encourages him." Thomas shook his head. His shoulders were tense, and it was a strain to stay airborne with the weight of the situation bearing down on him.

"Yes, I know. Someday we may understand Warren's motives, but not in his current condition. I had hoped the parents would change. Maybe the mother will, someday. She would have to disengage from the bottle, and that is never easy."

Thomas felt some relief. "I have been worried this whole time that I have missed something. I am glad to hear you do not know, either."

"You have missed some things, but you see the situation pretty clearly. There is no explanation for hate that any angel understands. In the meantime we need to encourage these girls to find that pay phone."

"I wish we could tell her." Thomas scanned the area. It was all clear.

Zelina smiled and pushed her hair behind her ears. "Me too. Although I do believe the phone might have connection issues at times when she calls the wrong people."

Thomas smiled back at Zelina. "That I understand."

"Let us go and light the way," Zelina said as they carefully followed the two girls into the darkness.

When a small light appeared to Lynn, she followed it, and Stacy followed her. Thomas grinned. *Nice.* He was learning from the best, and he felt more hopeful again.

CHAPTER 8

"There, that oughta cover it," Warren said smugly.

"You can't pay off the entire department. Some of those men can't be bribed," Gus insisted.

Warren held his hand up. "Ah, but there are enough like you who need those extra funds."

"You didn't use to be like this." Gus immediately wanted to take those words back. When was he going to learn to shut up?

"I agree. Your training was subpar. But, luckily for me, I had someone whose interest was real."

"Your family didn't lift a finger to keep you out of prison." *Shut up, Gus.* Why couldn't he let the truth go and just ride this through? Why did he feel it necessary to get through to Warren? *Because the lives of those two girls depend on it, that's why.*

"You know nothing about what went on," Warren snarled.

Gus tried to control the tremor that moved through him. "Yes, I suppose I don't. Sorry, Warren."

Warren adjusted his green polo shirt. "I will accept your apology once again. I hope we are finally done with this conversation. You are no longer my boss. I answer to someone else now. You'll do the same, or I'll have to remove you from the picture. You got that?"

"Yes, buddy, I got it. I'd like to know who I'm working for, though." Gus lit a cigarette, hoping Warren would finally tell him the truth. The steely blue eyes looking back at him with contempt showed Gus there wasn't any hope of reaching the Warren he had known. He didn't exist anymore.

"I owe you nothing. And you know the rules: No smoking in my car. Put that out, and listen closely to me."

Gus crushed his cigarette in the ashtray, which was littered with several other butts. Warren was playing with him now. Gus swallowed hard and tried to smile. He wanted to shout at Warren, to make him give up the name of the person they were working for. It scared Gus that Warren wouldn't tell him.

Warren reached over and picked a small piece of lint off Gus's button-down shirt. It was short-sleeved, perfect for the warmer fall weather, but at that moment, Gus wished he was wearing one of his warm plaid winter shirts to counter the chill he felt from being near Warren.

"Thank you. Now, understand, all you need to know is you work *under* me. As for my family, you must mean my father, because the rest of my family is none of your business, fat man. My father is a drunken loser who gets up every day and goes to a job he hates. The only money he has—which I want—belongs to his wife. My father's a man who follows all the rules. He was a good soldier in the war and didn't cheat on his wife. His weaknesses are his temper and his drinking."

"I'm sorry you grew up with that, buddy."

Warren's eyes narrowed, and his shoulders tensed. "I paid for that weakness, let me tell you, but I do not require or encourage your pity. Remember that."

"I will remember. But what about your stepsister? I haven't questioned you framing her. But do you really need to kill her?" Gus knew Warren was hiding something more—something worse.

"You obey orders, or you might find yourself in the same predicament as those drug dealers. Dave and Todd were trying to make money on the side. Dumb move. Our boss is a powerful man, and

Gus, if you were really a good cop, you'd know who you were working for."

"Understood." Gus started cracking his knuckles, a habit he thought he had rid himself of. "And yes, I do know."

"Good. Then quit your silly game of trying to get me to say it. Your pathetic life could end at any moment if you mess up." Warren's eyes almost looked red in that moment, and Gus could have sworn there was a black mist swirling around him. He rubbed his eyes. He needed some sleep.

"I understand, and I will follow orders. But don't you feel bad for your stepsister?" Gus tried one more time. He knew he had gone too far when a wide grin lit up Warren's face.

"I feel nothing, dear friend." The words were cold and hard, making Gus's entire body tense. Warren nodded his approval and continued in a bright tone. "But since we have her friend, she'll do whatever I want. You'll see how much fun that's going to be. Maybe you could indulge your—how do I put this? How you find pleasure with the fairer sex?"

Gus turned bright red. How did Warren know about that? He had never told anyone. He shrugged.

"No response? Didn't think so. I wouldn't admit to being tied up and beaten by a woman for gratification, either. Well, as they say, to each his own. Now, back to the young women at hand. How they end up dead doesn't matter. As for my family, my dad is off-limits, but my stepmother isn't. Won't take much with her. A little extra something in her booze, and she'll be a goner. No one would question a drunk's death. And Gus, you mean less to me than my stepsister or stepmother. I don't want you to ever forget that."

Gus nodded, his mouth so dry he couldn't even swallow. He realized one of the women who serviced him had to be a talker. He paid good money for their discretion, and when he found out who it was, he would make her pay painfully. That idea did not make him feel the same excitement that his sessions brought him, but he felt an arousal that needed to be explored. That new feeling surprised him. Unfortunately, he had other things to worry about.

It unsettled him that these girls faced death no matter what he said or did. He would soon follow, the moment he was deemed unnecessary. All he could do was try to make himself useful until he and his family could get away. Next to him was a man who had snapped and embraced his inner psycho. Maybe that was who Gus had always been dealing with, and he just hadn't seen. Warren pointed, and Gus turned down a familiar street. "Your father's house?"

"Home sweet home. Don't worry, they aren't there. Down at the bar until no later than ten because, you know, it's a work night, and they can't stay until closing."

"I wasn't worried, but shouldn't we be keeping a low profile, buddy? I don't understand why we're here." Gus knew he wasn't getting through to Warren on any level. There was not an ounce of good left in him. Kissing Warren's ass was about all he had left.

"I have my reasons." Warren pointed to his chest.

"Of course."

"Here's the deal, and I'll give it to you straight. It seems like you need to understand about my stepsister, although I have no idea why she is so important to you, and that is concerning to me." Gus nodded impassively and waited as Warren held his gaze. "Why Lynn has to die along with her mother is because half of the money her mother inherited goes to Lynn. Half goes to my father, then me. Our boss wants me to use it to branch out in this organization. Can't borrow it and have debt, ya know? My lifestyle requires all the money I make, so this fits my needs. My father won't mind me removing all his extra funds for myself." Warren paused and laughed. It wasn't a happy laugh. "Besides, it'll be fun to see him broken and broke at the same time. Might help his disposition, don't ya think? Plus, it would make me happy and might make up for some of that trauma I suffered as a boy."

Gus responded carefully. "Yeah, I understand. Thank you for telling me. You don't have to worry about me, buddy. I'll tell no one."

"You'd better be telling the truth."

"I am."

"Great. But right now, old friend, we need to look for the key." Warren smiled and studied Gus's reaction. He managed to keep his face as blank as possible. Warren shrugged. "I said, a key that our boss wants."

"Yes, you're looking for a key, Warren. I'll help you."

"You don't sound really interested, but it's important, and it's a very old key. And my father has it. Odd thing is my old man ain't got the brains he used to, but he's managed to hide this from me. Could you imagine if he put it in a safe deposit box? That would be out of character for him, although I'm sure I could handle that too once I get him to myself."

"I'm sure you can handle him." Gus wiped his sweaty hands on his pants.

"That's right, I can," Warren said with a sly grin. "You know what an honor it is that our boss has asked me to handle this whole situation. Says I can do whatever I need to, although he was very insistent that these deaths happen by tomorrow. And you know loose ends are frowned upon. Just know our boss has wants that we aren't required to know about, including this key. Once this job is done, then we can get back to making money. I can see me being able to buy a mansion in, oh, two years. Can't you, Gus?"

Gus grimly nodded. He would do what he could to keep his family safe.

"I need you to make sure no one is around, if you know what I mean. Then meet me inside. I'm gonna try some new hiding places for the key."

"Done."

"I'll be waiting." Warren strolled away, whistling. Gus shuddered and started checking the perimeter.

"I GOTTA STOP FOR A MINUTE, LYNN," Stacy said, breathing hard and holding her side.

"'Kay. I think we're far enough. You see all the strange lights?"

"Must be reflections off cars somewhere. I think we're getting close to civilization again and away from psycho stepbrother." Stacy waved back in the direction they'd come from.

"I'm sorry he did this to you, Stace—"

Stacy shook her head. "Don't apologize to me about him. He ain't even your blood. Although he makes your parents look perfectly normal, doesn't he?"

"What if they're in on this?" Lynn asked, turning pale.

"Your stepdad is an asshole, but he isn't a killer. He's a mean drunk with some issues left over from being in the war. I've seen men like that before, but never anyone like Warren. It's like he enjoys hurting others. You gotta wonder about those neighborhood cats that disappeared when you were growing up. And all the pets you guys had that ran away, plus those two hamsters that vanished out of their cage? What if it was your stepbrother doing something to them? Sorry, Lynn, I can't imagine how you're feeling. We can rest a moment while you tell me everything." Stacy sat on a stump.

Lynn sat on the ground next to her and quickly caught her up on the events since that night at the bar. It felt good to be able to share all of this with her best friend. They made a plan to get to Stacy's parents and took off into the night, guided by a small light. Lynn didn't want to think too hard about where it was coming from, but it wasn't from any distant cars.

* * *

THE EVILDWEL GRINNED WIDELY. She loved the fact that Gus had got a glimpse of her. The fear in his eyes was delicious. Her host was filling her with pride and had been for the past five years. He was so much fun. Getting him his current job had extended that fun. While her host and that scared little man talked about boring things, Dian reflected on her achievements and possibilities.

The kill was always the high point for her, and this host was no different. One human taking another's life was perfection, although the small animals her host had enjoyed killing held her interest for a bit. Those acts had drawn her to him and showed her his potential.

Then there was the euphoria Dian felt when her host randomly killed a stranger, but he enjoyed it as much as she did. Killing his stepsister and her friend was going to be the sweet topping to all her host's terrible deeds.

The only irritation was those insects buzzing around her perfect recipe of fear and hate. There was nothing the angels could do to her personally, but they were always trying to prevent all the fear and anger she required. That annoying Zelina had been a bother for years. Once or twice, that green-winged do-gooder had ruined a plan or two by sowing some of that repulsive love.

Although Green-Wings couldn't take away her host, that angel had found ways to wreck Dian's carefully thought-out plans. Not this time, though. Not with that pathetic sidekick, Thomas, who had tried to confront a fellow evildwel, Aten. Dian's mist darkened contentedly, thinking of the absurdity of Thomas appearing to that human—as if he could protect it from Aten, one of the strongest evildwels. Angels were foolish and bothersome, but they were willing to clean up after her, much like any good servant would do, by taking care of her broken hosts after she was done with them.

Dian grinned, thinking of how Aten loved to tell the story of when Thomas had helped a human drive off a cliff. It always made her laugh. She had learned a lot from Aten over the centuries, and she was almost as strong as he was, but she chose not to absorb the hosts' souls like he did. He had an ongoing tea party with perfect evil, she had to admit, but it was not her style. Too much baggage—she liked to have fun and enjoy every moment fully. How her race disposed of their meals was a personal choice, but when it came to creating and feeding off a human's fears, she was as skilled as Aten.

Her centuries of wisdom allowed her to see how truly naïve angels were. They were always trying to change the basic makeup of human beings, even after death. Showing them the error of their ways—how preposterous that was! Humans were naturally bad. They didn't really need much encouragement and were there for evildwels much like a herd of cattle. Dian and her kind only fed on the best, the ones full of fear and anger. When they were done, they moved on, while the angels fluttered about any souls left behind, as though trying to make a meal out of a rotten apple.

Dian felt a change in her host's mood and switched her attention back to him. He was heading to his father's bedroom. Her black mist swirled in anticipation. Finally, her host would learn the truth about his mother, and she would feed on the first course of a decadent banquet.

* * *

"Hurry up and close the door, Gus, or you'll make the neighbors nervous."

Warren almost seemed playful, like his old self, but Gus knew better. "I didn't want the people in that car to see me sneaking around a dark house. I wanted to come in like I was invited; otherwise, I'd look like a burglar, ya know?"

"You look more like someone's grandpa than a burglar. Might wanna lay off all that fast food. You carry your weight like a pregnant woman."

"Ha! My old lady calls it love handles," Gus replied, playing along. A few hours ago, he would have been hopeful. Now, looking into Warren's eyes, he saw only cruelty and mood swings so drastic he was getting whiplash trying to keep up. How did no one else see how bad he was? Or maybe they did and were as afraid of Warren as he was.

"Fat handles are more like it." Warren smirked. "Hurry up, fat man. I want to check under the shoes. I remember my father saying he was going to make a place to store his money there once. You know, in case he ever needed bail money. Not that he would ever break the law, mind you—I know he directed that at me. Know what I mean?"

Gus grunted back.

"Hand me the flashlight, would you?" Gus's heart was racing, anticipating the other Warren returning. "I have to be careful to put everything back like I found it. Nothing escapes my father's notice, even when he's drunk. Did I tell you about the time I took his car out for a drive when he was out of town? I guess I missed the tape he had placed on the wheels. Well, you know how he blew his top. One time, I might have deserved it. But it also taught me to pay attention. See? Right there? That ruler with the tape over it? Got to put that back just right, but you know what that tells me?"

"Something there that he wants to hide," Gus mumbled.

"Bingo! Right on the money! See where the carpet is cut? Let's pull it back." Warren carefully lifted a strongbox from the hole cut into the floor. "Very clever for an old drunk, huh?"

"Yes." Gus hoped Warren had found what he was looking for.

The grandfather clock chimed eight in the living room while Warren expertly pried the box open. His face showed visible disappointment when all he found were old papers.

"Just a bunch of old crap. Where could he have put that key?"

"Looks like newspaper clippings. Must have a good reason to hide them under the floor."

"Yeah, well." Warren glanced down and saw a familiar name. "What the—"

Gus recognized the name. Oh, no, it was about his saintly mother. This wasn't going to be good. Warren's mother was supposed to have died soon after he was born. Complications of a tough birth, he'd been told. Warren lived with his aunt until his dad remarried and he went to live with his new family. The move didn't change Warren's perception of abandonment by his father, and his father made it a point to beat the bad out of his son. Warren believed that his father blamed him for his mother's death, but these clippings told a different story.

"My mother died in a boating accident when I was one? So my old man *is* capable of telling a lie."

"I didn't know your family had boats." Gus tried to change the subject.

"We did at the lake. I learned how to fish and ski, but I never knew about any boats on the bay. This says the boat sank and everyone on board died, including my mom."

"Strange," Gus replied, his chest tightening again.

Warren continued as if Gus hadn't spoken. "I'm reading it, but I don't believe it. Foul play was suspected. Valerie Heath and Steve and

Dora Telly were the guests of Brad Smith. That's the dude who owned the boat, I guess. Why was my mom there under that name and not home with me? It says here that she was a special friend of this Brad. So my own mother left me? None of this makes sense. I don't like that. I don't like learning that my mother abandoned me for some guy. This could explain some of my dad's anger. Wait, here's her obituary. 'Loving daughter and mother of son'—finally, they mention me. Damn right. Doesn't mention being married or her name change."

"Maybe something else in there explains it."

Warren didn't respond as he pored over the documents, including divorce papers dated four months before the boating accident. There was a picture of Warren at a week old, his smiling mother holding him while his father stood proudly behind them. What had happened in a year to change all of that? Had his father's temper pushed her away? Did she meet someone else? Was Warren someone else's son? No, he looked exactly like his dad—it wasn't that. The answer appeared in a letter Gus read over Warren's shoulder, holding the flashlight as steadily as he could.

DEAREST HARRY,

I first want to thank you for marrying me and saving me from being deported. You know you didn't have to, and I understand that you loved me. I am grateful for that and for the son we had together. I know a family is what you always wanted, and now you have a son to raise. I hope that makes it easier when I'm gone. I am not cut out to be a housewife and raise a kid. Your sister will help. Someday you'll meet a woman who will love you as much as you love her. I've already met with the lawyer. The papers were drawn up after I got pregnant. I wanted to see if I'd change my mind after I had Warren. I didn't. In fact, the first week home showed me I couldn't live that type of life. I tried, for your sake. Please understand, and tell our little Warren that I died in childbirth. I don't want him to think I abandoned him. Find him a new mother—a good mother. I will change my name to Heath and move away soon with Brad. I am a better mistress than a wife. I'll send money for Warren when I can. Take care of him, and don't let your temper get the best of you. I've seen that you can be a good man.

Love, Valerie

"No wonder my old man was so angry all the time, although that still doesn't excuse it. This Brad Smith—that name sounds familiar, doesn't it?" Warren rubbed his jaw.

"I remember that boating accident, actually."

"You do?"

"Yes. I was still a rookie. Everyone was talking about it because Brad Smith came from money. Dirty money, in fact. That was your mom. I never made that connection. Sorry, buddy." Gus put his hand on Warren's shoulder.

"You're saying my mom was dating some punk gangster?"

"Mr. Smith was suspected of doing some illegal stuff. When he died, his wife and kids got a lot of money from the insurance policy, and they moved to the East Coast. No foul play was ever proven, but they sure tried. That's all I remember. Sorry." Gus shrugged, leaving out the part about the hot girlfriend who happened to be Warren's mom. He added, "Your dad was an asshole, but at least he took care of you, buddy."

"If you can call that being taken care of. I don't. And don't call me 'buddy' anymore. I'm not your buddy. This changes nothing, except to show me how screwed up everyone is. At least I finally found my place in life. I would never allow myself to fall in love or trust a woman, that's for sure. When I want a family, a woman will be necessary, but I won't let her control me in any way. She'll have babies, run the house, and mind her own business. I'm going to be a good provider and take care of my kids. They won't know about my loser father or my pathetic slut of a mother."

"I completely understand."

"Good. I don't want this mentioned to anyone. Understand that?"

"Yes. You want to keep searching?"

"No. Let's get out of here. We have a couple of girls to attend to. Unless you don't have the stomach for it, then I can drop you off with your wife."

"Well…I…" Mentioning his wife, especially in that tone and with no emotion in his eyes, wasn't a good thing. Gus had seen Warren vulnerable, which might make Warren trust him even less. *Great.* He wasn't sure if he could kill those girls. He might be a bad cop, and he could kill a bad guy when needed, but he had his principles. And that comment sounded like a threat to his wife. Gus had to regroup.

"You're a weak man."

"I have a daughter close to their age," Gus protested.

"Yes. You do have daughters, at least for now," Warren interrupted with a grin.

"Are you threatening my daughters?" Gus blurted out before he could stop himself. He really didn't want to hear Warren's answer.

"I would never threaten the daughters of a loyal employee. Are you a loyal employee?"

Gus sighed. "Yes, Warren, I'm a loyal employee."

"That's what I thought. How about you start calling me 'sir' now?"

"Yes, sir," Gus replied between clenched teeth. He came to a quick decision. As soon as he got the chance, he'd kill Warren. No one threatened his wife or daughters and lived. No one. Until then, he would play along with this psycho's game.

CHAPTER 9

"This is some friggin' crazy shit," Stacy said as she smoothed her hair down and adjusted her ponytail.

Seeing Stacy outside without makeup was a rarity. It made her look younger than her almost twenty-one years, but she could still turn a guy's head in her direction.

"I know it is, but at least we found each other and got—hey, isn't that a pay phone at that gas station?"

Stacy squinted. "I think so, but I'm kind of afraid to cross the street. What if your brother drives by, right then? He's gonna come after us, Lynn."

"We have to take the chance. You wait here, and I'll go. Run if anything happens. Promise?"

"I don't want us to separate. Besides, it would be better if I called my parents, not you."

"It's my stepbrother; I'll take the chance going to the phone."

Lynn had never felt so alert. The gas station was dark, but the phone booth was lit up like a beacon. She had no choice. They had to get help because they were dealing with a crazy person. Yet her feet were firmly planted, not moving, like something was holding her in place, and the phone booth was growing dimmer. She knew she needed to get to a phone, but she couldn't bring herself to move. *How crazy does that sound?* She listened for the voice or a warning. Nothing.

"No way. We stay together, no matter what. We need to call the police too," Stacy replied with her hands on her hips.

"We know Warren has a cop friend. How do we know who we can trust? And what if the ones we can trust think we killed those guys? I mean, I didn't tell them, after all, and with the break-in at our apartment, who knows what they'll come up with?"

"I don't agree, Lynn. If we explain, they'll understand—" Stacy broke off as a Cadillac sped by.

"It's Warren!" Lynn gasped, recognizing the car. *If I'd been crossing the street...*

"Good. At least we know where he is," Stacy said.

"Right. Maybe we can call the authorities anonymously and let them know what's going on—after we call your parents for a ride. We can have them drop us off somewhere neutral. Let them think my car broke down, and we've been walking after it got towed, or something. That keeps your parents out of it and gives us time to decide what to say to the cops. We don't have much time before Warren starts looking for us. Come on!"

They darted across the moonlit two-lane road toward the pay phone, which appeared to be glowing again. Lynn shook her head, wondering if the dimming before had been an optical illusion. Well, whatever it was had prevented her from being in the middle of the street when Warren drove by. The gas station was a two-pump operation with a repair shop. There was nothing else visible but the road and trees. Lynn quietly prayed that the phone wouldn't be out of order. It wasn't. The first call to Stacy's parents went unanswered. They weren't home! In a panic she tried her parents' number. It also went unanswered.

"Now what?" she asked.

* * *

THOMAS WATCHED Lynn dialing phone numbers with a smile. "Let me guess. They will not be able to reach the parents."

"Can I help it if Stacy's mom had a sudden urge for Italian food and Lynn's parents are so into that dice game at the bar that they lost track of time? Now, to get Lynn to find that phone number that she does not remember putting in her pocket."

"You are a big fan of Kent."

"I am. He is already worried about her."

Thomas peered into the darkness. "So how do you get her to call him? Or is he already looking in the area?"

"No; he is a good investigator, but not a mind reader. Lynn might have been inspired to grab that number this morning—it was her choice to do it or not," Zelina said with a small smile.

"Oh, yes, encouragement. You do take this to a new level. I do not remember seeing Lynn do that this morning."

"She did, right after her shower, while Warren was drugging her breakfast. You were watching him while I was with her, remember?" Zelina asked with a mischievous grin.

"Yes, I do."

"Little details make a huge difference."

Thomas smiled. "They do." The smile disappeared. "They still will not be safe with him."

Zelina held her hand up. "Kent is her only chance of surviving the night."

"What is so special about him? I do not see it." Thomas frowned.

"A lot, when it comes to Lynn. Together they are much stronger, and when you are dealing with criminals that do not usually let people escape…you get what I mean."

Thomas nodded and shifted his weight on the gravel driveway to get a better view of the phone booth. "I get it, but Lynn is not calling him."

Zelina's face lit up. "No, she is not. This is one of their friends she called before, but the line will cut out. Oh dear, still a bad connection."

"Is her pocket glowing?"

"Just a little, and it might be slightly warm too." Zelina's eyebrows knitted together as she bit her lip. Thomas had never seen Zelina do that before.

He shook his head, but Zelina did not notice. "She barely knows him. I am not so sure she will call."

"A small part of her wants to. That is enough, along with the song in her head and their kiss."

"You were responsible for that song in her head too?" Zelina shrugged without answering. "You tried to tell her he was her Prince Charming."

"No, wrong story. In *Sleeping Beauty* it is Prince Phillip." Zelina spun around as if she was dancing, startling Thomas, who stepped back and slipped on the gravel. He was lucky he did not fall.

He regained his balance. "Okay, Prince Phillip. But kissing does not always mean trust for humans."

"But once she realizes—okay, I will give her a hint: *Pocket*."

Thomas watched Lynn look around outside the pay phone booth. She conferred with Stacy, who shook her head. "She really looks confused now."

"Watch."

Thomas did just that as Lynn pulled a piece of paper from her pocket. She immediately showed Stacy, who just shrugged. Lynn inserted a dime into the phone and held the receiver to her ear. She gave Stacy a thumbs-up and started talking.

"He should be on his way soon. If the timing is correct, they should be able to get out of here unseen. I am going to send them some protection and love. You should do the same. It will be out of our hands when the evildwel finds her prey missing and figures out that we fooled her. That will be scarier than the entire drug ring."

"Sending it. That evildwel is starting to irritate me. Where will they go?" Thomas asked, hovering near while Lynn spoke to Kent.

"Many options. Let us see."

* * *

Lynn couldn't believe how upset Kent was. "I'm okay. I'm sorry I haven't been able to call. Yes, I did find Stacy, but things are kind of weird."

"What do you mean, weird?" Kent demanded.

"We had to escape. I'll explain more later. Can you come get us?"

"Give me the address from the pay phone. I'll find you."

Lynn could hear paper shuffling in the background. She gave Kent the address and the name of the gas station.

"I know where that is. My uncle used to take his car there. I'll be right there."

"We'll be behind the building."

"I'll flash my headlights twice so you know it's me. Don't leave. If I see anyone, I'll circle around and come back."

"We're not going anywhere, I promise. Thanks, Kent." Lynn hung up before he could respond. She felt her face grow hot as she flashed back to their kiss.

"He's on his way," she told Stacy as they headed behind the white stucco building.

"I hope you're right about the bartender, Lynn. I mean, he was cute and, well, a bit nerdy. I know he didn't seem like a criminal, but neither did your brother before he went to prison."

"Yeah, I'm fairly sure about him. I mean, he did save my life once already." Lynn stepped back, making sure they were in complete darkness.

"True," Stacy admitted as she sat down. She pulled off her sneakers and shook them out. "Nature stuff."

"Yeah, me too." Lynn did the same thing, even though she hadn't felt anything in her shoes. *Good way to keep busy,* she thought. She felt a knot in her stomach, knowing her belief in this one person could mean the difference between life and death. Hearing the voice again pushed her confidence up when it came to Kent. She worried about bringing him or anyone else into their predicament, but what choice did they have? Plus, he did have an uncle on the police force. She didn't want to think too hard about the fact that the paper Kent's phone number was written on had been hot or that she couldn't even remember putting his number in her pocket.

"Shouldn't we call the police too? Why wait? I mean, we can hear a car coming and get back here before they would see us." Stacy double-knotted her red Keds.

"Not sure who we could trust. Maybe we could report the kidnapping, who was responsible, and where the house is?" Lynn shook her shoes. Only a small leaf fell out. She retied them, ready to move swiftly if she had to.

"Yeah, we'll be out of here by the time they get here. Even if they just questioned Warren, maybe he would think twice about chasing us." Stacy nibbled on her bottom lip while tapping her feet.

"All right, you win. I'll be right back. Stay here and keep a watch."

Lynn carefully approached the pay phone and dialed 911.

"What is your emergency?"

"I would like to report a kidnapping," Lynn started.

"A kidnapping?" a female voice repeated.

"Yes. We just got away from him, but his name is—" The phone went dead.

WARREN WAVED at the security camera on his way into the main house. He was excited for what was coming next, but first he wanted to eat. *Can't kill on an empty stomach,* he thought, grinning. A simple peanut butter and jelly sandwich for now; later, he'd enjoy a nice dinner of steak and lobster to celebrate. He would so enjoy killing Stacy after he got his stepsister to do what he wanted. He could envision Lynn calling the police and confessing to the murder. Oh, the story she would have for them. But Lynn wouldn't be through yet. No, she would kill her own mother, who always took her early morning walk at Lake Chabot before work. If it hadn't been for Lynn and that mother of hers, his dad would have been a better father. Warren was confident of that.

Besides, he saw how men reacted to Lynn, like that Kent. He didn't want one to try to rescue her. His ugly stepsister had grown into a beautiful swan, and swans always had people admiring their beauty enough to want to keep them around.

Killing Carrie was doing the world a favor. There was not an ounce of maternal instinct in her. Once old Gus helped him out with all the details, then he would have to do away with him too. He'd seen those looks Gus was giving him. His "yes, sir" didn't fool Warren—Gus had to know the only reason Warren confided in him was because his time was limited. Getting rid of Gus's body would be easy; he'd use the incinerator in the safe room. He had already learned how well it worked for disposing of bodies. Smiling at Gus, Warren flipped a switch in the kitchen.

"The phones, sir?"

"Yup! Working again, like magic." Warren grinned and pointed to the switch.

"Oh, yes. I see, sir." Gus had that forced smile in place.

"I'm sure you do. Now I would like a nice PB&J and a glass of milk. You don't mind, do you? I mean, I'm sure you can make a sandwich, right?"

"Of course. My pleasure…sir," Gus said through tightly clenched teeth.

A few minutes later, Warren was handing Gus an empty plate. He did make a mean sandwich. *Might keep him around just for that—or not,* Warren thought. He chuckled. "You don't mind washing the dish and glass, do you, Gus?"

Gus rubbed his chest. "No, of course not…sir."

The "sir" thing was becoming more labored. *Better try harder, Gus; your death is becoming more painful by the moment.* Warren watched Gus roll up his sleeves to wash the dishes.

Gus was gentle with the dishes. Warren knew he wouldn't do anything to upset his boss now. "Done, sir."

"Well done. I like when things are in their place, don't you?"

"Yes, I do, sir."

Warren smiled at his witty remark. The old Gus would have had a sarcastic comeback. Warren didn't like the old Gus. "Why don't you call Peter and get the house staffed up again? Then we can head down and have some fun."

Ignoring any response from Gus, Warren headed for the bar and made himself a drink, heavy on the bourbon. He watched Gus talk into the phone. He was sweating and looked uncomfortable, which was good. Warren was enjoying breaking Gus bit by bit.

Gus hung up the phone after confirming that the house would be fully staffed by midnight. Warren gulped down the rest of his very expensive bourbon. He saw Gus flinch. *Bet he wants a stiff drink too.*

Warren tossed his glass to Gus, who fumbled it. He loved seeing it shatter all over the floor as much as he loved watching Gus jump right in to clean it up. He grabbed another glass and filled it to the rim with the smooth whiskey. "Make sure the staff keep out of the way when we move our guests." Warren paused, but all he got back was a nod as Gus finished cleaning the broken glass. He gulped his drink and slammed the glass down. No point in throwing it at Gus; he would be ready to catch it. "We'll leave this glass here and hope next time your hands work better and you don't break it. You ready?"

Warren smiled as Gus dropped the last shard of glass into the small white trash can. There was no broom in the bar, so he'd had to use a towel. Luckily for Gus, the glass broke into large pieces. Warren knew the staff would get anything he missed. Gus slowly stood and brushed his hands against his pants. He moved like a man in pain. *Little does he know how much pain he'll be in later.*

Gus responded without making eye contact. "Yes, sir."

Warren hit the button to open the wall to the elevator. He pushed the elevator button, and the doors opened immediately.

"So how are we handling this, sir?"

"I think you'll like what I've come up with," Warren said as they entered the elevator. He studied Gus, who looked like he was about to pass out. Maybe a little bourbon would have helped this weak man, but he was more entertaining this way.

"What is that, sir?"

"You'll see. Just follow my lead."

"As you wish, sir," Gus replied, studying the sterile metal walls.

"Something bothering you, fat man? You can be honest with me."

"No, sir. I will follow your lead," Gus said with a small sigh.

Warren watched the doors open and then held them but didn't step out into the tunnel. He turned his cold gaze on Gus. "Good. I didn't want to have to make that call regarding your family. I'm so relieved." He smiled broadly and stepped into the tunnel, holding the door and waving Gus along.

"Thank you, sir," Gus mumbled, trailing Warren out of the tunnel. He rubbed his hands together in a manner that seemed aggressive to Warren. Then the idiot started to crack his knuckles.

"FYI, I have people watching my father's house and Stacy's parents' house in case the girls need any motivation. You know how important family is, like your own. You'd do anything to keep them safe." Warren was smiling. He knew Gus was getting his message loud and clear, but he enjoyed adding the exclamation point.

"I understand. But how will these girls know men are in front of their family homes?"

"Good question. I'll have them call their respective parents and send the men to the door during the call, saying they need to use the phone because their car broke down. That way, they'll know what we can do and that our reach is limitless."

"Yes, that would work."

"Glad you approve," Warren replied with thick sarcasm.

"What, um, do you want the girls to do, sir?"

"Another good question. I'm not going to rape them, if that's what you're thinking. I'm not a monster. I want to watch their pretty faces turn ugly with fear. Just a little pinprick and a small cut here and there—you know, fun stuff. My goal is to get them to hurt each other to protect their families. My plan is for everyone to be dead by morning. Then we can celebrate with a late breakfast—I know the best place for pancakes. My treat." Warren smiled.

Gus just nodded. He looked pale.

"Speechless, huh? It's the least I can do for you, after all you're about to do for me," Warren said, like he was comforting a small child.

He was comfortable with Gus's sudden silence. He knew Gus would do anything he wanted, right up until he killed him.

Warren lifted the key to the heavy steel door, but the keyhole was gone, and the door opened with a push.

"They're gone, sir," Gus whispered.

Warren's eyes narrowed. "No shit. How?"

"They shot the lock out, sir." Gus pointed a shaking finger. "Look. The room wasn't really designed to keep people in so much as keep them out. The lock wasn't very strong on either side, and it allowed for escape, I imagine. It was the bar that provided the security of no entry on the other side, so—"

Warren stopped him by holding his hand up. He wanted to snap Gus's fat neck, but he held back. He would be useful in the search. "That is why they were tied up. I believe *you* tied up Lynn. You'll take the blame for this if they aren't found."

Gus gulped audibly, and his face turned an odd shade of red. "They can't have gotten far. There's no place for them to go. The only thing around for miles is that gas station."

"Yes, that gas station—where there's a pay phone. Make the call; get a search going. Say these two girls attempted to kill their boss. I want them alive, if possible. You and I will wait at the station. It's the only place they can show up, if they haven't already."

In a matter of minutes, teams were on their way, including a helicopter. They would find them, Warren was assured. He ran to his car with Gus trailing behind him. A painful death wasn't going to cut it now; he had to think of something special for Gus, possibly involving his family.

They drove in silence and parked behind the auto shop. Gus silenced the engine, and they waited. Soon three Ford Broncos passed by. Warren's team was there. The phone booth stood empty and well lit. If they were out there, this was the only place they would go. They couldn't miss it if they were headed back to civilization.

Warren glanced at Gus, who was sweating profusely and seemed to be having trouble breathing. *Don't die on me before I kill you.* This was a man who wasn't going to live to eat another breakfast. "You go back up to the house, and get someone to wait there. I'll keep an eye on things until you get back, and then we're going to search."

Gus put the car in reverse as Warren got out. "Yes, sir."

Warren frowned as he watched Gus drive away. He smoothed his hair where the wind had ruffled it and breathed in the scent of eucalyptus. Just a kink in the plan. He'd still get his fun. The helicopter flew slowly overhead and shone a light down, blinding him. He waved it off, but the light continued for a few more moments before the helicopter moved on to search the trees next to him. He stepped into the shadows again and waited. He had some ideas on where to look. He knew their friends and family. But he was more interested in that guy he'd met at Lynn's apartment—Kent.

Headlights were coming down the road toward him. He had a mess to clean up, and he would do that gladly. He smiled as he learned that a white Honda Civic—Kent's car—had been spotted nearby.

CHAPTER 10

Kent asked no questions as Lynn and Stacy jumped into his car. He peeled out of the gas station, loose gravel rattling behind. Lynn updated Kent while he sped down the dark road. The car radio was off, and his silence was heavy as she kept talking. She looked back at Stacy, who shook her head. It did sound crazy, Lynn realized as she finished. She wiped her sweaty palms on her jeans, wondering if her trust in Kent was misplaced. Shifting in the car seat, she tried not to put pressure on the gun tucked into the back of her waistband. She'd prefer not to have it there. What if it just went off—or worse, what if she had to use it?

Kent made a sharp turn into a crowded movie theater parking lot. He parked and turned toward Lynn with a sigh. He appeared to be weighing his words carefully—or was he stalling? Why wasn't he talking? Lynn wanted to scream, and her heart was racing. What if he worked for Warren too, and his interest in her had all been an act?

Kent spoke softly. "Okay, you're safe. No one will think we'd stop this close by. This isn't good, Lynn."

"Yeah, I know, but I'm glad you believe us," Lynn said. A rush of relief shot through her.

"I do." Kent's brown eyes seemed to penetrate her soul, calming her. He was the person between them and Warren now.

Stacy held up a hand. "I vote we go to the police."

"I agree, Stace. We should at least report Warren as a kidnapper. I know there could be a bad cop there, but your uncle…" Lynn raised her eyebrows at Kent.

"Yeah, about my uncle." Kent frowned and looked away.

Lynn wanted to turn his face toward hers, but not with Stacy sitting in the back seat. "You don't think he's one of the bad ones, do you?"

Kent's head snapped back toward her, and Lynn was afraid she'd made him mad, but he smiled weakly at her and shook his head. "My uncle, bad? No. Shot. He's okay, but he'll be in the hospital for a couple of days. I got the call right before I talked to you. He's probably wondering why I'm not there, but I don't think we should involve him. And you should know he isn't the first good cop to get shot in the last few weeks."

Lynn gasped and covered her mouth for a moment and then reached out and grasped his hand. "Oh, I'm so sorry! You should be with him, not me."

"I'm where I should be. My uncle will understand." Kent squeezed her hand and released it with a quick glance at Stacy. Lynn knew she hadn't missed that.

Stacy frowned at Kent. "So you're saying cops are getting shot?"

Kent turned around to face her. "Yes. The good cops answer calls, and someone is there waiting. There's a theory that a person with a scanner is shooting at cops when they arrive at the scene of a crime, but I believe someone is sending them a warning."

Lynn shook her head. "Oh, that's terrible."

"Even the cops aren't safe," Stacy muttered.

"They'll figure it out, but for now, my concern is keeping you both safe."

"Yeah, well, I would prefer never to see Warren again." Stacy grimaced and added, "Um, thanks for getting us, Kent."

"No problem. And you both should know—I'm a private investigator."

"You're a what?" Lynn gasped.

"I started out helping my grandpa as a teen in the summer. Then he got to the point where he couldn't keep up with his caseload. After three years of full-time work with him, I got licensed and became his partner last year. He, um, he died a few months ago. Heart attack. I took over."

"Sorry," Lynn said.

"Yeah, thanks."

"Why were you working in a bar, then, Kent?" Stacy asked.

"I used to help out a friend if things got slow at work, which they haven't been for a long time. I was there to observe some…bad people. I have an older client who goes by the name Mr. Justice who's been a client of my grandfather's for years. I've never met him, but he believes our local police need help breaking up a drug ring."

"So were we a part of your investigation that night?" Lynn crossed her arms.

"Of course not. Well, not until you hooked up with those drug dealers." Kent shrugged.

"Did you see me leave the apartment that morning?" Lynn studied her hands. She couldn't look at Kent or Stacy.

"No, sorry. Wish I had been there."

Lynn frowned and looked Kent in the eye. "That story about your mom—part of your cover?"

"Well, yes and no. What I told you about my mother was true, although I really had to leave to keep an eye on those guys." Kent blushed.

Lynn's eyes narrowed. "So you lied to me about wanting to go out. What a surprise. Showing up to save me was part of your job, I guess. That…well, you know…just collecting information, I suppose?" Lynn felt tears trying to break free from her eyes. She was determined not to cry in front of this liar. She frowned at Stacy, who took a moment to glare at Kent. Everyone had lied to Lynn except Stacy.

"You have this all wrong, Lynn." Kent grabbed her hand, but she pulled away. "I hated not telling you the truth, but I couldn't break my cover. When I came out to talk to you and gave you my phone number —well, I was drawn to you the moment I saw you. That isn't like me, seriously. I was breaking my rules of not getting personal on the job, but it was worth it to me."

"Whatever," Lynn muttered, picking at her cuticles.

"Lynn, I promise you, it was and is real. I was hurt when I saw you guys leaving with the two drug dealers. I can't explain to you how I felt seeing him take advantage of you in your condition. You were so out of it. I blamed myself for making your drink too strong at first. Now we know someone drugged you at the bar. Then, when I found out your real name and how you were related to Warren—I admit to having investigated your past, but my instincts were right about you. I hope you can forgive me."

"You investigated me?" Tears flowed down her face. Her emotions had come out, and he had stepped on them. This was exactly why she kept a wall around her heart.

Stacy reached over the seat and put a protective hand on Lynn's shoulder. "You may have saved us, but you are a huge dick."

Kent didn't respond. "Lynn, that kiss and my feelings are very real. I have to be cautious in my line of work. You need to understand how it looked to me—I didn't know which side you were on at first. Then, after talking with my boss, it became my job to keep you safe. After the attempt on your life, I knew I shouldn't have let my feelings for you come out like that, but I won't apologize for how I feel. Now my goal is to get all the bad guys in prison and keep both of you safe. Warren has outsmarted me in the past, like disabling my car so I couldn't follow when he left with you. I won't let that happen again. You called me, so you have to trust me on some level, right?" Kent gazed into Lynn's eyes and reached for her hand again. This time she didn't pull away.

"I kind of get what you're saying, but you shouldn't have kissed me until you told me the truth."

"I know. You're right about that, Lynn. And Stacy, I didn't mean to hurt your friend. And you can be mad at me all you want, but I plan on keeping you both safe."

"Not cool at all," Stacy remarked.

"I know."

"You could have been honest with me," Lynn replied.

"I was going to tell you, but Warren walked in right after. I've been trying to find you both since then. And since we are doing full disclosure, there is one more thing."

"Great, now what?" Stacy asked.

Kent glanced back at her. "Well, Warren works for his father's brother—a man who seems to stay just above the law."

Lynn's mouth fell open. "His uncle? Wait—I remember my stepfather calling his brother a crook. Is my stepfather in on this too?"

Kent shook his head. "No."

"Well, I guess it's a relief that he's not a criminal, just angry. It doesn't make him any better, in case you're wondering."

"Sorry, Lynn," Stacy said.

"And Lynn, when I researched you, I kind of learned about your stepfather's temper—I'm sorry."

"All you had to do was ask me. I was there. I'm the one who stood by her," Stacy said.

Kent smiled. "Yeah, you were, Stacy, but you weren't around to ask. And I'm very glad she has a friend like you."

"It doesn't matter. I'm out of there now." Lynn wiped her eyes.

"It does matter," Kent said, shaking his head. "No kid should have to deal with what you did. The neighbors knew about it but said it was none of their business. Your family kept up their yard and were good neighbors, and that was all they cared about. I don't understand people."

Stacy pulled away from Lynn and sat back in her seat. "I'm glad we can all agree that her parents sucked, Kent, but shouldn't we be getting out of here? We have people trying to kill us."

Kent scanned the parking lot. "Yeah, we should, but I didn't want you guys to run from the person trying to help you. I hope you understand that's all I'm trying to do. I'm sorry for not being honest. It goes with the job, which I know is no excuse."

Lynn's tears had dried up, and she was getting some of what he was saying, even if she didn't like it. "I have one more question. You seriously couldn't find my step-uncle's mansion?"

"There are many houses, not all of them in his name, in addition to all the businesses he owned. I'd only started to check out the list but wanted to be near the phone in case you called. Glad I did."

"There has to be one police officer you trust," Stacy insisted.

"There is, but what if Warren and his team are watching for you guys to try to contact someone at the department?"

"Another department?" Lynn asked.

"I wouldn't know who to talk to." Kent bit his lip. "I could take you to a hotel I know that takes cash and asks no questions. Not the best place to visit, but it's safe."

"I'm not going to ask how you know about this place." Stacy smirked.

"Good, because it's an undercover thing." He smiled.

Lynn rolled her eyes at him. As scared and mad as she was, if Stacy wasn't in the car, she'd be kissing Kent right now. Or she'd be out the door, running. She was a little conflicted.

Stacy broke the awkward silence. "Could you two please stop making eyes at each other and get us out of here? I've gotta pee."

"We're not—" Lynn started to say when a helicopter flew above them, its light illuminating the parking lot.

"Get down!" Kent yelled.

It passed over the car, lighting up the interior. Lynn was sure they couldn't see anything from above. What if there was someone on the ground following along? She held her breath until the light passed them by. She heard footsteps outside their car, and a flashlight shone in.

"Hey, over here!" The light disappeared.

Lynn carefully peeked out the window and saw two men pulling a man and two women out of a similar Civic. Thankfully, white Hondas like Kent's were common.

"Stay down!" Kent warned.

"It's two men holding a gun on the people from a white car like yours. It's a man and two women—like us," Lynn whispered, glancing back at Kent. He signaled for her to get down.

Lynn sank onto the black floor mat, which was remarkably clean. She saw Kent retrieve a gun from under his seat. She remembered hers and reached for it.

"They suspect you're with me. I need to get a new car. I know one that isn't being used—my uncle's."

They heard tires squeal and a man yell, "Hey!"

"They must have another lead. We got lucky that time. Let's get out of here." Kent gunned the engine and raced out of the parking lot with his lights off.

"Lucky? Maybe they got lucky not finding us. I was ready to take them down." Stacy held up her gun.

"Yeah, I noticed Lynn's gun. Guessing you found them at the mansion?"

"We did. I'm a good shot."

Kent turned to Lynn. "You a good shot too?"

"Just point and shoot, like Stacy says."

He chuckled. "So I'll take that as a no?"

Lynn shrugged and looked away. "Um, yeah, I suppose."

"Maybe you should give it to me, then."

"No way. We both stay armed," Stacy said.

Kent stopped at a red light, watching behind them. "Have it your way, but be careful where it's pointed is all I ask."

"Duh," Stacy replied as the light turned green and they merged onto the main street.

Lynn glanced back, seeing a brown-haired man hugging a blond woman. The other woman was a brunette. She shivered. *That could have been us, and we'd be dead now.*

She still couldn't believe that she'd grown up with a killer. How powerful was Warren's uncle, whom she'd never met, and what did her stepbrother do for him? And who was Kent's Mr. Justice? Could she forgive Kent for lying to her? She had no answers. She tucked her gun into the pocket of the backpack; it had been digging into the small of her back. Her mind was swirling like a storm, and there seemed to be no escape from the turmoil.

* * *

"I'm sorry, sir. I'll deal with that personally. Mr. Stone has taken care of all of us, and we will take care of him. We won't stop looking until we find these people."

The short man, who had already lost most of his blond hair, looked sixty, but Gus had run into him at an A's game with his two sons a couple years of ago. He'd been celebrating his fortieth birthday. But Gus couldn't remember his name. Steve, Scott, Simon? Something like that. The man was nodding so hard it looked like he would strain his neck. Gus looked away.

Warren was busy smoothing his shirt down, but his expression reminded Gus of a predator playing with its dinner before eating it, holding it down and watching it struggle. He spoke slowly. "Good. I hope so, for your sake. These people can put us all out of a job and in jail. You get that? If they go to the police and we can't get to them, even with our people inside, it could be bad. And the fact that they attempted to take out your boss should be uppermost in your mind. That is why you are looking for them."

The little sweaty man's head was still bobbing like an oil pump. "Yes, sir. We have his license plate now. We won't miss them."

"See that you don't, or I won't have any use for you," Warren warned as the man hurried off into the dimly lit church parking lot.

"They're doing their best to find them," Gus said softly.

"Best isn't good enough. My uncle has taken good care of me since I went to prison. So I'll make sure things run smoothly while he enjoys himself on his island. Killing a few lackeys to get a job done poses no problem for me. I'm the only nonexpendable person under my uncle—I think I've mentioned that before."

Gus dutifully nodded. "You've made that very clear, sir. Will I ever get to meet your uncle, Mr. Stone?"

"You? Why would he want to meet you?" Warren laughed and hit his knee.

Gus held back the urge to punch Warren in the face. "No idea, sir; just wondering."

"I don't pay you to wonder. In fact, I think it's about time you hop into your car and head over to my father's house and keep an eye out for Lynn there. And to earn your life back, I'd like you to find this." Warren handed Gus a small, worn picture.

Gus ignored the threat. "This is the key?"

"Yes. It's bronze. Roman, I believe. Looks like a ring, huh? Not sure it opens anything, but you never know, right, Gus?" Warren paused for a moment, staring at Gus intently. Gus forced a grin, and Warren continued. "*My* uncle will reward you handsomely if you find that; plus, I won't have to kill you." He burst into laughter and slapped Gus on the back.

"I would like to live, sir," Gus said with an uncomfortable laugh.

"Yes, that seems to be a common human trait—until it isn't."

"Um, yes. So you want me to head over there now?"

"That is why I had you drive us to your car, fat man. But there is one more thing I require from you."

"What's that?"

Warren's eyebrows lifted, and his lips pressed tightly together. "Rethink betraying me, Gus."

Gus felt the blood drain out of his head. "Why do you think I'd do that?"

"I know you, remember? You taught me all you knew. Your pride makes it hard to take orders from me. I see it in your eyes. You know who will pay for it. Now you may go. Do check in when you learn anything. Oh, and Gus, let the team watching the house go on to their next assignment, would you? They know where to go next, don't worry."

"Yes, sir, but you're wrong about me. Yes, I trained you, and all I was doing was making a living. You've figured out how to go beyond that. I'm proud of you, buddy."

"Don't make me remind you again. I am *not* your buddy." Warren's hand snaked out and slapped Gus across the face, leaving a bright red mark. "Are we clear now, Mr. Williams?"

"Yes sir," Gus mumbled, rubbing his red cheek as he walked to his car. His pride stung more than his face.

* * *

WARREN WATCHED another car drive into the parking lot. A tall, thin man with a baby face and cold eyes opened the driver's side door and slid in next to him. Warren immediately disliked him. An expert sniper, he had been assured. He would give him a chance, though. It was the least he could do.

The man started the car and said, "We have the men in place, sir, like you asked."

Warren gave him a pleased expression to start their working relationship off right.

"Good. Thank you, Perry. You made sure the team at my father's house knows to head over to Mr. Williams's house when he relieves them?"

"Yes, I personally contacted them."

"Good man. We need to keep an eye on Mr. Williams in case he decides to do something stupid. Can't have that. Our boss requires respect, and so do I. I mean, after all, I'm his second-in-command. That position deserves respect, doesn't it?"

Perry nodded quickly and checked his mirrors. "Yes, sir. You are very well respected."

"Of course I am. If I ever think otherwise, that person dies. I hope all of you know that. If you're loyal and respectful, I will reward you with riches. It's a simple choice that some people don't get." Warren laughed.

The man's blue eyes filled with hate—or was it fear? Fear was acceptable; hate was not. "Understood, sir."

"Good, let's get going. Lots of places to search, and I'd like to start with Kent Stuart. You have all his information?"

"Yes."

"Good. I think starting with the hospital where his uncle is makes sense. We'll go from there. Drive, please."

Warren could feel the driver's emotions radiating off him. He decided the man was terrified of him. They all were, and if they weren't afraid of him, they would soon learn to respect him. That made Warren happy, yet he felt sad that this caper with his stepsister, stepmother, and beautiful Stacy would be ending so soon. But good times had to end—like his uncle's life.

His uncle had been more angry than fearful when he'd killed him. Warren had accepted his anger since he was family. The best part had been shooting his aunt and cousins first, with his uncle watching. It was nothing personal, he assured them. It didn't make a difference, he could tell, but he made it quick for them. For his uncle it was personal, and he let the pain linger for as long as he could. He cut and stabbed him until he begged to be killed. Warren finally took pity on the soft old man and shot him, even though he didn't deserve it after treating Warren like just another employee all those years. The only downside was how long it took to burn all the bodies.

He'd had plenty of time to make his plans in prison—thanks to his uncle. And now taking over the reins of the business was so satisfying. No one had a clue—nor would they, if everything went to plan. Soon it would come out that his poor uncle and family were lost at sea— during a storm, if Warren got lucky. Authorities would have to declare them lost, and the wreckage would never be found. The funny thing was that the boat *was* at the bottom of the ocean—just a different one. Everyone who knew about it was dead. He was in the clear and would soon be playing the part of the grieving nephew forced to take over the family business and all the money. His uncle had changed his will, leaving it all to him—just in case.

He smiled, remembering his uncle's last garbled words as blood poured from his wounds: "You will be judged. There is justice."

His uncle was not a religious man, but that was the only thing he could come up with. Not that Warren cared. He had all he needed from the man. Passwords, accounts, all his thugs—it was a great life. It was going to be even greater soon, once he had that key that his uncle had wanted so badly. Warren was important now, and the things his uncle had longed for had become the things Warren wanted. Maybe the key would open something cool. If not, he could always sell it. Warren Stone was the perfect boss, and no one could touch him, not even the police. He was too powerful.

CHAPTER 11

"We're staying here?" Stacy said. "You've got to be kidding me."

The No-Tell Motel, as the locals called it, had seen better days—like before Lynn was born. Weeds covered the filled-in pool. The fence around it was only standing on two sides; the rest lay rotting. The old wood front was freshly painted, though, and lines were drawn clearly in the parking lot under the dim lighting. The vacancy sign was lit. Lynn was pretty sure that no one bothered with a reservation because it was off the main highway and its business was mainly people cheating on their spouses and high school kids trying to get lucky. Lynn had heard the motel charged by the night or the hour, and any drug you wanted was available, but she'd never been here. The back of a car had always been fine with her, or a blanket out in nature.

"It, um, it isn't all that bad," Lynn said.

"No, it's bad, but at least they change the sheets after each occupant," Kent said.

They pulled in under a cluster of eucalyptus, oak trees, and tall golden weeds. The helicopter wouldn't see the car there, Lynn noted, and it was hidden from the road.

"We're running from criminals by hiding with criminals?" Stacy asked.

"What, you never came here in high school?" Kent joked.

"I did not," Stacy replied hotly.

"Me neither," Lynn said. "You?"

"No, it wasn't on my list of places to…you know."

Lynn was positive he was blushing. "You know about it from your investigations, then?" she pressed.

"Exactly. The night manager tolerates my presence because I 'cut him in,' as he says."

"Wonderful. You have a crooked friend, and we're hidden under some trees. I feel *so* safe," Stacy said with her trademark eyeroll.

"Safer than when you were running away from criminals on foot? I'm doing my best." Kent turned off the engine.

"Yeah, I'm thankful you came and got us. It's just that I've been tied up, drugged, and saw someone killed in front of me. So excuse me for questioning our safety," Stacy huffed. Tears threatened to overflow her eyelids.

"I'm sorry you were pulled into this mess, but I'm doing the best I can on short notice."

Lynn knew her friend was ready to melt down, but that wouldn't help them now. She quickly changed the subject. "So we're getting your uncle's car?"

Kent smiled briefly at Lynn. "We leave this car here and take a taxi. Pay them cash and get another car—my uncle is only one of our many options. Anyway, there's a vending machine around the corner if you're hungry. It's filled often, if you're wondering, and it has some good stuff in it."

"I have some nuts and water in my backpack, but I wouldn't say no to a candy bar or maybe some chips," Lynn said.

"I should be hungry, but I feel sick to my stomach." Stacy wiped her eyes with the back of her hand.

"Yeah, probably the drugs. Food might help. I'll see what they have, but you two stay here. I'll let the manager know I'm working a case and leaving my car behind. He'll let me use the phone so I can check in with my uncle, let him know I'm okay." Kent smiled. Lynn grinned back while Stacy quietly studied the night outside. "Be right back."

As soon as Kent disappeared around the corner, Stacy reached for Lynn. "I'm sorry. I know we need to keep it together, but it kind of just hit me. This sucks!"

"It does. I'm not sure how I haven't lost it. I guess trying to stay alive is a good incentive." Lynn patted her friend's hand to reassure them both.

Stacy's smirk was back. "Yeah, that it is. It's like we've been thrown in some crazy movie, huh? And it's up to us to save the day. You and I, we can—you know. I mean, we already got away from the bad guys."

"We did. Now we're packing guns and on the run. And Stace, it's been about finding you the entire time, and I did. We got this."

"Yep," Stacy agreed. "I wish I had my makeup so I look better doing it."

Lynn shook her head. "You look fine, as always. I have my lip gloss, and here's a brush in the car door."

Stacy took both items and got to work brushing her hair. "Lynn, when did you have time to sleep with him?"

"It was only a quick kiss," Lynn said, feeling her face redden.

"Well, there's some explosive chemistry going on between you two, but, your libido aside, I hope we can trust him."

Lynn looked away. "I think we can. He's been there for us so far."

"Yeah, I totally thought we were going to get shot in that parking lot or have to shoot them. I was glad to see he carries a gun. If his gun doesn't get pointed at us, we won't point ours at him. This whole thing friggin' sucks." Stacy glossed her lips. She almost looked like she was ready for a day at the lake, makeup-free but still pretty. Even her pink nail polish was perfect. Stacy was a girl who could look good no matter what.

Lynn nodded. It did suck. That summed it up perfectly. She ran the brush through her hair while Stacy gave herself a side ponytail. It felt like the first normal thing she had done in a while.

* * *

Gus pulled up to the front of the house and relieved the other observers. The Stones weren't back from the bar yet, but he would do as he was asked and watch the house until morning. He knew Warren's father kept a loaded gun in the bedroom, and Gus didn't want to get caught on the wrong side of that. He took out his anger on the dashboard. His hand throbbed from Warren's arrogance. Gus had been the one taking care of Warren all those years, and now he was treated like this? He had been the father figure when the real father wasn't there. Gus shook his hand. It hurt and was already beginning to swell. Not a good sign, but at least he'd been able to make that call.

His wife had been confused, but she ultimately agreed to go visit her mom in Florida with their kids—on the next flight out.

"Okay, I guess. I mean, what about my job? And the dog?"

"No questions now. I'll take care of both," he had told her. "This is job-related, and you're not safe. Grab what you can in the next five minutes for all of you. Stuff it into the large blue suitcase and go. You'll find an envelope with cash and a bank account number in it. Use it to get what you need, and take the kids to Disney World. Understand?"

"Okay. Please take care of yourself," she added.

"I always do. I'll meet you there in a few days. I love you." He hung up before she could respond.

She had been wanting to visit her mom, and they were always welcome there. Gus could relax; his family was safe. He made another call to the neighbor who usually took care of Pogo, their black Lab. She always enjoyed watching the dog and would bring the paper and mail in too. *Perfect.* Now Warren's threats would only affect him. Warren had gone too far—he had to die. He was sure the boss would appreciate getting rid of that traitor; Gus could tell something Warren was saying didn't add up.

No one would let a beloved relative rot in prison for two years for burglary. Warren's uncle was using him to get at his brother. That part had always been clear to Gus, but he'd keep playing the game, for now. He needed to figure out exactly what game Warren and his uncle were playing, and quickly. Tomorrow morning, he'd make another run-through of the house. If he found the key, he'd have an in with the boss and would finally get free. He had a few ideas of where it could be that he hadn't shared with Warren. Gus always covered his bases. He knew the guys he relieved here were heading to his house, but they would find it empty—he'd checked before coming here. He pushed his seat back and closed his eyes as his chest tightened again. Tomorrow was going to be a very long day. After that it was time to see a doctor and get his heart checked out.

* * *

"Gus stopped and made one phone call, sir, and took a rather long route to his assignment," Perry reported.

"Thank you. Checking in on the little woman, I suppose. Keep an eye on him. The unit at his house?"

"En route, sir. They were stopping to pick up some food."

Warren slammed his hand to his forehead. "I don't pay them to eat! They better hope the family's still there."

Perry nodded as he turned onto the winding road. Warren adjusted his collar and ripped out the tag, which was irritating him. In fact, everything was having that effect on him. "The hospital was a waste of time, but I want the unit to remain there just in case. I imagine Kent will try to contact his uncle, one way or another. Make sure they understand I want them to find a way to observe his phone calls. Keep the unit at the uncle's house. Go ahead and let them know now."

Warren heard his instructions being repeated on the radio. When Perry was done, he continued. "It's a shame all those 'good' officers keep getting shot, huh? Maybe they might want to rethink whose rules they follow." He smiled. At least something was going right. They passed through the gate. *Nice to be home again.*

"Yes, sir. Your message is getting across."

"And that white Honda?"

"I was told there's no sign of it."

"That is not what I want to hear. I want a different answer next time. Make sure they know that."

"Yes, sir."

"Well, that's all. You can open my door now."

Perry put the car in park and jumped out. Warren glanced at himself in the rearview mirror before he got out. Even at his worst, he always looked good. Soon everything would be done, and he could relax. It made him grin, imagining all the ways he could kill someone. With everything he had at his disposal, he'd never get caught and could fulfill all his fantasies.

* * *

THOMAS WATCHED the taxi turn the corner. "Well, they got rid of the car, and the taxi is taking them away, but they are not safe."

"No, they are not. Kent's car will be found soon, and the taxi driver will be talking about where he dropped off his fare. The only lucky thing is that Kent is not taking them to his uncle's car, because that would not be safe for any of them. He did not want to scare the girls, but he is not taking that option."

"I assume you had something to do with him changing his mind?"

"It was completely his idea. I had him remember something he had read about a while back, in a case where the killer used a man as bait. When this man's nephew and wife went to check on him, they were all killed. It was thought to be a burglary. It was not. The nephew was the target."

"Oh, I suppose that would work. You did the same thing with Lynn and her high school memory." Thomas hovered by the car window.

"I did. It is only a reminder of things that have already happened. A good tactic to use. The humans choose what to do with it."

"So where is he getting a car?"

"He has to steal one." Zelina shrugged.

"He is breaking the law, then? Should we not stop him?"

"No. This was something he remembered from when he rented a car at the airport after his own broke down. He had thought how odd it was that they left the keys in the car, especially with how easy it would be to bypass the spiked rods. This small infraction can be overlooked in this situation, and he will be forgiven. It is in his nature to come forward and offer to pay and accept the consequences. Luckily for him, the place he is thinking about right now is owned by his boss, so you see—"

Thomas interrupted. "He knows he is taking a car from the guy he works for?"

"Oh, no."

"This is not okay."

Zelina looked Thomas in the eye. "No, it is not. But he is doing what is right to save those women from a horrible end. Like I said, this is not a simple thing we are doing. It is not up to me to judge him."

Thomas nodded in agreement. He had been judging Kent. Another thing to watch out for. He watched them get into a vehicle. "They seem to have settled on that one."

"Yes, a Chevy Blazer. I think it looks more like a family car, does it not?"

"Yeah, I suppose it might fool them for a bit. How long before Warren figures out where they went?"

"Not long. First, it will be assumed that they flew out. Gives them some time, I hope. Rather clever plan." Zelina looked up at the sky and pointed. "Look, there go Gus's family to safety, boarding the plane to LAX, where they will spend the night and then head to Florida in the morning. Although Gus..." She shook her wings. "Right now, we prepare. Hopefully, Kent, Lynn, and Stacy will be ready for the showdown, as the humans call it. We should check on him."

* * *

STACY PUT her hands on her hips. "I'm not comfortable doing this. What if we get caught?"

Kent sighed. "It's a rental, and I'm renting it. I promise to pay later. If I leave them my information now, we'll be found. You understand?"

Stacy shook her head. "Yeah, well, this isn't your uncle's car, like you first suggested. If you had let us in on the plan instead of just driving us to the airport, you know, we might have found a way to do this without grand theft auto."

"Yes, maybe I should have been more forthcoming, but I wasn't sure until I saw the taxi driver. I let him know where to go before you got in, sorry. It's just that I had a bad feeling about going to the hospital or my uncle's house, and I remembered renting a car from here a while back for a case when my car was in the shop. I'll make my nightly call in to my boss at three. I hope he'll have some suggestions; if not, we'll figure it out."

"This doesn't sound very promising," Stacy said.

"Being alive is always promising," Kent countered.

"Yeah, well, let's keep it that way."

"I'm trying." Kent grinned.

Lynn threw up her hands and said, "Do or do not. There is no try." She cracked her first real smile in days. "I can quote movies too."

"Gee, this isn't nerdy," Stacy said.

"It isn't. Lynn is right. There is no try at this point." Kent merged onto the freeway.

"Of course I'm right." For the first time since waking up next to a dead body, she felt like everything was going to be okay.

* * *

"HAVE you located them at the airport?" Warren spoke into the phone through clenched jaws.

"No, sir. We are checking all the airlines, but there aren't many flights this late."

"Well, check the departed flights, the hotels nearby, and the restaurants. Do I have to think for you too?"

"No, sir. We're looking."

"Call me back when you find them. We know who they're with and what they're driving. Can't be that hard to find in the middle of the night." Warren slammed the receiver down before his lackey could answer. He would make sure he paid for that. They all would pay. This was getting out of hand. Too bad they weren't here in front of him, then he could have relieved his rage quickly by stopping someone from breathing. He stood for a moment, reflecting on all the things he planned to do once he found the trio. The bloody images filled his mind and pushed the rage away. Calm, he sank onto the cool leather couch.

Maybe he was going about this all wrong. He knew Kent was a PI working for an elusive boss who was the root of all his problems. Maybe he could kill all the birds with one stone, including Mr. Justice, the man who had given his uncle so much trouble. Time to take another look at Kent's grandfather's papers. There had to be something that would point him in the right direction. Warren picked up the receiver and barked out his instructions. He poured himself a glass of champagne at the bar and then plopped back onto the couch, put his feet up on the glass table, and smiled.

"Cheers to me." Warren quickly emptied the glass. He closed his eyes to rest them for a moment and fell into an exhausted sleep.

CHAPTER 12

"Okay, he is asleep, but that evildwel is not," Thomas noted. "It always makes me uncomfortable to feel its heat flowing off of Warren, but I think we are making it just as uncomfortable."

"That is why I keep my distance. You seem to tolerate it better than me, and I am glad if you can make that creature uncomfortable."

"One of those things."

"Yes, it is. I like when Warren sleeps because it means he cannot add anyone to his kill list, no matter what that thing wants." Zelina grinned slightly while pushing her black hair behind her ears. She shook out her wings.

"True. Hey, are you going into full angel mode? Do we need to get back to Lynn?"

"Yes, there is a chance right now." Zelina paused, as though listening, while biting her lip. She glanced in both directions. Thomas did not see or hear anything but extended his navy-blue wings. Then, as suddenly as Zelina's green wings had opened, they closed again. "I guess not."

"What happened?" Thomas closed his wings too.

"Kent changed his mind. That idea would have been a trap for them." Zelina kept glancing around like she expected something to happen. Thomas had not seen her this agitated before.

"You have to teach me how to do that."

Zelina nodded her head. "You are almost there. You will naturally tune in to it when you concentrate."

"I have tried. I will keep at it. Mr. Justice will help?" Thomas felt the stress of the moment and started to feel for absent pockets. He was definitely going to suggest a change in the basic angel wardrobe.

"Yes, he will try," Zelina said. "Certain things will have to happen for this to resolve. Good, Kent is taking them to the ocean."

"Why is that good?"

"It is closer to where they need to be, but they do not know that yet."

Thomas paused for a moment and took a deep breath. He saw a log house with two cats. "I see where they need to be."

"I have had that faith you would." Zelina smiled. "Come on, we need to get back to them. We do not want to be here when Warren wakes up."

Zelina took off, leaving Thomas no time to respond to her compliment or her cryptic statement. He suspected this was intentional and quickly followed her.

* * *

"Where are we going?" Lynn asked as they headed to the toll crossing of the Bay Bridge.

"I thought we'd be heading in the Sacramento direction, to Lake Tahoe or somewhere north, to get out of here," added Stacy.

"I started heading that way, to be honest. I was going to a friend's cabin, but then I changed my mind. I think the safest place right now is the ocean. Harder to sneak up on us, right?"

"Yeah, that makes sense. I suppose you have a friend who has a house on the ocean too?" Lynn yawned.

"Not this time. But there are a couple of motels on the beach, and I have a credit card that isn't in my name, so they shouldn't find us from that. We'll stay there. I'll make my call while you guys get some sleep. I'll make sure it's a place we can get out of quickly if we need to."

"Which beach? You gonna share where we're going?" Lynn asked.

"I'll tell you when I know," Kent replied. "I'm kind of following my gut on whether we go north or south once we get through the city. Always worked for me in the past. In the meantime, get a quick catnap in while you can."

"I've gotta pee again," Stacy said.

"Use this coffee cup they left in the truck. There's nowhere to do that for a bit," Warren said.

Stacy looked mortified. "I can wait."

Lynn smiled. She knew her friend would give in and use the cup soon. "Chips?"

"Yeah, it'll soak it up." Stacy laughed.

"I'm thinking it will be better if you lie down now, Stacy. Cover up so they don't see you at the tollbooth."

"What? Why?"

Kent glanced at Lynn. "Because they're looking for a man and two women, not a couple. Not sure how far their hand reaches. There are cameras too. And Lynn, if you don't mind trying to look at me like an adoring date, that would sure help."

"I'll do my best." Lynn glanced back at Stacy, who responded with an eyeroll.

Lynn settled in next to Kent with her head on his shoulder. She thought she should still be mad at him, but he was warm and smelled of musk, and that cancelled her negative feelings. He smiled down at her right as they got to the tollbooth. Lynn didn't move after they drove through, and Kent seemed fine with that.

It kind of killed the mood when she heard Stacy use the cup and then put it in the cupholder. Lynn avoided looking at Kent so she wouldn't burst out laughing and make Stacy mad. Instead, she closed her eyes for a moment, and that scene from *Sleeping Beauty* came back to her. Was Kent her real-life prince? Too soon to tell what he was to her, but he and that story sure seemed connected. She wondered if he would sit through that movie with her.

She could hear Stacy lightly snoring in the back seat as they drove through the tunnel. Lynn wasn't close to being able to sleep yet, so she turned her attention to her favorite city without moving away from her comfortable spot on Kent's shoulder. It was a clear night, and Lynn felt like she could see forever. She wished she was on one of the piers looking out on the bay instead of driving across it to hide. San Francisco always held good memories for her, maybe because it was not a place her parents liked to go. One of the few times they'd visited was for her mother's birthday. They'd had reservations at Alioto's on Fisherman's Wharf, thanks to Lynn's urging, but they only made it as far as the deep-fried cheese sticks and first round of drinks. Her step-father complained so much they left before ordering the main course. The cheese sticks were cold, the drinks too watery, the napkins dirty, slow service, he couldn't understand the waitress's accent—and the list went on.

None of it was true. The place was perfect. But her stepdad hated change, and they ended up back in Castro Valley at the subpar restaurant they always went to. No promised ice cream at Ghirardelli, no walking around the streets or going to Pier 39, nothing. Her mother got a scoop of vanilla ice cream with a candle and a diamond bracelet from her stepdad, and Lynn got heartburn and a silent ride home. She had plenty of time to replay what she'd heard her mom mumble to herself in the bathroom stall at the restaurant: "Why did she have to come and ruin it for us?" That about summed up Lynn's childhood after her stepdad entered the picture.

Lynn had had great times in the city with Stacy. Last year was her favorite, when they rode BART to Union Square at Christmastime. She loved looking at all the decorations in the Macy's windows and the tree in the square. They waited in line for lunch in one of the hotels because Stacy claimed it had the best onion soup around, and they were served champagne in line!

And then there was Tammy. Her mom took the girls to the city, and those were some of Lynn's favorite childhood memories. She felt a heaviness on her chest when she thought about her best friend. She had all those amazing memories of things they did together, yet she could never think about them without feeling sad. Instead, she always thought of that morning when the phone rang and her mother answered. She could still remember her mother's face—there was no emotion as she informed Lynn that Tammy and her family had been killed in a car accident on the way home from an uncle's funeral. Her mother didn't even look at Lynn as she shut her bedroom door. Lynn never learned who had called to give them the news. She sat in stunned silence the rest of the morning, and that afternoon she grieved with Stacy. They learned from Stacy's mom that the car swerved to avoid something, maybe a deer, and went off the steep road. They hadn't been wearing their seatbelts, Stacy's mom added grimly.

Even now, the tears threatened. She got a concerned glance from Kent, and she forced a smile. He tightened his arm around her as they merged into another lane. Lynn knew this wasn't the time for that particular trip down memory lane. She wanted to tell Kent these things someday, but not now. Her eyes suddenly felt heavy. She let them close, and for the first time in a long while, she felt safe as she drifted off. A small smile flickered on her face as she swirled into her pleasant dream of dancing in the forest.

* * *

THE EVILDWEL COULDN'T HAVE BEEN MORE pleased with how things were going. The thrill of the hunt was exhilarating, thanks to Lynn. Dian couldn't wait for her host to catch up to her. Too bad that man let her get away. Calling all the local hotels could pay off, along with watching all the roads leading out of the Bay Area. These ideas would come to her host, thanks to her subtle suggestions. He was always good with the small details, unlike some of her hosts. She was impressed at how quickly they'd found Kent's car, which led them to the taxi driver. Too bad the driver got away with only a broken hand.

Next time, she thought with a smile, she would push for a less happy outcome.

Dian filled her host with enough doubt for him to realize that the three fugitives likely hadn't flown out of the airport but had driven away in a rental. He caught on quickly that there would be no paper trail if the car had been stolen. Dian pondered. Would Kent go to a friend's house, a hotel, leave the area, or hide in plain sight? That question would soon be answered with all the power at her host's disposal and a little help from his killing muse. She smiled at that term, pleased with herself for coming up with it. It was perfect, and the story created was all hers to enjoy.

One fun subplot was dealing with all his employees. Their fear radiated off them when they had to give him bad news. That alone could feed her for months. Dian felt a satisfying bolt of energy shoot through her every time. Although it was positive for her, she knew her host was spinning out of control again. Time to rein him in so she could enjoy this more fully. She gently encouraged him to pull some strings, get those calls made, and find out if a man and two women had checked into any hotel within a fifty-mile radius driving a rental car in the middle of the night. *Look for the places off the beaten path, like on the ocean.* Maybe the people on her host's payroll would encourage more cooperation from business owners if a reward was offered for finding these criminals.

With all options covered, it would happen soon. Even without her guidance, Kent was easy for the humans to read. If he did something as stupid as going to someone he knew, her host's people would be there, waiting. But that wouldn't happen because he was a complete do-gooder who would never put anyone else in jeopardy. She wasn't a fan of that trait, but it certainly made planning easy. Then, once they got hold of Kent, Lynn, and Stacy, her host could finish it for her with a massive kill and get rid of the bodies too. *Wonderful fun!* The best part was that the killing list was growing.

* * *

"WE'RE HERE."

"Huh? What? Where?" Lynn felt suddenly shy about falling asleep on Kent. She sat up and rubbed her face. A glance at her watch told her it was one thirty.

"Hey, sleepyhead. We got lucky; the guy usually doesn't take guests after midnight. He fell asleep at his desk."

Stacy kept snoring.

"You're sure this is safe?" Lynn asked.

"No, not really. But like I keep saying, it's the best I can do for tonight. And heading south was as random as I could come up with."

Lynn opened the car door into the brisk night. The smell of the salty ocean hit her immediately. The full moon lit up the night sky, illuminating the waves hitting the sandy shore. She would leave a window open so she could listen. They got Stacy up and headed for Room 4. *Great—an omen?* Lynn remembered waking up to a dead guy in Apartment 4A. She shuddered as they entered a plain room with two double beds. There was a TV with a small antenna, a desk, and a tropical couch. Nothing fancy, but she didn't care. She watched Stacy go into the bathroom like a zombie. She came out and fell into the closest bed—dead to the world, as her grandma used to say. She sure missed her grandma and knew she would have loved Kent.

Lynn studied him. She wondered what would've happened with the sleeping arrangements if Stacy hadn't been there, but Kent wasn't paying any attention to her as she slipped in next to Stacy. She had hoped. Oh well, maybe she had misread everything. She had a sudden urge for a smoke; she hadn't had a cigarette since she found Stacy. She knew she should get some more sleep, but she didn't want to close her eyes yet. She wanted to watch Kent. Which might sound creepy if she said it out loud.

Kent turned his face to her, and the moon lit up his smile. He mouthed, "Come here," and smiled. She didn't hesitate. She wrapped a blanket around herself and followed him outside.

"I got you a pack of cigarettes at the No-Tell Motel. Sorry I forgot to give them to you until now." Kent placed them in her hand. Even that slight touch sent chills through her. It was crazy.

"Thanks. I keep meaning to quit these things, but, well, ya know…"

Kent smiled. "I hope you do. I'd like to see you stay healthy."

"I'd like to see me stay healthy too."

The tension between them was overwhelming. His misleading her at first was forgotten. She turned her face up to him, inviting another kiss. She couldn't tear her gaze from his lips as she reached up to push a stray lock of hair out of his eyes. It seemed like forever before he bent down and gently kissed her. Soon things progressed from gentle to intense as their bodies pressed together. His hands slid down to her lower back, and he pulled her toward him. She pressed herself against him, and he quickly responded.

With a small sigh, he pulled away, a question in his eyes.

"The beach," was all she had to say.

He surveyed the area and tugged on their motel door to make sure Stacy was secure. Satisfied, they walked hand in hand to the sand and waves. Out of sight of the street, parking lot, and motel, they quietly laid the blanket on the sand. Their clothes were scattered before they even lay down on it. The moon lit up every muscle on his body, much to Lynn's satisfaction. He was beautiful. She shivered in anticipation.

Quickly, they were intertwined. His mouth left her lips and began to explore her body. She had never felt so much passion from any man before. It was as if her body had been created for his touch, and her reaction was immediate and intense.

* * *

ZELINA HEARD Thomas sigh as she took in the view of the full moon illuminating the ocean. She realized he was trying to pretend he didn't hear the sounds coming from the blanket on the beach and was about to speak when Thomas said, "They are really going to do that now, with all that is going on?"

"Yes. That is love that you are seeing. Note that it is different than anything she has ever been around. Their love is important. Come on, we do not need to be here now. This is a private moment. Let us check on Stacy." Zelina smiled.

"Yes, it does feel strange being here now. Thank you."

"Sorry, but I was enjoying the ocean. One of Earth's special delights that I wish the humans would all care for and enjoy."

Thomas kept his gaze on the ocean. "Yes, the splendor of the ocean, the forests, and deserts. There is so much beauty, but they seem to want to ruin it all."

"Some do, but not all of them. There are those who can be reminded to look and enjoy."

"Not the people coming after them."

"No, not those people. Those are the people who throw their trash and do not look back." Zelina imitated a human throwing something down and then stomping on it. That always made her mad. Thomas smiled at her acting efforts.

"They are coming soon?" Thomas entered the motel room.

"Yes. They only have a few more hours of peace before the end." Zelina glanced back to the beach. "It is going to get busy soon."

"I keep seeing that house."

"That is the goal."

"I hope—" Thomas started to say.

"So do I," Zelina finished with a smile.

She put a lot of faith in Thomas. She watched him settle in next to Stacy and wrap his wings around her. For that moment she was safe. Zelina stood outside the motel door. She watched the couple return, hands clasped, surrounded in a pink aura of pure love. *Here is your prince, Lynn—you have found one of those rare true loves that happen here on Earth.* It was beautiful to see. Zelina looked at the front office and sighed. He was the one she worried about, but it had to be.

* * *

"That was amazing." Kent kissed Lynn's cheek.

"It was," replied Lynn, feeling shy. Raw, new emotions were surging through her, and she felt exposed for the first time in years.

"I could do that every day for the rest of our lives."

"You could?" Lynn asked in amazement. Most guys would be

trying to wiggle their way out of a commitment after that. She usually did, but this time she didn't want to.

"Yup. You better get some sleep. I'll make my call and then see what our next step is. And Lynn?"

"Yes?"

He bent down and pressed his warm lips against hers. He took her breath away, just like in all the stories. Talk about bad timing, if they got caught; but at least she'd finally experienced love. It made sense that she kept seeing Sleeping Beauty dancing in the forest with her prince. Lynn had found true love too. *Who knew?* Now, if only Kent felt the same way.

"Sleep well, Lynn."

"I will." Lynn beamed up at him as he opened the door and surveyed the room. Just Stacy, snoring away.

Lynn glanced back at Kent's body, silhouetted in the doorway, as she stepped into the shower. She rinsed off all the sand she'd accumulated on the beach. She used the flowery shampoo and soap the motel provided, humming the Disney song that she had thought was so silly a few days ago when it came to her in the bar. Perhaps on some level, she had already known about him, and for once she was going to go with this new feeling because it was so amazing!

Finished, she threw her wet towel down, put her clothes back on, and tried to untangle her hair with her fingers. She didn't want to wake Stacy up looking for her backpack and Kent's brush. She was disappointed to find that Kent hadn't come back from making his phone call.

She slid in next to Stacy, leaving Kent the other bed. *Don't want things to be weird in the morning* was her last thought before she fell asleep.

* * *

Kent dialed the phone number from memory. A familiar voice answered but didn't ask the usual question: "What do you have to report, young Kent?" Instead, he was asked, "Is Lynn Hill okay?"

Kent was thrown by his question. He couldn't figure out why his boss was so interested in Lynn, but the moment he heard her name, he had insisted on her protection with no offered explanation. Maybe he didn't want an innocent girl involved.

"Yes, she is with me right now, and so is her roommate. They called me earlier, and I rescued them from her stepbrother, Warren. His goons have been looking for us ever since, even using helicopters. I was able to ditch my car and borrow a rental, for now. I hope we're safe here, but I'm worried." Kent watched the dark parking lot. He saw a light go on in the office.

"You need to tell me every detail since your last report, when she was staying with her stepbrother in an unknown location."

* * *

"WE HAVE three confirmed late check-ins with rental cars in our area. There have been two more reported outside of San Francisco, sir," the nervous man told Warren.

"I assume you are checking into all five of those possibilities?" Warren downed another glass of champagne. That would be his last. He pulled out his coke stash; he needed to clear his mind.

"Yes, sir." The man gulped loudly.

Warren wiped his nose carefully and smiled. "Get on it. I expect a report within the half hour."

"We're on it." The man rushed out of the room.

"You bet you are," Warren said to himself with a smirk. "I have the world under my control. Soon, little sis, soon." He stripped his clothes off in front of the lackeys who remained. He was glad he'd had Gus call in the standby employees a few hours ago to get the house in working order for him. No more guest cottage.

"I would enjoy a swimming partner," he said as he strode to the pool and dove in.

The cool water woke him up. He didn't want to miss a thing tonight. It was going to be epic. He found a towel waiting next to his neatly folded clothes. He smiled. His uncle had trained them very well. He rinsed off in the warm water of the outdoor shower and wrapped the plush towel around him. He waited to see how the staff would accommodate his request for a swimming companion, and soon there was a beautiful, dark-haired woman smiling at him from the living room.

He wondered where they had been hiding her. The girl was stunning. Her clothes signaled a houseworker, perhaps a cook, although her tight-fitting top over a generous bust indicated something else. He signaled for her to join him. She seemed eager to please him, shedding her clothes with each step. Her body was perfect. Every inch of her was at his disposal. He prided himself on staying in great shape, and he knew how to please a woman, so she was in luck.

No words were necessary as he satisfied her under the full moon. He could tell she was having the time of her life. He patted her playfully on her firm bottom when he was finished. She smiled and bent down to arouse him again, but he held up his hand. As much as he would have enjoyed another round with her, he had things to do. He pulled her in for a quick kiss, then pushed her away with a hard slap across the face.

"I have other things to do," Warren told her. "Leave, now."

She looked at him with tears in her beautiful brown eyes. He hoped he wouldn't have to mark up that lovely face. *She'll learn to read my moods soon,* he thought with a smile, watching her hurry off with only a towel covering her. He hoped she'd remember to pick up her clothes later. Warren hated a mess.

Another quick dip in the pool, and then he was dressed and ready to finish what he'd started. He watched for the woman to return, but another one twice her age was tidying up. He would get back to training the first one after this was all over. A couple of sessions would make her more attentive. He ran his fingers through his hair and sat back down on the leather couch to wait. It was almost three thirty.

"Sir?" A timid older man entered the house.

"You better have good news. I've just been sitting around here waiting, you know."

"We believe we've found them, sir. A man with two women and a rental checked into the Whirlwind Motel on the coast near Pacifica at one thirty. We ruled out the other leads we have. We feel confident this is them, sir."

"Ah, some good news. Wonderful. Do we have men on the way?" Warren asked, suddenly wanting a cigarette for the first time in months. He wouldn't do that to his temple. He didn't like it when the women he was with smoked, either. *Like kissing an ashtray.*

The man looked at the ground. "No, sir. We wanted to get your instructions first."

"I believe I've made it pretty clear that I want them. You really didn't need me to tell you that again, did you?"

"Uh, no, sir. We'll get them."

"You'd better. I want to be airborne in an hour. I want to greet them at sunrise. You figure out how to make that happen."

"Uh, yes. Of course. Thank you, sir."

Warren waved his hand in dismissal. "You are quite welcome. Don't disappoint me."

The man shuddered and ran out of the room, already on his walkie-talkie. That gave Warren some extra time. Maybe he should call for that sweet girl again. He would make it up to her. It wasn't long before he found her room in the servant's area. The staff had been very obedient in keeping to their quarters unless he needed them. He knew his uncle demanded loyalty and obedience, and it showed. It also helped that most of them weren't in the country legally. When he got some free time, he'd talk to each employee personally to see if they were a good fit. He had high standards too, when it came to the upkeep of the house. Right now, this brunette beauty was one gem he wanted to keep around. He barged into her room without knocking. He saw fear in her eyes. He would soon replace it with longing. He made up for that slap, and he could tell how grateful she was.

"You may sleep now. I want you to always be here for me. And I'll always take care of you, I promise," Warren said with a crooked smile.

"Thank you, sir," she replied.

"When we are alone, I insist that you call me Warren. Save all that 'sir' stuff for around the rest of the staff, please."

"Yes, Warren."

"There, now get some sleep, my beauty." He glanced back one more time. He saw fear again—or was it hate? It was gone quickly, replaced by a beautiful smile. Maybe he was tired. If he saw it again, he would make sure it was the last time. As soon as this thing with his stepsister was done, he would find out her name and see how much they were paying her. Perhaps that was the problem. His uncle was a cheap man. Yes, it was probably about money, but she had to be happy he was in charge now, instead of his loser uncle.

CHAPTER 13

"*H*urry, we leave in five minutes!" Kent called loudly outside the bathroom door.

"I am. You just woke us up! Shit!" Stacy protested from the shower.

Lynn grinned at Kent as she stepped out of the bathroom. "She's always crabby in the morning."

Kent nodded with a smile that didn't reach his eyes. "I got us ready by going over the map and loading the car."

"How could he find us?" Lynn asked. She was glad of the small bottle of Scope in the bathroom; at least her breath was minty clean.

"No idea, but the light came on in the front office while I was on the phone, and I heard the phone ringing. Could be a coincidence, but who would be calling a hotel at this hour? I think it's better to follow Mr. Justice's suggestion to stay with him. It's why I'm pushing so hard to leave. We barely have time for this." Kent quickly pulled her into a kiss that left her breathless and then just as quickly pulled away, holding her gaze. "And no time to tell you I'm falling hard for you, either."

Lynn blushed but didn't reply.

"We're supposed to drive to a point where he'll send us a helicopter. After that we'll be relaxing in a mansion." Kent smiled—too brightly.

Lynn knew he was trying to keep her calm, and she was, except for her racing heart, which had nothing to do with being chased by bad men. At least they were safe and together for the moment. She matched his cheerful smile. "Gee, another helicopter on our behalf—we're popular."

"Yes, we are." Kent winked and then yawned. "Mr. Justice's concern is for the safety of you girls in all this craziness."

His beautiful eyes that she could get lost in couldn't hide his worry. Then there was the whole matter of the dark smudges under his eyes. He hadn't slept. She'd have to make sure he didn't fall asleep at the wheel. "This is crazy."

"It is. Right now, the best thing we can do is get out of here. Would you mind hurrying Stacy along?" His smile seemed forced now. It reminded her of when things were bad at home and they had guests. Everyone pretended that everything was fine.

"Yeah, got it."

She opened the bathroom door and was greeted by a burst of steam. Lynn wondered about this secretive Mr. Justice as she worked on her tangled hair. Was he really just some dude helping to put bad guys away? She hoped it was that simple, but she knew that nothing ever was. One thing seemed simple *and* scary: Kent was amazing. She splashed water on her face and grabbed a towel for Stacy. But if he was lying, well, she wasn't sure she had a second forgiveness card.

"We have to go, Stace," Lynn urged. She draped the towel over the rod. It quickly disappeared, and the water flow stopped.

Lynn was using the "facilities" just as Stacy burst out from behind the shower curtain wearing the short white towel. Within a second she was dressed. "Ready!" she declared. She pulled her shoes on. "See, I told you I could take a fast shower!"

"You did," Kent agreed. "Let's go."

They hurried to the truck as Lynn glanced at the office. "Light's still on. Maybe he can't sleep."

"Maybe," Kent replied as he backed up the Blazer. The light went out, and a man peeked out the window at them.

"Okay, that was weird." Lynn frowned at Kent, who was too busy driving to notice. She scanned the parking lot. She didn't see anyone, but she kept looking. The feeling of being watched was strong.

"What was?" Stacy asked, pulling the front of her hair into a side ponytail.

"The dude in the office was watching us leave."

Kent glanced back at the dark office. "I have a bad feeling about this."

"Me too," Lynn whispered.

"Thanks, Han Solo. So I got woken up because some dude can't sleep? Maybe he was wondering why we were leaving in the middle of the night." Stacy shook her head.

Kent looked in the rearview mirror and met Stacy's gaze before pulling onto the dark road. "I'm trying to keep you safe."

"And I appreciate that, Kent, but I don't see how anyone could find us here is all."

"I can't take any chances. Besides, Mr. Justice wants us with him. He's providing a helicopter. Once we get there, you can sleep all you want."

"Yeah, well, cool. I've always wanted to ride in a helicopter. But, um, are we going to drive with our headlights off?"

"Yes, we are."

Stacy shrugged at Lynn and bent down. "Not big on cleaning their cars out," she muttered, holding up an opened pack of gum.

"Huh? Yes, well, they probably hadn't gotten around to that." Kent kept looking in his side mirror. Lynn knew he was worried about being followed. So was she, but she didn't see anyone. "Fortunately, the moon is full."

Stacy looked out the passenger side window. "Highway 1, with steep cliffs and the rocky ocean shore below—what could go wrong?"

"Nothing while I'm driving, I can assure you of that, Stacy," Kent replied in a dark, sarcastic tone Lynn hadn't heard before. It gave her chills as they went into a sharp right turn. She still didn't see any cars following. Maybe they were okay, but now she was wondering if there was a side of Kent she wasn't aware of.

Lynn glanced back and shook her head at Stacy, who responded with an eyeroll. She knew Stacy needed all eight hours of her beauty sleep or she got irritable. Being drugged didn't help, either. Lynn heard loud pops as her friend took her frustration out on her gum for several minutes and then threw it out the window. The silence was unnerving as they drove down the dark and empty road with the ocean on one side and rolling hills on the other. Kent was watching the left side as they traveled further south. After a long period of tense quiet he finally made a quick turn onto another road.

"What are we looking for?" Lynn asked.

"The pay phone Mr. Justice told me we'd find along this strip of road."

"Pay phone? Aren't we meeting up with a helicopter?" Lynn asked. She heard Stacy open another piece of gum and begin chewing loudly again. She was going to hurt her jaw if she kept that up, but Lynn wasn't going to be the one to tell her. They were all on edge. At least the gum chewing broke the silence of the last several miles. It was like the ticking of a clock; each pop took them a little further to safety, Lynn hoped. She studied the fancy radio with a cassette player. They couldn't use the cassette player, but they could certainly use the radio. Her only concern now was keeping Kent awake without distracting him. Of course, he wouldn't have to stay awake if she hadn't called him. A sudden wave of guilt flowed through her. There were two people on the run with her, and she was the only one Warren wanted. She was the reason the two most important people in her life were in danger. And they weren't getting along. *Great.*

"I call, and then he sends the helicopter, was what he said to me. He wants to make sure no one is following us, Lynn."

"I'm watching for that. I don't see anyone but us out here."

"I know. Doesn't mean they aren't there, though, but thanks for keeping a lookout." Kent grinned and winked at Lynn, reminding her of Han Solo's cockiness and moodiness. She found that endearing. How could she think he had a hidden, dark personality? *Oh yeah, because I grew up with crazy people, that's why.* Kent was definitely nothing like them.

"You didn't mention having to call first. Why do our plans keep changing? I don't like this." Stacy sighed.

"Plan changes are the only thing keeping you alive right now," Kent said quietly.

Stacy didn't respond, and the silence grew heavier. Lynn gave up on the uncomfortable, unsaid words and pointed to the radio. "You mind?"

"No. I prefer music when I'm driving. Wasn't sure how you guys felt about it," Kent shrugged.

"I'm all for it," Stacy said.

Lynn tuned the radio to an alternative rock station and found "One Thing Leads to Another" by the Fixx, one of her favorite songs. She didn't crank it up loud, like she normally would have done. She left it on low, like background music in a movie, because that was exactly how she felt, like none of what was happening was real.

* * *

DIAN WAS THOROUGHLY ENJOYING HERSELF. Her host putting that woman in her place with a slap was a tantalizing surprise. That charm and ruthlessness was totally her host. Sometimes he surprised her, and that wasn't easy to do. Everyone in the household was fearful of him, and that was a feeding frenzy for her. Of course, Dian's insight paid off when Lynn's location was discovered. She encouraged her host not to rush into anything this time, like when he'd taken it upon himself to kill Lynn with a gas leak. That was not the way she liked to do things. It had been a foolish mistake, not staying focused on her host. Lynn would have been dead, but not in the most gratifying way.

Now to meet Mr. Justice. Dian was already making plans for his demise. The first report came in. She laughed along with her host when hearing their targets were driving on a dark highway without their lights on. Like no one could spot them.

The next update came after several long minutes. They had

stopped at a pay phone. Dian had to calm down her host's spinning thoughts and push him in the right direction. He told one of his nameless lackeys that it was a good sign they were contacting the person he suspected was Mr. Justice. *Great insight,* she thought proudly. Yes, they would be meeting up with him soon. Once Lynn, Mr. Justice, Kent, and Stacy were within her host's grasp, they would pay dearly. The downside to this lovely outcome was that her host might not survive.

Of course, Dian had a plan in place for her next host. Serial killers were always at the top of her list. Some evildwels preferred abusers over killers, but either way, it wasn't hard to find humans who functioned in fear or hate. Even the ones who claimed to have no feelings worked well as hosts.

Dian would certainly miss this host when the time came. He was everything she looked for. He'd have been an amazing find during World War II, on the German side. She could imagine his rise to power and everyone he would have taken down to get there. She had been a part of that war, but her human host had been weaker than she had hoped. She would never again make the mistake of entering anyone who had even a shred of good feeling. That German soldier killed others to survive, but he didn't enjoy it like she did. When she was done with those weaker hosts, she encouraged them to do something that would get them killed—or kill themselves. That soldier had killed himself when they lost the war, like his leader.

The host she remembered most fondly had been executed in an electric chair. Of course, she left before all the pain, but his fear right up to that moment was more intense than that of his victims because all his hope was gone. The victims had hung on to a small shred of faith that they might live.

As much fun as the past several days had been, she was beginning to see small signs of her host losing the control that had served him so well, especially in prison. But it wasn't over yet. The helicopter hit turbulence, and she fed on his fear of flying. *Soon.* Her mist darkened in excitement. This was going to be amazing. If anyone had looked at her host, they would have seen her bright red eyes glowing in excitement. But no one was paying any attention to the boss, and even if they had, they wouldn't have believed what they were seeing. Dian wished she could hug herself. She certainly deserved it.

* * *

"THERE'S THE PAY PHONE. I'll be right back; keep the car running." Kent squeezed Lynn's hand before running to the phone.

"I wish we had some coffee."

"Yeah, me too, Stace, but they aren't open yet. I wish you wouldn't like…well, ya know, be so…at Kent. I mean, after all he's done for us."

"Yeah, sorry. I was kind of a bitch back there. I like the dude. I mean, after all, he quotes Han Solo. I'm, um—well, just kind of freaked out, ya know?"

"I know. Me too. I think we're going to be okay now. And I'm glad you like him." Lynn turned the radio off. She didn't want to hear the DJs talking about their hot girlfriends instead of playing music.

"Yeah, we're gonna be cool now, and yeah, I don't hate him. The way he looks at you, I can tell it's real, ya know?"

Lynn turned away. "I know, I see that too, and honestly, it's the first time I've liked a guy this much."

"I can tell. He's easy on the eyes too."

"Yeah, well, I can't disagree. I just want the two people I care about to get along."

"Got it. I will try to refrain from my usual amusing comments for a while, just for you." Stacy held up the pack of gum. "You want some old rental floor gum?"

"Well, who wouldn't?" Lynn helped herself to a piece of Doublemint. The sugar and mint hit her taste buds immediately, waking her up. "Thanks," she said right as Kent came back.

"His pilot is sick. But Mr. Justice is happy we made it to this point. He said there's a road through the hills that will lead us to his house." Kent grabbed some gum when Stacy offered it.

Stacy's form of apology was her brightest smile. "Cool."

"Thanks for the gum. Oh, and Stacy, Mr. Justice recommended we use our headlights from now on. That should make you happy."

"I'm ecstatic," Stacy said. She looked at Lynn and added, "Yeah, that will make me very happy. Thanks, Kent."

"You're welcome."

Kent glanced at Lynn, who grinned and then asked, "You sure we can trust this Mr. Justice?"

"My grandpa did, and I trusted him. Never had any reason not to, but, well, right now, the only ones I trust are you two." Kent stumbled through his words while rubbing his eyes.

"The three musketeers."

"That we are, Stacy." Kent smiled at Lynn. She was pretty sure she blushed, and she hoped Stacy hadn't seen, but she had.

For the first time in years, Lynn heard that term and didn't feel like crying. It was what she, Tammy, and Stacy used to call themselves—before. That had to be a good sign. Maybe it was time to be able to remember her like she wanted to. If they survived. Otherwise, she would be seeing her old friend soon.

"Could you two lovebirds tone it down a bit? You are making the back seat people uncomfortable. You think I didn't notice you two sneaking off together?"

Lynn couldn't remember ever feeling this embarrassed about having sex, maybe because, for the first time, it had been more than that. "I, um…you were sleeping, and we just…"

"You slept together—no big deal. Never seen you embarrassed about it before."

Lynn gave her friend a slight headshake as Kent put the Blazer in reverse and headed back down the road into the hills. Stacy seemed to get it because she shut up, even though Lynn knew she was trying to be nice at this point. Kent mouthed "Sorry" to Lynn when she looked over. She smiled.

She wasn't sorry, but she didn't want to make him uncomfortable. She was crazy about him, and for some reason, against her better judgment, she trusted him as much as she trusted Stacy. She felt like the three of them could do anything, like those roommates on *Three's*

Company, except that two of them were a couple now. Or so she hoped, if they lived through this bizarre crap.

* * *

"Almost at the log mansion," Thomas declared.

Zelina glided next to him. "Yes. This can go two ways, one not promising at all. Unfortunately, Warren has found the information he was looking for. He was not happy to learn who Mr. Justice is."

Thomas frowned. "Warren knows?"

"He does. Do you?"

"I do, and of course, the other part. Warren does not know that, does he?" Thomas's eyes narrowed.

Zelina quickly shook her head. "No, he does not know all of it, just enough to cause some trouble. We do not need that information in the mix of things right now. I am not sure what Mr. Justice will share with them. He certainly does have a lot to answer for, but that is up to him. We will see."

"Yes, I could see where too much information at once would make matters worse, but it all has to come out someday."

"Yes, it does. I am hoping I can convince Mr. Justice to be careful in his sharing. My thoughts are also on Lynn's real parents. Her father is now recovering, but he has a lot of anger to resolve, as you know. He did not appreciate the family who adopted him. He only dwelled on why his parents did not want him. He found out who his father was, but that reunion did not go well. His mother wanted to keep him but did not. She died young, from cancer, or I believe she would have approached him. All his anger attracted that evildwel to him, but, as you know, bad men do not always have an evildwel directing them. Some are plain bad. Like Warren's uncle, whom he ended up working for." Zelina sighed.

"I worried more about him and not about Carrie and Lynn, like I should have. I deeply regret that and hope what we do next helps."

Zelina looked concerned. "I am saying this now not to make you feel bad but to help you understand what is about to happen."

Thomas shook his head. "I see what secrets do. None of it is good right now."

"No, it is not. I am glad we are here together to fix this mess these humans have created."

"Me too."

CHAPTER 14

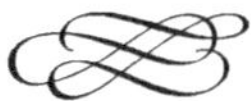

The two-lane highway narrowed, making Lynn glad she wasn't driving. The rock wall on one side and the cliff on the other, with no shoulder, allowed no room for driver error. Lynn watched Kent, who kept his hand out the open window, a trick she had used before to stay awake while driving home late at night. Stacy had fallen back to sleep, her gum fallen onto her arm. Lynn wondered if she should remove it before it got in her hair, but she didn't want to distract Kent. Instead, she slid closer to him. She loved the front bench seat and decided it was a must for when they drove together—if they ever got another chance.

"You okay?" he asked quietly.

"I guess so. You?"

"Next to you I am, but I'll feel better when we get off the road."

"Me too."

Lynn nuzzled her head under his shoulder. He had to readjust his arm, but in the end, they fit perfectly together. She almost fell asleep, but something she saw made her bolt upright. "Is that a guy standing next to that car ahead? Do you think he needs help?"

"He's in front of a big black gate; that's what Mr. Justice said to watch for."

"So are you planning to stop? What if it's some type of trap?"

Kent reached under the seat and pulled out his gun. "I'll be ready if it is a trap, and you and Stacy are armed." Kent slowed and parked, blocking the black Mercedes but angling their vehicle so that they could get out of there quickly. Lynn reached over and grabbed her gun out of the backpack. She gripped it tightly, praying she wouldn't have to use it, knowing she would if she had to. Maybe she wouldn't make such a bad detective if she had the right partner, like on *Hart to Hart*. Kent carefully opened his window as a grandfatherly type with wild white hair and a long brown raincoat approached them holding a flashlight. Lynn saw PJ bottoms peeking out and slippers on his feet. Someone had gotten him out of bed.

"Mr. Stuart, Miss Hill, and Miss Kelly, I presume?" he asked, shining the flashlight into the car. Stacy didn't stir.

"Yes, who are you?" Kent asked.

"I work for Mr. Justice. You may call me Alfred—and before you bother, yes, I know, like Batman," Alfred said with a crooked grin and a heavy British accent.

Lynn immediately liked him. He had a full white mustache and a beer belly, although he looked too refined to drink beer, so maybe he just ate well. His skin was tan, like he spent a lot of time in the sun. Could he be Mr. Justice himself, checking them out before talking to them?

"So I guess that means you're his butler?" Kent asked.

"I'm his assistant, but I'm known to answer the door for him or lay his clothes out too. Would you mind following me? The house is set back a ways."

"You're taking us to Mr. Justice?" Kent asked.

"What else would I be doing at this awful hour—besides sleeping?" Alfred winked.

Lynn glanced back at Stacy. How was she sleeping through all of this? She snuggled against Kent as they slowly drove down an unlit, narrow lane lined with tall redwoods. They made a right turn into a large, circular drive in front of a rather imposing log cabin.

"A place where I could spend some time," Kent said.

"Me too. I love log cabins." Lynn took in the size of it.

"This is more like a log mansion," Kent replied.

"It's amazing. I hope the guy inside fits his home."

"You mean a rich mountain man? Living off the land, aided by his butler named Alfred?" Kent chuckled.

"Naturally," Lynn replied as they parked next to the Mercedes. There was an enormous satellite dish off to their right, along with a radio tower and several large solar panels. Mounted cameras pointed down at them. This was a man who took his privacy seriously. She hoped that was good for them. Kent got out while Lynn woke Stacy.

"We're here? Sorry, I should have stayed awake with you guys. I think all those drugs they fed me are still roaming around my system." Stacy smoothed her hair down and shook her head, trying to wake up.

"I understand, Stace. No problem. Come meet Mr. Justice's assistant, Alfred."

"Alfred? Like Bruce Wayne's butler? Really?" Stacy grinned.

"Yup. Just like him, English accent and all. He claims he even answers the door."

Stacy got out of the car and looked around. "This place is awesome, Lynn. I never knew log cabins could be this big! I bet that porch goes all the way around. You see the pool and the firepit? This dude knows how to live."

Lynn smiled. *Look out, Mr. Justice.*

Alfred informed them they weren't to meet Mr. Justice yet. He would show them to their rooms to get some rest. Lynn frowned at Kent when she heard it would be best if they didn't leave their rooms until morning to give their host some privacy. *Are we guests or prisoners here?* she wondered. *At least we're alive,* she concluded.

They entered a dimly lit room with tall ceilings and a plaid couch with two black cats on opposite sides, both ignoring their guests. Alfred was pointing out the amenities as Lynn took in the beauty around her. A bearskin rug lay in front of a handsome stone fireplace big enough to cook in. She imagined lying there with Kent on a cold night, drinking hot chocolate; and… She smiled at Kent, who grinned at her like he could read her mind. *Maybe he can.*

Photos of nature adorned the walls. Maybe Mr. Justice was a photographer; that was the only clue she could find about the owner other than that he liked cats and bear rugs. She liked this place much better than the mansion where she had been held. This was cozy, with hardwood floors and everything in warm, sunset colors.

"The kitchen and dining room are through there." Alfred pointed at some western-style swinging doors. He indicated the wide wooden staircase. "Upstairs are the bedrooms and exercise room. The basement is Mr. Justice's private area for his office and hobby room. Follow me, and I will show you your rooms. Do you girls want to share a room?" he asked.

"Sure," Stacy replied. "Unless they want their own room. I don't mind either way."

Lynn blushed, unable to make eye contact with Kent. Why was she acting like a silly teen with her first crush? She was a woman who'd been with many men, yet this was the first one to make her act so goofy. It unnerved her a little.

Alfred had a slight grin. "Very well, you decide your sleeping arrangements. There are three available rooms for you; take your pick. Although we don't have nightwear for the ladies, I did put out some large shirts that might work for you. If you leave your clothes outside your room, I'll put them in the laundry for you before I go back to sleep. Can you think of anything you might need before late morning? There will be a hearty, country-style breakfast served when you rise."

"Thank you, we're fine. Don't worry about washing our clothes, either. Thanks, though," Lynn added.

"Yes, thank you. We're fine for tonight—I mean, this morning, really," Kent said.

"Yes, it is morning, but it's still dark, so it doesn't count. Well, then, sleep well." Alfred grinned and walked down the hall, making a left turn. He was soon out of sight.

"Stacy!" Lynn hissed.

"What? I thought you two might want more time alone."

"Yeah, well, I'd feel better if we stayed together," Kent said. "I'll sleep on the floor, if necessary."

Lynn opened the door to the first room and was amazed again. It contained a king-size bed, a fireplace, a desk, and a couch next to a picture window overlooking a brightly lit pool framed by redwoods. She peeked inside the other two rooms; they were the same.

"It's like we're on vacation!" Stacy exclaimed.

"Yeah, I'm not going to complain. This is so cool," Lynn said.

"This is nice, and I'd like to enjoy it more, but we should sleep while we can. I have a feeling that today will be interesting," Kent warned. "My gut tells me we're safe here. My grandfather trusted Mr. Justice, and I'm going to trust my grandfather, but I'll remain on alert, just in case."

"I can agree with that," Stacy said.

All three fell asleep quickly in their clothes, the two girls in the bed and Kent on the couch.

Alfred peeked in and saw that they were sleeping. He smiled as he noiselessly closed the door, and the faint *click* of the lock failed to rouse the sleepers.

* * *

"Yes, sir. We have a location."

"And?" Warren was feeling testy. He wasn't a fan of flying, and a helicopter was even worse than a plane. The lights below didn't interest him, nor did the ocean. He was in their area, ready to pounce on them and their benefactor. He took a long swig of scotch to steady his nerves and hoped they would be landing soon.

"It's an hour's drive from their last location, sir. They were met by a man and went into a gated area. They were clueless they were being followed; we're positive. No one has left since they entered, and there is only one road in and out. There's a high fence all the way around with state-of-the-art security. We've checked the entire perimeter and seen a large house, pool, and communication equipment. The grounds are surrounded by redwoods, and there doesn't appear to be any other houses or structures in the area. We believe we can breach the wall and get near the house. How do you want us to proceed, sir?"

"I'll get as close as I can with this flying contraption. I don't want you to alert them to our presence yet. I would prefer that you keep gathering information. Get all our power there, with our best going in first. Let our contacts in the police department know to avoid this area if they get a call. I want my stepsister back, and I want you to figure out how to get us in there to do that—the quieter, the better. I don't want to have to call in too many favors. I'm sure we can come up with an explanation to suit everyone after the fact."

"Yes, sir. We're on it. Are we allowed to kill any of the occupants, sir?"

"Only if you must. I'd like my sister alive, and our so-called Mr. Justice. I'd suggest a fire to lure them out, but that would draw too much attention, and I don't want to start a forest fire. Stick to knives and gas unless you can't. Let me know when it's secured, and I will meet you inside. I'm counting on you. All your training had better pay off. If it doesn't…"

"Understood, sir."

* * *

THOMAS FELT uncomfortable sitting by the sleeping trio. "It is going to happen soon."

"Yes."

He fidgeted with his hair and almost began biting his nails. He had not done that in decades. "Should we wake them up?"

Zelina's attention was on the door. "No, they need to sleep. It will be a long day for them."

"I see it ending below."

"Mr. Justice is prepared for many things. His home being attacked is one of them. You see that bookcase over there next to the armoire?" Zelina pointed.

"Yes."

"It is a passageway that leads to either the basement or other rooms. The basement, or the 'below' you are talking about, is a room much like the one Stacy was kept in. It can withstand almost anything." Zelina wrapped her wings around Lynn.

"I feel like we should be doing something." Thomas fluttered his wings.

"Yes, we will. Good call with your wings."

"Alfred?"

"Yes. He needs a wake-up call."

"He is—"

Zelina interrupted him. "He is. You go knock some books off a shelf."

"What about you?"

"I will keep an eye on these three. We cannot take the chance that they will find their way out of this room in case Alfred does not make it here to help them."

"He will make it here—I will make sure." Thomas flew off.

Alfred was lightly snoring when Thomas knocked over three books.

"What? Who's there?" He sat up and peered into the darkness. He flipped on the light and saw books sprawled on the floor. "Earthquake?" he murmured, picking them up. He glanced at the two monitors on his desk and saw two men creeping in the darkness by the back wall. "The alarms didn't go off."

He pulled on his clothes, watching more dark figures gathering around the wall. He retrieved a gun from the desk drawer and switched to another view. Lynn, Stacy, and Kent were still sleeping. Thomas could feel his guilt for having locked them in their room but understood why. He had some explaining to do before they found out. The good part of that was the intruders would need a key to get into their room. That would briefly slow them down.

He hit a red button under the desk and pulled out a picture of a smiling young girl. "No one is going to ever hurt you again, sweetheart," he assured the picture. He stuffed the picture into his pocket and pulled on his coat. He opened the bookcase and entered the tunnels.

The alarm system indicated that they were safe, but they certainly were not. Thomas followed Alfred, thinking he would go to Lynn's room, but instead, he entered a large room that looked like it belonged on a movie set. Every monitor was ablaze with activity. Men were surrounding the house but still not triggering the alarm.

"Trapped," Alfred muttered. "Good thing I sent the staff home earlier, or I'd have to worry about them too."

Thomas watched Alfred push a few buttons. Lights came on outside, and steel shutters covered the windows and doors. He set off several explosions, which took down a few of the men, but they kept coming.

Alfred picked up the phone and quickly set it back in its cradle. "Lines are dead. I hope the panic button was operational. Not that it matters—I can't wait for help now."

He bent over a panel and pressed a button, holding his finger in place to be scanned. "Please state your name," an electronic voice requested.

"Alfred," he replied.

"Do you like mountains?"

"No, hills," Alfred said.

"Thank you, Alfred. Do you like revenge?"

"No, I like justice."

"Confirmed, Mr. Justice."

"Activate full defenses on outer rim. Be on standby for total defense of safety."

"It is done," the voice confirmed.

He rushed out of the room, headed for the tunnels. Thomas glanced back once to see bullets and arrows flying from the defense system, but nothing seemed to stop Warren's men. They had a large metal object like a snowplow on the front of a pickup truck to ram the front door. *They will be in the house soon,* he thought grimly. He hoped Alfred could get his guests safely into this room before that happened. But to his surprise, Alfred was not going in the direction of their room. He was gathering cats.

Thomas heard the pickup revving its engine and slamming into the front door while Alfred placed his cats in a carrier stored behind the couch. The door bent but did not break. It would not hold through too many more attempts. The truck backed up, no worse for wear, and revved its engine again. Alfred was moving at top speed now; he deposited his cats in the safe room and headed for Lynn's room just as the front door cracked. Something was thrown in, and an oily smoke began to rise. Thomas understood that the cats wouldn't have survived the gas attack, but still, the old man was cutting it close. He watched Alfred sprint toward the bookcase upstairs and push it open.

Lynn was dreaming about Kent. They were lying on a warm tropical beach, wrapped around each other. She felt safe under the moon and stars with her head on Kent's shoulder. She was breathing in his musky scent when her stepdad yanked her up, calling her a sl*t and a wh*re. He began hitting her, as he'd done so many times in drunken rages. She looked to Kent to protect her, but he was gone. She felt the same helplessness she'd endured growing up, when she heard a voice yelling, "Let's go!" Was Kent saving her, after all?

"Kent?" Lynn sat up with a shiver.

It had been a dream. Well, really, a memory in a dream. She hoped it wasn't a warning. *Can I really not trust Kent?* Stacy was sitting up next to her, looking as confused as Lynn felt. Kent was already on his feet with his gun in hand, pushing his feet into his shoes. He caught her eye at that moment, and she felt safe again. Then there was the matter of the breathless butler standing in their room, looking like he had just run a marathon.

"Come on! There's no time. They're in the house!" Alfred said.

"Who? What?" Stacy asked.

Kent pulled Lynn and then Stacy out of bed. "I can hear them. Let's get out of here!"

"Our shoes," Stacy protested. Lynn grabbed them. "I thought we were safe!"

"No more time!" Alfred watched their door. "Follow me."

They heard the crashing and yelling getting closer. It would only be minutes before they were found. They followed Alfred into a narrow tunnel behind the wall and watched the bookcase close after them.

"I can lock this door; that should slow them down. Please try to be quiet so they don't hear us," Alfred warned.

The white concrete tunnel sloped downhill. Its small, round lights suddenly began flashing.

"The power is down, and the generator is coming on." Alfred was out of breath.

Kent grabbed Lynn's hand and squeezed. Together they ran, with Stacy following behind. The lower they got, the louder the sounds became. It sounded like the men were tearing the house apart. How soon would it be before the intruders discovered they weren't in the house anymore? *And those poor cats!* She hoped they'd found a good place to hide.

They went deeper below the house until finally they entered a large room, where the two cats waited expectantly in their carrier. Once the door was secured behind him, Alfred opened the carrier. The cats darted out and settled on the couch.

"I think you understand what's happened and can see for yourselves what's going on outside on the screens. Let me update you, and then you can ask questions. We are safe here. I apologize for my last-minute retrieval of you." Alfred seemed to have lost his British accent. "And yes, I saved the cats first, but in my defense, they were in the line of fire. Your room was still safe."

He paused and took a breath. "I told you my name was Alfred and I was Mr. Justice's assistant. That part wasn't true; I *am* Mr. Justice, but my real name is Alfred Hill." He watched Lynn's face as realization dawned.

"You are..." was all Lynn got out.

"Yes, now I recognize your voice, Mr. Justice," Kent said, looking puzzled.

"Sorry I used a fake accent, but I had to be careful."

"*You* are Kent's boss?" Stacy asked. Behind them, the monitors went black.

"I am, but I'm also Lynn's grandfather. I'm her dad's birth father."

Lynn, feeling a little dizzy, sank onto the couch between the cats.

"You need to explain." Kent sat next to Lynn and putting his arm around her protectively.

"We have nothing but time. At least, until we don't. There is one more exit to the outside, if we need it. Hopefully, the cameras will come back online, but I am doubtful of that. So we wait, and I'll explain," Lynn's newfound grandfather said.

"I can't wait for this." Stacy sat next to Lynn and began petting one of the cats.

* * *

Thomas's mouth hung open. "He is not going to tell them the rest, is he?"

"No. He is too ashamed."

"He should be. She is barely able to understand this. Are they safe here?"

"Doubtful. He has a plan, though."

"Plan?" Thomas folded his wings.

Zelina shrugged. "Well, they are not done with Warren."

"I think I see that."

"It is not a pleasant future, but it could be a survivable one. Right now, we need to be patient and let it play out before we can help them."

A frown crossed over his face. "This is the part I do not like."

"I do not like it, either. It always depends on everyone's decisions." Zelina stood close to Lynn, her wings touching her.

"But they are more prone to do one thing over another."

"Right, with a bit of help."

"That is our part." Thomas smiled. He would not make the same mistake twice. He hoped these humans were capable of learning too.

* * *

ALFRED SAT down in a brown leather chair and started to talk without looking at the people in front of him. "Let me explain this to you, Lynn, before you pass the judgment that I know I deserve. I was a selfish and greedy young man. I came from money, and when the wrong woman became pregnant, I insisted she give the baby up for adoption. My ego was huge, and I wanted him to keep the Hill name—with, of course, a nice bit of cash for the adoptive family. My own father was a partner with the wrong people—the Stones. I made tons of money and did a lot of bad things with that family. The woman I eventually married was a Stone, but she couldn't have kids. So I decided to become involved with my son from a distance.

"I watched him get married and have you, Lynn. I was proud. He was slowly making his way up the ranks of our organization. I was going to bring him into my circle when he proved himself and tell him the truth. That never happened because his drinking got worse and I was embarrassed by his actions. I decided that bringing him into my life wasn't a good idea, so I turned my back on him and my grand-daughter. When my wife died the next year, I swore I would marry again and produce a real heir. But when I found out my only son had also died six months later, everything changed for me." He wiped a tear away.

"Changed?" Lynn squeezed Kent's hand when she heard a loud crash.

"It was like everything I had done in my entire life came back at me. I could barely get out of bed. I was living in a black-and-white world, and the only color left was you. I had more money than I knew what to do with, yet it meant nothing. I lived in a world where killing was no different than taking your trash out to the curb. I was going to make a move and get myself free. Then I would come to you and your mother and be a part of your family. I planned my death after moving all my money around. Most people thought I'd died broke in a boating accident. My remaining assets went to pay off all the outstanding debt from the life I used to lead.

"I changed my name and waited. I was ready to approach you, but then your mother got involved with a Stone and married him. It took me a while to realize your stepfather wasn't a part of the crime organization, but in the meantime, I filled my emptiness with the bottle, just like my son had. I had to find a purpose for myself again, so I turned my attention to helping the police put this corrupt family—and many others like them—away. My finances were solid, and only one man knew I was alive—Kent's grandfather, my best friend from childhood. I became the Mr. Justice the Stone family hated. At one point I was going to turn myself in, but your grandfather talked me out of it. He insisted I could do too much good, but that also meant I couldn't be a part of your life, Lynn. I will always regret that and the weak shadow of a man I had become."

Lynn swallowed hard and nodded, unable to speak. How different her childhood could have been.

"I wish my grandfather had told me," Kent said.

"He was protective of you, son, and I think he always planned to, but life gets away from us sometimes. You are the spitting image of your grandfather. It broke his heart to walk away from his job in law enforcement, but he couldn't pretend that the bad cops hadn't taken over, with the Stones involved."

"Yeah, he was a good guy," Kent replied, squeezing Lynn's hand tighter.

She looked her grandfather in the eye with a frown. "Okay, so you gave up my dad, you were a criminal for the same people my stepbrother works for, you wanted my dad back, then you didn't, then you felt bad and pretended to die, you started drinking, and then you became an undercover superhero. Now you want to be my grandpa while men are tearing your house apart looking for us? Did I miss anything? Like, how about saving me, when I was growing up, from my stepfather's drunken rages?"

"Yes, you got it all right, except I quit drinking several years ago. As for your stepdad, I honestly didn't know about that. I heard you had food poisoning at fourteen, but that's all. I didn't know that you'd tried to kill yourself until much later. I was heartbroken, and if I had known, I would have found a way to get you out of there; I promise you that. I'm very sorry, Lynn. I may have been a bad man in the past, and I did many things, including turning to the bottle, to escape my reality, but if I had known, I certainly would have protected you."

"Yes, *food poisoning*. That's what they told the neighbors to explain why an ambulance came to our house. My mother and stepfather were and still are good actors, and they are cold and cruel drunks. I understand that my stepfather was abused as a kid to toughen him up, like his brother. It backfired, though, and only made him a crazy man who beats his children and his wife but turned his back on his family's business. Being a soldier added to his craziness. I understand why he was the way he was—doesn't make it okay, though." Lynn folded her arms defensively. "And as for my mother, I've heard that her father was the same as my stepdad, so that was normal to her. Never met the guy, though—he took off. So now that we know each other's history, I'm not going to fall into your arms and cry about how wonderful it is to find my grandpa."

Alfred sadly shook his head. "I don't expect that, Lynn. I hope that someday you'll give me a chance to prove myself and fully forgive me for everything." He looked away. The room was tense with unspoken words. Alfred finally broke the silence with a forced grin. "I never expected to find my detective and granddaughter in a relationship, though."

"We aren't in a relationship," Lynn replied. "Yet."

"'Yet'? I feel hopeful," Kent said with a smile.

"I feel like I've been watching *All My Children*," said Stacy. "I'm waiting for a twin sister to pop out from behind a door. This is some crazy shit, Lynn." She gave her friend a quick hug.

"They do say truth is stranger than fiction, don't they?" said Alfred.

"They do. I understand why you needed to tell her all of this now, just in case." Kent glanced at Lynn, who was staring off into space, and added, "Anyway, I can't see them giving up and leaving, even though it has quieted down out there. I'm sure this room is earthquake-, fire-, and bombproof, but I've always found that things aren't always perfect. So do we have a plan besides recounting family history and sitting around with two cats in a basement?"

Alfred stared at Kent. Lynn felt the tension and was worried that a fight might be brewing between them. Alfred only smiled, though, and said, "Young man, you are so much like your grandfather. He was the only one I allowed to take such a tone with me. He'd be proud of you."

A large crash came from outside the door. Warren's men had found the tunnels.

"Can they get through that door?" Stacy asked.

"I was assured it would withstand even the strongest explosion."

"I don't see how they could set an explosion off and not cave in the tunnel," Kent replied.

"Yes, that's my take on it too. But I'm sure they'll come up with something. I do wish the cameras would come back online so we can see what's going on outside. In the meantime I believe we should eat something and fill one of those backpacks with supplies. We are going on a hike."

"A hike?" Lynn repeated with a frown.

"One thing you will learn quickly about me, Lynn, is that I'm a planner. I want an exit strategy from any situation. Hopefully, my call for help is being answered, but if it isn't, then we can still get to safety. There's a car and another exit that I'm sure they won't find. You might compare this to the Batcave, if you will, minus the crazy outfit." His grin scared her a little.

Lynn didn't know what to make of the man in front of her: a wealthy criminal turned do-gooder, her grandfather. She had gone from drunk, abusive parents to a superhero grandpa. It was almost funny, or would be if her stepbrother wasn't currently intent on killing her. A small part of her worried that her mother and stepfather would be next on the kill list. No matter how bad they were, they didn't deserve to die like that. Everything she had seen growing up made sense to her now. She was the only sane one in her messed-up family. She too wished she could see what was going on outside. It wouldn't have surprised her to see Warren leading the charge.

She watched Alfred make them a huge breakfast without offering to help. He opened cans from the shelves of food. The room wasn't all that much different than the other safe room she had been in, but this one had a higher level of fortification: thick concrete walls that, she was told, were reinforced with steel plates and a few other things to keep it all stable. Lynn choked down the fried hash and scrambled powdered eggs with some coffee and canned orange juice. It wasn't the best breakfast she'd had, but at least she wasn't hungry anymore.

"There are showers and toiletries over there if you'd like to clean up. Sorry I don't have any women's clothes here, but you can use my shirts and sweatpants, if you like. They are all clean, I assure you. Then you can grab a weapon and some food and water, and we'll get going, unless the cameras come back on and tell us another story."

"Uh, thanks," Stacy said. She headed for the showers, and Lynn followed her.

Lynn quickly stripped off her clothes. She didn't really need a shower, but she wanted to wash off the information she had just been given. It was all too much for her.

"You okay, Lynn?" Stacy asked from the shower next to hers. The setup was much the same as the one at the gym they had gone to a couple of times to play handball.

"Yeah, why not? I mean, I have a rich superhero for a grandpa."

"That's true," Stacy replied.

Lynn focused on the tasks at hand. At least she had her own clothes, so she didn't have to wear an old man's sweatpants. She grabbed an oversized, fluffy brown towel and brushed her teeth and combed her hair like it was any ordinary day. She barely recognized the girl looking back at her. With the lack of sleep, being drugged, and death all around, she seemed unfamiliar to herself. *Strange feeling.* She heard Stacy get out and returned to the main room, where she found Kent filling his backpack. He was taking two guns, she noted. He winked at her and left to shower as Stacy came out.

Lynn's grandfather was cleaning up their mess from breakfast, but she still didn't feel inclined to help him. Instead, she threw a few things into a backpack, picked out a new gun that looked simple to her, and sat down next to one of the cats. Mystery snuggled against her, and Magic curled contentedly into a ball. The purring soothed Lynn as she tried to make sense of it all.

* * *

WARREN WAS happy to be out of the air and safely in the back of a black truck. He would drive home later—no more flying. He snarled at the man opening the car door. "Report."

"We've searched the house from top to bottom. We found evidence of cats, but the cats escaped or were taken with the targets. We found a tunnel system that runs through the house, but it was empty. We did find a solid door with no locks, and we believe the targets to be on the other side in a safe room. After firing several rounds, it was concluded that bullets would not penetrate the door. We want to try dynamite. Experts believe an explosion might collapse the tunnel, so we would do it from a distance and then dig our way in to them." The man gulped loudly and tugged on the red collar of his security uniform. His eyes gave away the fear that each breath he took might be his last. *He's right,* Warren thought smugly.

"So you're telling me that we had them surrounded and you let them escape?"

"Um, well, we know where they are, sir. We can't access them. We wanted to confer with you about our use of explosives first." The man ran his fingers through his thinning blond hair, making parts of it stand up.

"You have failed me again. It should have been easy to catch them sleeping. I know there's security, but we overwhelmed that quietly. Pounding the door down alerted them, but you went directly in. I assume you went to the bedrooms first?"

"We cleared as we went, sir. Once the downstairs rooms were clear, we went upstairs."

"So you are telling me you surprised them and then spent time wandering around downstairs instead of going to where they were? You gave them time to flee to the safe room."

The man was sweating profusely. He looked like he was going to faint. "I…um…we had to clear each area before carrying on. That is standard, sir."

"I don't want 'standard.' I want people who can think beyond that." *Too bad I never caught the name of this loser.*

"I am sorry, sir. It won't happen again. I promise they will get into that room."

"I wanted this done before noon. Can you promise me that?"

"Noon? Well, we can try."

Warren held his hand up. "I do not like to have to wait for anything." He pulled out a small handgun to end their conversation. He aimed it at the man's head. The man turned pale and started to run. Warren pulled the trigger before he got very far. He watched him crumple to the ground, resembling a large sack of garbage.

"Now, who's next in charge?" A smaller man stepped forward with a fake smile pasted on his face. He kept his beady eyes forward as he deftly avoided his predecessor's body.

"I am, sir."

"Your name, please?"

"Rich," he said as two other men dragged the body off and tossed it into the back of a pickup as though a murder hadn't just happened. But it had, and the consequences of failure were clear.

"Yes, you will be treated the same way if you don't get this done. That fellow had many chances; don't worry about that. I'm not that cold if you make one mistake, but many? You understand that must be punished. How would anything ever get done? Now, although you managed to stop all communication from the house, I think our Mr. Justice is a resourceful man. So we will back off, except for keeping someone posted at all the doors and possible exits from the house. I don't think collapsing the tunnel will help us, and I don't believe they will exit from that door again, but I do believe they will come out—somewhere else. We'll be there waiting. I'll even help with the search, and I want every available body looking for that exit. I need someone searching the records on the house. Who the builder was, plans—things like that. Might get lucky. It's doubtful he would allow such a record to exist, but you never know. People do miss things, occasionally. So get going, Rich. I recommend that next time we meet, you have some good news for me."

Rich bowed his head and wiped the sweat off his brow. "Yes, sir."

"Our boss will be pleased to hear of your loyalty, Rich. Thank you."

Warren watched the man run off. *I say jump, they ask how high.* He'd never understood why his father didn't want to be a part of this. That drunk was toiling away at a job he hated for a boss who didn't appreciate him. That was more criminal by far—and beneath them.

"Perry, I want you to have Gus pick up my father and stepmother. Keep them alive. Lynn won't let them die, no matter how badly they treated her. Tell him Alternative Site B is where I want them kept, in sleeping mode. Then call Unit 2 and tell him Cover C, Site B. Got all of that?"

Perry nodded. "Yes, sir."

"Good. Remind Gus to keep it quiet. I don't want a messy cleanup around all those nice middle-class families. Make sure I'm kept updated," Warren said with a grin of anticipation. *What a family reunion this will be.*

He tuned out Perry's monotone voice relaying all his instructions. He wanted to think about Lynn. If she survived, she would watch all her loved ones die slowly, including her mother, Stacy, and Kent. He would want Mr. Justice to watch it all, of course, and he wouldn't make his death easy, either. It would be just like his uncle's end.

"It's done, sir," Perry said, not looking at Warren. *What a lack of respect.* Too bad the scrawny driver didn't appreciate his brilliance.

"Now let's take a tour around the property. I think anything the right size could be a possible exit. Pass that on."

"Yes, sir."

Maybe, after this, it would be time to get a new driver who would appreciate him. Tie up the loose ends his uncle had left. He was glad to put Cover C in use or kill Gus slowly after the parents were taken care of. Letting Stacy and Lynn get away—there was no way to come back from that one. Unfortunately, Gus's family had escaped, but that was okay. Warren didn't really hate them, just Gus. He smiled and closed his eyes as he heard his last order being relayed over the radio.

"Where do you want to go?" Perry started backing up the truck without making eye contact. His disapproval was irritating Warren.

"We are looking for anything moving or a hidden tunnel or exit. I'm not sure. I'll know when I see it. I want to make a few loops around the property, and we might want to keep our distance from the main house in case something happens to it."

"Happens to the house?"

"Yes. I can't see the old man leaving it intact if he escapes, can you?"

"No, sir. Good thinking."

"I know. Now drive." Warren beamed at his own cleverness.

"It will be bumpy, sir."

"Understood. Let's go four-wheeling."

"Yes, sir."

Warren smiled. His trashy sister would soon do what he wanted to save the very people who'd treated her so badly. *My brand of karma*. It was going to be the perfect ending to that part of his life, and then he would begin his new life as the head of this family.

CHAPTER 16

"*K*ent, could you please help me move this shelf?" Alfred asked.

"Sure, Mr. Justice, uh, Hill," Kent said.

"Alfred would be better. Let's keep the Mr. Justice part between us during work. I'll have to make another name change. I certainly can't go by Hill, and now Alfred Johnson is gone. So Alfred is my preference, Kent."

"Sure, Alfred." Kent pushed the shelves of canned food.

As the wheels glided across the floor, Lynn could see this was a job a child could have done. *Trying to make us feel useful?* Kent rolled his eyes at her when Alfred wasn't looking, and she quickly grinned back. There was a hidden door behind the shelves. It was a plain gray door with a simple lock that opened into what looked like a giant drain. *Not much security*, she thought, until she saw that the other side was even more fortified.

"Where does this go?" Lynn asked.

"To a fake drainpipe by the stream."

"A stream? I didn't see a stream on the way in." Lynn peered into the darkness.

"No, it's below the house and not technically on my property, which is useful."

"Does it come out at a road?" She was sick of all these vague answers.

"No, it's not visible from a road. I know you think I'm not telling you everything, but trust me, I'm being as honest as I have ever been in my life. We all know this house isn't safe anymore, so I'll make sure it's destroyed when we exit. Remember I said I always have backup plans for any situation? It's because of the people I have had to cross, and this situation is the grimmest of them all. I can take the insurance money and move on. I have many places to go, although this was my favorite hideout." Alfred lifted his disgruntled cats back into their carrier.

"How well do you know Warren?" Lynn asked.

"Too well. I wasn't happy to hear he'd made contact with you again. I admit I didn't think he'd try to hurt you, though."

"He's evil."

"He's totally crazy too," Stacy added.

"He is both," Alfred agreed as he pushed a button that started a countdown.

"How long?" Lynn stepped back from the tunnel and rubbed her arms.

"We have thirty minutes to get clear. Won't take us that long, though. Everyone ready? Guns loaded?" Alfred slipped on his backpack and picked up the cats.

"Yup, ready," Stacy confirmed.

"Yes," Kent replied. Lynn nodded and held up her gun, making sure not to point it at anyone.

"It will be dark for a while. When you see the light, please remain quiet until I can check out our surroundings. Follow me."

They entered the murky tunnel, the only light coming from their flashlights once they closed the door behind them. *If he's going to destroy the house, why bother?* Lynn wondered. She immediately stepped in a puddle that splashed all over her pants. Not so much a fake drain, after all. *Great.* What if there wasn't only water in the tunnel—what if there were rats living in it? She didn't see anything moving; but that didn't convince her that they were alone in there.

"Lynn, you need to know one more thing about Warren," Alfred said, puffing in the lead.

"What?" Lynn's mouth went dry. How much worse could it be?

"Ew!" Stacy suddenly stopped.

Kent, who had been in the rear behind Lynn, pushed around her with his gun drawn. "What is it, Stacy?"

Alfred had turned and pointed his flashlight at the ground. Lynn could see he was smiling when they all noticed the partially decomposed rat.

"A dead rat! I almost stepped on it." Stacy's beam of light pointed to the ceiling where thankfully only spiders dwelled.

"Yeah, well." Kent kicked it behind them.

"There might be one or two in here, sorry. But Lynn, you need to know that Warren wasn't exactly his uncle's most trusted, or he wouldn't have gone to prison. He certainly wouldn't make that person his second-in-command. I kept a very close eye on Warren while he was incarcerated. He was very talkative in prison. I learned a lot, actually, including about your childhood."

"Better late than never—not." Lynn shook her head.

"I know. That is one thing I'll always have to live with, and so will you. I can't say I'm sorry enough, but right now you need to know what Warren is capable of. I'm positive that he killed his uncle and the rest of the family."

"Sick, but that doesn't surprise me," Lynn admitted.

"That makes sense. Mr. Stone hasn't been seen in a while," Kent added.

"So you figured out Warren killed his family quickly, but you couldn't figure out your granddaughter was being abused before now?" Stacy said. Lynn was always grateful for her friend's loyalty.

"Yes, I blew that. I didn't know until after she moved out and it was too late. I can't change history, though, as much as I would like to. Apologizing doesn't seem like enough. But now we need to focus on Warren. Killing is a game to him, and that type is the worst."

"Are you sure?" Kent asked.

"I would say I'm 99 percent positive. I've had other detectives working for me, Kent." One of the cats let out a small cry. Alfred stuck his finger into the cage, which seemed to soothe it.

"Other detectives? What did they find out?" Kent asked.

"Warren's outside activities."

"What outside stuff?" Stacy asked.

"The other people he killed."

"Oh," Stacy said in a small voice.

Alfred quickly changed the subject. "If I had made the connection between Lynn and that girl named Andrea, we might have protected you better, but…"

Lynn didn't respond, but Kent did. "Yeah, I thought you reacted rather strangely when you heard Lynn's real name."

"Yes. I was prepared to help a girl named Andrea, but when I learned it was Lynn! You won't like to hear this, Lynn, but I already had someone following you—for your protection. Although he didn't do much of a job—he left his post the night you got drugged at the bar. Left you alone, and I never connected you with Kent's Andrea. Stupid of me."

Lynn refused to comment. The man was having her followed, and he was worried about the names she used? *Whatever, coming from a man who uses fake names too.*

"So you help all girls in distress?" Stacy asked.

"I try to help where I can. I have a lot to make up for. Plus, I have a granddaughter who was fairly careless about her safety."

"Whatever! Don't pretend you care now, because you had someone following me around," Lynn replied.

"I won't apologize for that, Lynn. I will, though, for him not doing his job. As for caring, I never pretend." Alfred glanced at Lynn.

She refused to meet his eyes. "Well, maybe I don't care."

"I don't blame you. I can only hope that someday…"

Kent grabbed her hand. "Do you have any proof Warren killed his family?"

"I do. He isn't as careful as he thinks. His uncle's boat was sunk far from where it was supposed to be. I have divers in the area collecting evidence. I doubt the bodies will turn up, but it will make Warren a liar. In the right hands, it will take him down."

Kent sighed. "And my job is to chase drug dealers around for you."

"Yes. It's important to get them off the streets, if I can."

"Okay, so Warren is a killer," said Stacy. "We all know that. He sank a boat, his uncle and family are missing, Kent works for you, and Lynn is your granddaughter. Cool, but none of this will matter if we're dead. Aren't we on a timetable here? I mean, I'd like to get as far away from your exploding house as possible, thanks."

Alfred stopped. His white hair and mustache glowed in the low light, making him seem more like someone's sweet old grandpa. "I like your directness, Stacy. You are a loyal friend to Lynn. Thank you. Yes, the timetable is intact. We're fifteen minutes into this, and there's the exit, see? Once outside, we'll be safe from the blast because we're below the house and farther away than you realize. We'll be safe from the explosion, but not from Warren's crew."

"Okay, well, you're welcome." Stacy's tone indicated an eyeroll.

Alfred trudged on, and his puffing grew louder as he continued through the tunnel. The cats had to weigh around forty pounds with the carrier. "Lynn, I want you to know that I have tried to protect you. I failed your father, and I don't want to fail you now. When you needed me the most, I wasn't there. Know that the man who left his post was fired. If he had done his job, perhaps things would have gone differently. Not much else I can say right now. We'd better be quiet the rest of the way, until I can check my camera."

A stalker grandfather—what next? A better question was did she want to learn anything else. She watched Alfred set the cats down and then move toward the light shining through a grate. Lynn brushed a cobweb out of her hair. There was her killer stepbrother who supposedly murdered his uncle and family and wanted her dead. On the other hand was the man who had people follow her around. He was the lesser of the two evils. She preferred another option for people in her life and hoped Kent was it. She watched Alfred study the camera and then quietly peek outside.

"All clear, but let's stay quiet just in case." He slid the gate open and grabbed his cats. Kent, Stacy, and Lynn followed him.

There was the creek. It was beautiful, with several waterfalls near the exit. Redwoods surrounded them in all stages of growth. There was no road or even a visible path. Lynn relaxed a little bit, hoping they had finally gotten away. Kent had his arm around her, and Stacy held her hand. It was like they had found a perfect picnic spot. She wanted to lie down by the creek, but of course, they weren't safe with Warren around.

Alfred broke the comfortable silence after a quick glance at his watch. "I know you have questions, Lynn, and there's more I want to say, but we need to focus on escaping. I promise that we will sit down and talk this all out once we're safe. Question what's going on around you now—that will keep you alive."

"Yeah," Lynn grumbled.

Alfred set the carrier down and rubbed his temples. "I will protect you with my life, Lynn. I promise."

Lynn didn't respond. He couldn't make that promise to her. Besides, after her childhood of drunken false guarantees, she'd learned not to trust what people said. She trusted Stacy and maybe Kent, but her so-called grandfather had not earned a spot on that list. She smiled, thinking about the list she'd made only a couple of nights ago. At least she could answer her questions now, although she'd probably never see the list ever again. She hoped Warren hadn't found it and had a good laugh at her expense. She was going to make sure she got the last laugh on him. Maybe her button's message, "F*ck Off & Die," would magically strike him dead. Not that she was a killer, but that was one human who shouldn't be breathing.

She sighed and pulled away from Stacy and Kent. She wanted a moment alone by the creek to regroup. Since neither followed her, she guessed they understood. She kicked a wrapper from a fish filet that someone had carelessly discarded. *Losers*, she thought; and turned around to pick it up.

"I hate litterbugs. How hard is—"

Alfred interrupted. "*Shhh*, I hear a car."

It sounded like a truck that was four-wheeling, but Lynn knew it had to be someone searching for them. It was moving slowly, but they couldn't see it yet. Kent ran to her and yanked her and Stacy back toward the tunnels. Alfred and his cats followed them. Behind the metal bars, they listened to the truck get closer. Lynn wasn't sure if whoever was in the truck had spotted the drain. She hoped they would move on.

She felt Kent's hand on her shoulder and was reassured. It was a good first step, although she had never given her trust quite so easily. It made about as much sense as seeing her own body years ago in the hospital before waking up from that coma. It was as if Kent was her soulmate, if she believed in that sort of thing. Or she could simply be losing it. *Crap.*

"Do you think they'll find us?" Stacy whispered.

"No, that's doubtful. This looks like an ordinary drain from the outside. Let's stay here until they leave. We can't take any chances," Alfred said, running his fingers through his hair as he glanced at his watch again.

"Are we safe when the house blows?" Stacy pointed into the darkness.

"We should be, but I'd like to not be in here, just in case. We have eight minutes."

Would the drivers be gone in time for them to get out of the tunnel? Lynn studied Alfred. *A lot of drinkers in my gene pool.* At least he'd quit, and maybe that would be a good idea for her someday too, before it got out of hand like what she grew up in. Maybe her grandfather had some sense, but he did look more like Batman's butler than an ex-criminal turned good guy. She hoped he had some hidden weapons that would keep them safe.

Lynn heard the truck move away, and then the sound faded to nothing. Now they could get out of the tunnel and, hopefully, to safety.

* * *

Thomas studied the landscape. "He did not leave."

"Yes, I know." Zelina nodded absently.

"He saw the drain's reflection. It is a trap. We need to warn them."

Zelina turned her attention to him. "We cannot. But Lynn can certainly have what she needs."

Thomas looked around. "What?"

Zelina pointed. "See that object over there?"

"That old pocketknife?"

"Yes. That is important."

"I do not like Lynn back with Warren. What if she does not make it? That is not fair," Thomas protested. A tear ran down his cheek.

Zelina put her wings around him. "No, it is not always fair, but we can give her a chance."

Thomas wiped the tear away as Zelina pulled back. "I know. I can see some of it but not the outcome."

"Because it is not for sure. You are doing so well. I am impressed."

Thomas had more questions, but he was fine with leaving their conversation there for just a bit. The hard-nosed angel had paid him a compliment. If he had not been so worried about Lynn, he would have smiled. Instead, he watched the group carefully.

Zelina tapped his shoulder. "See how the light is hitting the knife along with the feather?"

"Yes, nice work."

She smiled. "I take no credit for what I am able to do."

"Yes, well—look! Lynn found it. She slipped it into her back pocket."

"Now send love to them. They need to hope and keep fighting until the end."

"Sending it. There is Warren and another man. Wait, two other men. Where did they come from?"

"They are the backup."

Thomas wrapped his arms around himself. "What can we do?"

"Nothing, now. Just watch Warren's driver. He has training for this and a lot of bills."

"He is shooting at them!" Thomas yelled.

"Do not worry. He only shot the men and was careful where he shot them."

"We could not have stopped that?" Thomas protested.

"No. The shooter does not like his new boss. Those wounds will heal up nicely—if they survive this. Now watch the other two men."

"Well, getting shot is never good. They are sneaking up behind Lynn and Stacy, but—" Thomas jumped as the ground shook. "Hey, what was that?"

Zelina glanced toward the sound. "The house. It is rubble now. I believe the authorities will determine that it was a gas leak."

"Warren and his men did not even hesitate, like they expected it. It could have just as easily been an earthquake. They have a big one coming soon."

Zelina nodded, "Warren knew, or at least his evildwel did."

"What did they throw? What are they doing?" Thomas was hovering over them, wanting to help.

"Well, Lynn and Stacy were going for their guns when the men got shot, as you saw. Those canisters will put them all to sleep immediately—some new mix developed overseas. Oops! Stacy got a shot off."

"She hit a tree. That stuff works fast; they are all out."

"They are. Although I think Warren and his men wearing masks was overkill; the wind is blowing away from them. This ended up being clean and simple and did not involve anyone else. If they had run into the other search party, it would have been fatal to Lynn and Alfred. It really was the better of the two choices."

Thomas frowned. "I will take your word for it. Where is that other group?"

"They turned around after the explosion and went back to the house."

"Okay, so their chances of meeting were limited by the short amount of time?" Thomas scanned the area for more of Warren's men but saw nothing.

"Yes. Life is all about short amounts of time, and what happens in them."

"I guess that makes sense. It did not take them long to load them into the truck. Look, they even took the cats. Are they going back to the mansion?" Thomas fluttered his wings.

Zelina shrugged. "Yes, but they will not make it."

Thomas got a flash of Lynn holding a gun. He realized it might all depend on what she did after that. He still experienced a lot of confusion when dealing with humans, but he felt like he was starting to understand them. "It is up to Lynn. I understand now how her tolerance for the drugs will pay off."

Zelina smiled in approval. "Exactly. The other two are leaving. It is just Warren and the driver."

"And that evildwel."

"It is growing tired of us."

"Good."

The black truck drove back the same way it had come. Warren was smiling as the driver looked in his rearview mirror. He did not catch Perry's frown, but Zelina did. She nodded to Thomas. That look gave them hope.

CHAPTER 17

*L*ynn had spotted her stepbrother with a man she didn't recognize. She had no time to warn anyone before the shots rang out, and she watched in horror as Kent and Alfred collapsed. It felt like everything was happening in slow motion as she reached for her gun, Warren threw something, and there was a loud explosion that shook the ground—the house. A small silver cylinder at her feet released a smoky substance that stung her nose and made her eyes water. She heard a shot close by as everything faded away.

She awoke on the ground with a rock poking into her back. She wanted it so badly to be a dream, but she knew it wasn't. She tried moving but couldn't, and her eyes felt weighted. Everything sounded so far away, but she felt herself being carried. A car engine roared to life, and she knew Warren was going to kill her and probably already had killed Kent. She felt a tear run down her cheek as she faded out again.

Lynn wasn't sure how much time had passed. She replayed that moment of Kent getting shot over and over in the darkness. Finally, her surroundings came into focus again. She was inside a moving vehicle. In a panic she forced her eyes open. She was on a black leather seat in a vehicle next to Kent, Stacy, and Alfred. They were all unconscious but appeared to be breathing and very much alive.

Her arms were tied behind her back and her legs bound together. Unfortunately, Warren was there, directly across from her, and he appeared to be sleeping. A gun lay across his lap, begging for her to take it from him. Kent was next to him, his leg bandaged where he had been shot. He had been tied up too. Alfred was tied up next to her with a similarly bandaged leg wound. Their breathing soothed her. And there was Stacy, who was passed out and tied but didn't seem to be hurt. The cat carrier was on the floor under her feet. The cats had been knocked out too.

Lynn gently wiggled around, glad she could move her muscles again. She was careful not to alert Warren or the driver as she stretched her neck to see where they were being taken. Eucalyptus, pines, and oaks. It looked like they were on the road back to the mansion. She had a feeling that if they ended up in that room under the mansion again, there would be no second escape.

Only she and the driver were awake, and he wasn't paying any attention to the passengers. She had to stop him from getting to their destination. She closed her eyes in case the driver checked while she tried to come up with a plan. She attempted to release her hands—no luck. She almost sighed but stopped herself. Her back pocket felt hot, and she suddenly remembered what she had picked up right before she heard the shots. Was it still there?

She wiggled again and got her hand into her back pocket. It was. They'd missed it! It took her several tries, but finally she got the knife opened and went to work on cutting her ropes. The angle was difficult, and it seemed to take forever. If she could just get one hand free, she could get the gun and shoot the driver. And then they would crash. But if she shot her stepbrother first, then the driver would probably shoot her, unless she held the gun on him and got him to pull over. Well, she'd have to decide who to shoot first; all their lives depended on what she did next. *No pressure.*

Every second stretched into an eternity. It wasn't easy to adjust her position with her legs tied, but at last her right hand was free. It was now or never—she had to get that gun. She reminded herself that her legs weren't going to move the way she wanted them to. *Okay, Lynn,* she thought, *let's do this.* But before she could make her move, the truck hit a sudden bump and woke up Warren. She froze, keeping her hands under her and her eyes closed.

"How close are we, Perry?" Warren asked.

"About thirty minutes out, sir. I'm taking the back way in, as you requested, in case someone followed us."

"Good, I'm glad you listened. They are all still out."

"Yes, sir. I've seen no movement. They'll be out for at least another hour."

"Well done. You did well, but if you had killed a couple, I wouldn't have minded." Warren yawned.

"Yes, sir. Thank you."

"I think I'll take another nap with these sleeping beauties. I can't wait to remove the life from his cats slowly in front of Mr. Justice. First one cat, and then the other, and I'll top it off with his granddaughter. Always having to change my plans because of her, but it will be lots of fun. Don't you think?" Warren stretched and kicked the carrier. No response.

"Yes, sir. Do you want me to wake you up when we arrive?"

"That would be fantastic."

"Sleep well, sir."

"I plan to."

Then everything was silent. After several long minutes, Lynn peeked. He was asleep, and Perry had headphones on. Lynn closed her eyes again and quietly got back to work.

* * *

THE EVILDWEL WASN'T happy that her host had fallen asleep again. What a lazy human he had become. She thought about waking him but wondered if he deserved what was coming for being so careless. A gun on his lap? Sitting with the hostages? He should be next to his driver, although she knew he couldn't really trust him, either. What her host was missing was that the girl was wide awake. Dian almost admired Lynn for her strength. She wondered if the girl would kill her host or the other way around. The thrill of the unexpected prevented Dian from acting on her host's behalf for several important seconds.

This host had been a lot of fun, but his cockiness was making him sloppy. For old times' sake and the promise of things to come if he lived, she would make one final effort for him. Although there was that incessant snoring he always did while he refreshed his body. Why couldn't he be quiet like the others? She wouldn't miss that. She wasn't pleased with the two insects along for the ride, either. They seemed smug. She knew they couldn't touch her with all their drivel about love, but it was making her feel quite uncomfortable. On the other hand, she knew her presence made them just as uncomfortable.

So Dian hung on to that and her host. She knew someone was going to die, and she didn't want to miss that, no matter who it was. She set her mind back to the problem at hand. It was hard to think with *them* there, making it feel like all her bad air was being knocked out of her. She didn't breathe like the humans did, but after living in breathing beings for so long, she understood how it felt to be breathless. Dian's red eyes never left the angels, who seemed to be doing their best to pretend she wasn't right across from them. Suddenly, the girl's eyes opened. *Time to act.*

She willed her host to grip his gun, giving him a huge dose of fear. He only shrugged and snored louder. Too much drinking—and those drugs. She should have never encouraged that behavior. She tried to startle him with images of his father beating him as a child. He moaned in his sleep and thrashed. Maybe he would surprise her and react in time. Sometimes he was full of surprises.

She sent image after image and waited. Finally, she sent an image of the cheerleader in high school that he'd fallen in love with and later killed. That woke him up. Too late, though, because now he had a gun pointed at his head. It was his turn to feel fear, which she could feed off happily. She spotted the discarded knife Lynn had used to cut her bonds. That might work if she could get him to focus.

* * *

"Pull over, Perry!" Lynn held Warren's wide-eyed gaze. "I have a gun on your boss."

"Now, Lynn. You should never point guns at people. What are you thinking? What if we hit a road bump, and you accidentally shoot one of your friends instead? That would be horrible." Warren's soothing voice couldn't hide the terror in his eyes.

Lynn saw Perry glance back at them. She realized her stepbrother had told him to try to jar the gun from her grip. She prepared herself for the bump, but it was stronger than she had anticipated. She almost lost her grip on the gun as Warren reached for it. She squeezed the trigger. All she managed to do was shatter a side window and wake the cats.

"Sir?"

"I'm fine, but apparently, Lynn has figured out how to shoot a gun. Why don't we find a nice spot to pull over and see what she wants?"

"Yes, sir."

Lynn didn't plan on giving in to him. She held on to her gun firmly, knowing from what Kent had told her that it would fire five more times without having to reload or do anything else. It didn't matter what type of gun she had as long as it did what it was supposed to do. At least she hadn't shot one of her friends; she was proud of that. She would also be ready for another bump in the road.

Lynn felt like she was in control, but Warren's calm nagged at her. Was she missing something? Did Perry have a gun, and would she soon be dead? She watched her stepbrother nod to the driver as the truck slowed down. She was ready to throw herself to the ground if she thought he was going to shoot her, but that didn't happen. Instead, the truck stopped in a pullout surrounded by trees. There didn't seem to be anyone else around. She wanted to shoot Warren now but was worried that the bullet might hit Kent if she missed. By hesitating, she lost her one good chance.

"Leave them in the car," commanded Warren, like he was still in control.

"Yes, sir. I'll get the door for you."

"No—thanks, though, Perry. Why don't you wait here for us, okay?" Lynn cut her feet free without looking away from her stepbrother or taking her finger off the trigger.

"After you," Warren offered.

"Hey, no, thanks. You get out first and slowly. If you try anything, Perry, I will shoot him."

"I understand, ma'am," Perry said as Warren nodded again.

"Stop right there, Warren."

"Of course, dear sister. I know we can talk this out." He smiled brightly at her. *He is so full of shit,* she thought as she cut the ropes binding the others. Kent started to stir, as did Stacy, but both fell back asleep. Alfred didn't move as Lynn got out of the truck.

"I hope you don't get dizzy. That could happen, you know. I wouldn't want to get shot by accident."

"No, that would be horrible, wouldn't it?" Lynn replied, feeling the effects he was talking about. But she stood her ground. *See, partying does pay off,* she thought with a small grin.

Warren slowly raised his hands. "You know, I have authorized Perry to get his gun from the glove compartment. You shoot me, he shoots them."

"I kind of figured that one out, Warren. Which is why I want you in between him and me, if you don't mind."

Warren wove his fingers together. Was he trying to intimidate her? *Not working.* "No, of course not. Good planning, sis."

Lynn shifted her weight and adjusted her grip on the gun. "I think we can stop using that term, don't you?"

"Completely up to you. But you must know there's nothing personal in all of this, right?"

Lynn smiled and shook her head. "Oh, no. I'd never take it personally, you trying to set me up for murder and then kill me. Why would I do that? How stupid do you think I am?"

Warren just shrugged. If Lynn was a killer, he'd be dead already. Right now, she wanted answers and a way to make sure Perry didn't kill her friends. He smiled. "Yes, it's a tough call. Someone has to die today. You understand that, I hope."

Lynn glanced in the truck. She didn't see any movement. "As long as it's you, I'm okay with that."

Warren's eyes widened. "Now, that isn't very nice! After all we've been through together? Do you remember the beatings we endured? The belts, fists, and hangers against our young skin, until we bled? The cruel words and things breaking all around us?"

"Yes, I remember, but it didn't make me want to kill people when I grew up."

Warren glanced back at the truck. "It isn't that simple. I was just doing my job. I was following orders from my uncle. He wanted all these things done. I tried to stop him, but, well, since I'm not the boss, all I can do is what I'm told. This isn't on me. All he wants is a key that my father has. It opens something valuable. Have you ever seen it?"

She checked inside the truck again. She was on edge. It was too quiet, and she could have sworn that Kent had been in a different position before. *Weird.* At least the cats were quiet again.

"'Just following orders' is no excuse for trying to kill me. I don't know anything about a key, so why me?" Lynn held back the information that she knew Warren had killed the boss.

Warren rubbed his chin with his right hand, so she kept track of his left hand. "We can talk this out, Lynn. Let me explain it to you."

Lynn pointed the gun at his heart. "Explain away. I'm eager to hear why you're such an asshole."

"Language, please! And maybe you should point the gun at the ground for now. We both know you have no idea how to use it."

"Whatever. You saw I can shoot it, and I will point it anywhere I want. So please, do go on."

Warren gave her his best smile. "You see, the truth is—and be assured I am only telling you this because I was raised with you for a while—your mother inherited some money. I saw their bank statement once, and wow! You were so brave walking away from all of that and their control. The problem is that you're going to inherit half of that amount. I need your half. So really, nothing personal—just business."

"So you're saying you wanted to kill me because I was inheriting money that I clearly didn't want? Do I have that right?"

Warren cocked his head to the side. "Yes, and it's what the boss wants as well. He needs that key, but if they think you're dead, that would work too. You know, like your grandpa? And Lynn, you wanna know the difference between us?"

Lynn smirked. "Please enlighten me, Warren."

He put his hands on his chest. "I wouldn't stand talking like this if I had a gun pointed to someone. Want to know why?"

"No, please tell me."

"Well, for one, I would have pulled the trigger. While we were chatting, my plans have gone into effect. I took the liberty of taking my dad and your mom. They're all tied up waiting for us. If you don't do what I want, they will be shot immediately. Perry has already called that in. Do you really think I would let you have control over this situation?" Warren smiled like he had already won.

"Well, I could believe you, but I don't."

Warren laughed, and then his smile hardened. "That's your choice. Your button has Todd's and Dave's blood on it. Very incriminating, don't you think? Your grandfather is a traitor, so it goes without saying he will die. Kent might stand a chance. I am giving you one opportunity, due to our shared history, to live. Maybe even make a life with your PI in another country, as long as everyone here thinks you're dead so I can collect your money. What do you think, sis?"

"I will repeat myself. Do not call me 'sis' anymore. I don't believe you would honor your confused offer, Warren. Besides, what will your *uncle* think? Shouldn't you be calling and getting instructions from *him*?" Lynn goaded. If he thought she'd walk away from Stacy, he was out of his mind. Well, but of course he was.

"You're right. If my uncle was alive, I would be checking with him. Now you know how powerful I truly am." Warren laughed, but a slight frown crossed his face. "No, he's not dead, but you should have seen your face. And did you notice that during our talk Perry managed to leave? Now, let me sweeten the deal and offer to let Stacy go with you. Heck, I'll even throw in the cats. I have a plane on standby, and we could get you out of the country for good. And how about a hundred thousand dollars to get you started, and our parents get to live too? Best offer you're going to get. I suggest you take it, Lynn."

"No deal. Fact is, *I* have the gun on *you*."

"Don't say I didn't try to help you. The problem we have now is if I don't check in, our parents will be killed. Do you want to take that chance? I mean, they weren't the best parents around—am I right? I can understand if you want me to kill them. I assure you, Perry is nearby, waiting for my signal."

"Or there could be no signal, and I shoot you, and he takes off. Then no one else dies."

"You'll never get the chance to shoot me. He is a trained sniper."

Lynn surveyed their surroundings and risked a quick glance in the truck. Not only was the driver gone, but so was Kent. How did Warren miss that? How had she not noticed?

"Well, what'll it be?"

"Not happening, bro," Lynn replied.

Warren shook his head and smoothed his hair. "Too bad. I'll miss you, I hope you know that."

Stacy was moving around now.

"Well, I won't miss you. Turn around; it's your turn to be tied up."

"Who is going to do that, may I ask?"

"You may. Stacy! Bring some of that rope, and let's tie this dude up."

"Coming!"

"She'll regret that, Lynn. Tell her to stay in the truck, or she'll be shot." Warren's eyes were darting around.

Her stepbrother was sweating. *How very unlike him.* With Kent missing, Lynn felt more confident.

"You have no idea where Perry is, do you? Well, I do. He abandoned you."

"You're wrong."

"No, I am not. You'd never let our parents go if you really had them. Now get in the truck."

For the first time, panic settled on Warren's face as he scanned the tree line. No one. The silence was the one thing keeping Lynn sane. That meant they hadn't found each other—yet. Stacy tied Warren up, thoroughly and painfully. Lynn glanced in at her stepbrother and thought how good it felt to see him on the other side of a rope.

"You didn't need to tie it so tightly, Stacy," Warren said. "I hate to think how you'll pay for that."

Stacy laughed. "You're the one who is going to pay. You are a piece of shit."

"Language, please. Don't want to appear to be trashy, do you?"

Stacy turned around and punched a startled Warren directly in the face. "Careful, or you'll find out how much this trashy girl would enjoy beating the shit out of you for what you did to her."

Lynn had never felt prouder of her friend.

"You will both pay for this." Warren spit blood.

"Doubtful, Warren." Lynn winked. "Pretty impressive, Stace."

"Thanks. Can't say I've even punched anyone in the face before. It totally felt good."

"I bet."

He was secured opposite Alfred and completely helpless. The tables had turned, and he was backed into a truck's corner.

CHAPTER 18

*B*ang! *Pop! Pop!*

They all froze, turning toward the sound. Silence followed. Warren had taken all their weapons. She hoped Kent had found one before pursuing the driver. She scanned the tree line but saw nothing.

"We need to get out of here, Lynn," Stacy whispered.

"I'm not leaving without Kent." Lynn folded her arms.

"What if it was the driver who..." Stacy left the question unfinished, not looking at Lynn.

Lynn knew what she meant, and she refused to believe it. "You might have to go without me, because I'm not leaving Kent behind."

"I'd put my money on Perry. So what are you going to do, bring Kent's body along? It isn't what I'd do, but..." Warren smiled.

"Shut up, or I'll punch you again!" Stacy's rosy complexion transformed into an inflamed shade of red.

"I never would have guessed you to be so violent, Stacy. But Lynn—"

Stacy punched him in the face again. This time, his bloody eye and cheek showed the damage.

"Hey, that hurt!" Warren whined, shaking his head.

"Good. You are such a loser." Stacy slipped into the driver's seat, shaking her bleeding hand, and started the truck. Lynn had to admit that she enjoyed watching Stacy put Warren in his place. A smile crossed his face, and Lynn followed his gaze.

"Oh, shit!" was all Lynn could get out. They watched Perry run out of the forest. Kent didn't follow.

"We need to go, Lynn."

"I'm going to look for Kent—he might be hurt." Lynn tried to jump out of the truck, but she felt a hand tightly grasp her arm. Alfred was awake. He pulled her back inside next to him. "He'll be okay. He has training. Leave, Stacy."

"I will not leave him!" Lynn shouted, trying to pull away. *Surprisingly strong for an old man,* she thought. Alfred shut the door as Stacy started to drive away and did not loosen his grip on Lynn as he extracted the gun from her hand. Perry was standing beside the road, dazed. Why wasn't he coming after them?

"Circle around." When they got into place, Alfred shouted from the truck, "Drop your weapon, or I'll shoot!"

Perry raised his arms and dropped his gun. He sank to his knees and fell to the ground, his blood pooling around him.

"Is he dead?" Stacy asked.

"I'll go check. You girls stay here. And I mean *you*, Lynn."

"I need to find Kent." Lynn teared up.

They watched Alfred check the man's pulse and shake his head. He shrugged as he picked up the gun and walked away.

"Is he…" Stacy asked.

"He is. I'm going to look for Kent now. You girls stay here and lock the doors. If I'm not back in five minutes, go get help. Understand?" A determined glint was in his steel-blue eyes.

"I'm going with you." Lynn returned his look with the same determination.

"I don't have time to argue with you, Lynn. Stay—"

"Look!" Lynn pointed.

"Don't shoot!" Kent called.

Lynn almost passed out from relief. Warren turned away from the reunion in disgust. He kicked the small knife that Lynn had left on the seat and furtively picked it up.

"Watch him, Stacy!" Lynn jumped out of the truck.

"Got him! Go give your man a hug." Stacy glanced back at Warren, who was smiling.

* * *

THOMAS'S EYES WIDENED. "Warren has that knife! That was careless of them. Guess the evildwel is not done yet."

"It is not. Too bad about the driver. He should have run away from Kent. I had hoped for his survival." Zelina glanced back at the body. "He is already with his angel."

"Why is Stacy not paying attention? She is fixing her hair. Warren is almost loose."

"I would help her, but she might not survive if she is warned. See there?"

"What? Oh, another gun."

"Yes, it is better if she runs from Warren. But either way, the parents still need to be released. Only then will this be over."

Thomas nodded, wringing his hands. He could not believe what he was watching. "How could they let Warren get free again? Yes, there he goes. Poor Stacy, she has no clue. How does she not hear him? He is hitting her with the cat carrier. Really? But she is not knocked out; she is jumping out as the truck takes off. Oh, those poor cats! He tossed the carrier out of the truck. They are terrified—but not hurt. Kent and Alfred finally noticed. Now they are chasing the vehicle while Lynn helps her friend up. Wow, this is playing out like one of those movies humans watch." Thomas blushed when he realized he had said that all out loud.

"You *do not* have to recap the event for me. I am watching the same thing."

"Sorry. This part really surprised me."

"Yes, well, things surprise me too, and I might have gotten worked up a time or two. I thought we had Warren, but I knew there was a chance—wait. I think a glow would come in handy now. Right where the gas tank is. Nice shot, Alfred! Warren and that truck will not get very far. They still stand a good chance of escaping, and we are back on track."

"I see a big tree."

"Yes, definitely not the house. Warren does have help on the way, but right now, he will have to walk. A coward alone with his weapon. He is not much of a threat against four—well, three, who are also armed. Until his backup finds him—then it will be different." Thomas nodded. "I hope meeting her grandfather is good for her. I mean, once she finds out." Zelina pushed her hair behind her ears.

"It might be better if she does not find out," Thomas said.

Zelina sighed. "True, but if she does…"

"Yes, right." Thomas shook his head. Humans and their secrets did so much damage.

* * *

"He's getting away!" Lynn yelled.

"I think I hit the truck. If I'm right, it won't go too far, which means he won't get his help soon," Alfred said.

Kent started walking. "Let's follow him and see."

Alfred shook his head. "I'd rather we went this way."

Kent paused for a moment to rub his leg. He turned around. "Okay, I guess that makes sense. So we head away from him?"

"Exactly."

Stacy stood up, brushing the dirt off, while Lynn picked up the cat carrier. "Let's go, then."

The group walked slowly away, with glances back at the retreating truck. Just before the road curved out of sight, it stopped.

Kent smiled. "Good shot, Alfred."

"Look, he appears to be running from us. It's an act. I believe he will watch to see where we go. Let's make sure he sees us clearly." Alfred grinned as he rolled up the sleeves of his red plaid shirt. "I can take the cats, Lynn."

"I have them. Lead the way."

"Okay, come on."

"How did you get past us, Kent?" Lynn asked.

Kent laughed. "I thought you saw me. I heard the driver quietly report the situation to whoever is in charge, right as I was waking up. I got out behind the truck, and I had a gun strapped to my leg that they missed. I was going to surprise the driver, but he surprised me by leaving the truck. I followed him but hadn't counted on him retracing his steps and coming at me near an old abandoned house. He got one shot off and missed, and I got off two and didn't. Now I wonder if he even meant to shoot me. I guess I'll never know."

Lynn touched Kent's arm and glanced at his leg. "Perry was trying to survive. He shot you once already. All I know is I'm glad you're okay. Does it hurt?"

"Not really. It will heal fast. I think the bullet went through cleanly. Might have a scar."

Alfred chimed in. "Yeah, I've been shot before—this isn't bad. And Kent, you had to shoot Perry; you had no choice. It's Warren we should be focused on. He has as many lives as a cat. My hope is he's now on his ninth one."

Stacy sighed. "I'm sorry, this is my fault. If I had only watched Warren more carefully!"

"You couldn't know. I'm glad you're okay. You are, aren't you?" Lynn asked, a little out of breath. The cats were heavy.

"I just feel stupid and a bit bruised. I'm fine."

"Your punches made me feel good." Lynn grinned.

Stacy laughed. "Yeah, me too."

Alfred brushed a leaf off his jeans and looked over at Lynn. "Here, give me that. They're my babies, after all." He removed the carrier from Lynn's hand.

"I had it."

Alfred ignored her protest. "Let's put some run into our escape until we hit the curve, where he can't see us anymore. Then we can cut into the woods and head back in this direction. They'll be searching for us in the wrong place at first, and we can keep a close eye on our enemy."

"I want to get out of here." Stacy's voice was pitched high with panic.

"We will, Stacy," Alfred assured her with a hand on her shoulder. "It's not like we are going to go near him; we're just watching. We'll make sure you and Lynn are hidden in a safe spot first. Kent and I will survey what's going on. Once he abandons that truck, we might be able to use the radio and get help of our own. Then we do what we have to."

"We are not splitting up." Lynn looked at Stacy, who quickly nodded.

Alfred glanced at Kent, who shrugged. "Okay, we don't split up."

The group jogged around the corner with the expected pair of eyes watching them, then they cut into the forest. It wasn't long before they had a visual on Warren again. They made sure he couldn't see them. Warren's help quickly arrived, and they left the broken-down truck and rushed off in two new trucks in the direction the group had made sure Warren saw them go.

Alfred and Kent whispered intently together. "You know what to do?" Alfred asked.

"Yes, I got it. Wait here, Lynn," Kent said, before sprinting to the truck.

"I should make sure he's okay." Lynn started to follow.

"He said to wait here." Stacy grabbed her arm.

"He knows what he's doing, and I don't want to have to rescue you more than once. It only takes one person to operate a radio—if they left it working," Alfred said.

"I believe I was the one who untied myself and took down Warren. Thanks, though. Besides, I don't like being told what to do." Lynn threw her shoulders back.

"Yes, I admit you did save us. Thank you. But right now, I have a plan in motion. I know I have no right to tell you what to do, but I think you—"

Lynn's eyes narrowed, and she clenched her fists. "You have no right to tell me anything."

"I know. I'm trying to keep us all alive." Alfred looked away.

Kent's return intruded on the grandfather–granddaughter disagreement. "Okay, I got through. They're on their way to us. I let them know we'd be near that old abandoned house I saw earlier. We'll find some place to hide. In fact, I saw a grove of redwoods, and one looked like it might be hollowed out, but if not, we'd be inside a thick grove and out of sight from above. Hear that?" He pointed upward at the familiar rumble of a helicopter.

Lynn gave her grandfather one more disapproving glance before responding. "I hear it."

"Come on," Kent said. "You want me to carry the cats?"

"No, I've got them, young Kent."

"I love cats, but shouldn't we leave them behind for now?" Stacy asked.

"No. I will not leave anything behind. You lead the way, Kent, and we'll follow, won't we girls?" Alfred asked, not looking at Lynn.

"Of course we will." Lynn's reply was thick with disapproval.

Stacy gave Lynn her famous eyeroll and mouthed, "Sorry." Kent turned to look back at her, and she gave him a grin and nodded to Alfred. Kent smiled and shrugged.

This new man claiming to be her grandpa was overstepping his bounds. She'd let him know, when this was all over, that it wasn't okay. She'd been independent for quite some time now, and didn't need a replacement dad. Plus, her stepdad would start off conversations exactly like that, saying he had no right and then going on to say what he thought anyway, meaning he really did think he had every right to speak. Well, now she had learned to speak—and defend herself too. The words might not always come out right, but at least they came out.

The large tree Kent had noticed in the redwood grove was hollow inside, the perfect place to hide.

"How did you notice this, Kent?" Lynn asked.

"It caught my eye. Well, a feather caught my eye right before that driver, Perry, came at me. Lucky, huh?"

"Very lucky." Alfred's attention was on the path they had just traveled.

"Come on, grab some branches and stuff. Let's hide the entrance and our footprints," Kent urged.

"Yes, we'd better hurry. I can hear the helicopter getting closer," Alfred said, dragging a large branch.

Soon the four of them were sitting in a dark hole in a tree with a cat carrier in the middle. Would the cats give them away? The darkness seemed to keep them quiet. A dim flicker of light came through the branches that blocked the entrance.

"I hope there are no rodents in here," Stacy said.

"Um, doubtful," Kent said.

"Yeah, well, not being able to see is unnerving," Lynn added as Kent's warm hand found hers and squeezed.

"They should be here soon. You let them know there are armed people looking for us, right?" Alfred asked.

"Yes. I also gave them the code you told me. The truck is a good point of reference."

"My parents?" Lynn asked.

"They know, right, Kent?"

"Yes, I let them know."

"Warren won't hurt them if he can use them against you," Alfred said. One cat started to make noise; he calmed it down.

Lynn wished they didn't have unpredictable cats hiding with them, but if they had left the cats behind, she was sure Warren would have taken care of them in a bad way. "I hope so."

"And Lynn, I know you don't like me caring or my watchful eye. You can't fault me for wanting you safe. I know I have a lot to make up for. But I will try to tone it down, and I apologize if I offended you," Alfred said.

"Yeah…well, I don't need another father or someone to hire people to follow me around." Lynn felt Stacy's cool hand squeezing her arm.

"I understand, and I'm sorry we aren't safe now," Alfred replied quietly.

"I guess you aren't responsible for Warren and my stepfather, but then, if my own dad hadn't been so screwed up, maybe my mother wouldn't have met my stepdad and turned into what she is, so, yeah, pace yourself with me, would ya?"

"I will."

Kent put his arm around Lynn and pulled her closer. Lynn hoped Stacy wouldn't freak out about the dark or rodent. She hated mice and rats. Stacy scooted closer to Lynn again and grabbed her free hand.

Kent caught the movement. "We're going to be fine now. You doing okay, Stacy?"

"Yeah, super. As long as nothing is crawling near me, I'm cool."

"Good, because we're safe in this tree. All the crawling things need stuff to eat. What would they find inside a tree? And Warren's men, they wouldn't be smart enough to look in a tree for us. They expect us to keep running."

"I hope so, but what if one of the cats..." Stacy said. "Well, there's nothing we can do about that. I wish I had a flashlight. I feel like I'm surrounded by everything I'm afraid of."

"Yeah, this is totally creepy, Stace," Lynn agreed.

"Totally," Kent added, with a little playful mockery. Lynn smiled but didn't reply. "Does silence mean you're mad at me?"

"You'll find out later," Lynn said, with a smile in her voice.

"You two are making me sick." Stacy playfully poked Lynn's arm.

"Listen!" Alfred whispered, pulling the carrier up to him. His hand was inside now, keeping Magic and Mystery calm. All Lynn heard now was soft purring—and a helicopter.

"They have to be somewhere, Rich!" said a familiar voice from outside. *Warren.*

"We'll find them, sir. With no traffic on this back road, it's very unlikely they hitchhiked. The abandoned building checked out clean."

"What about the footprints that were found?"

"They passed through here, but I've no idea where they went. They might have retraced their steps and gone back to the road."

"No, they're too smart to go out in the open. They're close by—I feel it. You can't let them get away."

"Yes, sir."

Lynn started to tremble. Warren was only a few feet away. If one of them sneezed—or meowed—they would be found. If someone thought to look more closely at the pile of branches by the tree, it would all be over. Kent hugged her closer, and Stacy huddled on the other side. Three of them were armed, and she wasn't one of them, which was fine with her. Stacy had Perry's gun. No other guns had been found in the truck because Warren had left them behind by the drain.

A loud voice broke the tense silence. "I found something!"

"What is it?" Warren asked.

"A red button. Looks like it's off an old man's shirt. See?"

"I believe that belongs to our Mr. Justice. Like I keep saying, they're here somewhere. Spread out, and carefully search this grove. He isn't clever enough to outsmart me. They aren't getting away from us," Warren said.

"We'll go over this area branch by branch." The voice broke off. "Who is that, sir?"

"What? I don't recognize them," Warren replied.

A man's voice rang out. "We are here to pick up our boss. We do not want trouble, but if you will not leave, we will have to insist."

"This is a family matter," Warren replied. "I think it's best if you move on."

"We cannot do that, sir. We are under orders to retrieve four people, and that is what we are going to do. Step back so we can go check that house."

"Your choice, of course. Please do check out the house," Warren said. Lynn heard him say in a lower voice, "Take them out, Rich. This place is getting too crowded."

"Yes, sir; there are two more people over there."

"You're afraid of four people? There are more of you, by far, and you need to do what you need to do, like I said. Make this work, no matter what. Understood?"

"Yes, sir," Rich replied. They heard him run off.

"What's this? A footprint?" Warren said. "Why don't we see what's behind that nicely arranged pile of leaves and branches, shall we?"

Lynn felt Kent stiffen and pull away from her while Alfred carefully closed the cat carrier. She heard a gun click. Then several shots rang out beyond the tree just as Warren pulled away the branches to expose their hiding place. The light flooded in, almost blinding her. Kent reached out and pulled at Warren's legs, knocking him down. More gunfire, then silence. Warren wasn't moving.

"Mr. Justice? Sir?"

"Thank God!" Alfred said. "Dominic!"

"Where are you, sir?"

"In the tree. If you could clear our passage out," Alfred said.

"Done."

They carefully climbed out, squinting in the bright sunlight. There were four dead bodies and four very alive and heavily armed people in green standing in front of them, three men and a woman, all smiling brightly as if they were on a hike instead of a deadly rescue mission. And in the dirt by the tree was Warren, who was opening his eyes. He had a deep gash on his head that was bleeding profusely. The helicopter flew over them. After two well-placed shots, it careened away like a wounded bird.

"Some got away, but then, they didn't see too eager to engage. That helicopter won't bother us for a while." Dominic smiled at Stacy. She was returning it. Tall, blond, and now her hero. *If he has money too, they'll be all set,* Lynn thought.

"That leaves you, Warren, and the release of her parents." Alfred handed him a white handkerchief.

"Not going to happen." Warren gently dabbed his wound. "I have the upper hand here."

"Really? Is that why they left you behind?" Lynn asked with a grin.

"That is what they are trained to do—regroup. Like I said, I have the upper hand with our parents under my care."

"Funny, I was thinking the same thing with you under *my* care now. Seems like we have a good exchange. Don't you think?" Alfred brushed the dirt off his clothes. "Mind if I get my shirt button back, Warren?"

Warren scowled and didn't reply. Lynn wondered if this had been too easy, or if he was a terrible leader and his team had abandoned him. It was a shame he hadn't been killed with the others.

"What do you say we get out of here before they come back—if they do—with reinforcements?" Alfred smirked at Warren.

Warren didn't look defeated to Lynn. The fact that he was not trying to talk himself out of his position worried her.

"Sounds like a good idea to me." Kent smiled at Lynn.

"You could explain to my people exactly where you think your parents are being held, Lynn. We'll get right on that, right, Warren?" Alfred said. But Warren remained tight-lipped.

"I would think they are at the house in that safe room under the pool. Are we going to get them now?" Lynn asked.

"Yes." Alfred didn't take his eyes off Warren.

"Good, but I wish I didn't have to deal with them." Lynn stroked the closest black cat in the carrier. In gratitude either Mystery or Magic licked her finger and meowed.

"Done. I'll come up with a nice story and leave you out of it, but I'll make sure your stepbrother pays for all he did. Work for you?" Alfred said.

"Sure does."

"You, Warren?"

"You are never going to find them. You aren't very bright, are you?"

CHAPTER 19

"Didn't that seem too easy?" Lynn asked Kent as they walked back, hand in hand, to an already running black truck. Warren followed peacefully along with Alfred, who was lugging Magic and Mystery's carrier, to a white truck, while Stacy was busy flirting with Dominic. The rest of the team stayed behind in the woods to clean up.

"Nothing has been easy about this, but I am wondering what was going on in Warren's head," Kent admitted as he pulled her closer to him in a quick embrace before they got to the truck. Even after all they had been through, a thrill ran through her. She'd never felt this way about anyone in her life, let alone trusted someone so quickly.

"Right, but what? I mean, his men abandoned him. Unless that was the plan because he knew we'd use the radio…"

"Leaving him behind so we would let our guard down. Would be a smart move—or a stupid one. I'm not sure. Figuring on us splitting up would be a stretch. Who knows? Your parents may not be where we think they are," Kent said.

"I know, which is why I still don't trust that this is over yet. Even if we got away and got my parents back in a trade, what would stop him from hunting us down afterward and making us pay? Maybe we can get my parents back and turn him in at the same time, unless he dies. When you're dealing with Warren, you can't rule anything out. Not that any of my rambling helps you." Lynn chuckled.

"I am very fond of your ramblings." Kent winked. "I think we need an in-between plan to cover us and your parents and at the same time stop Warren from acting against us in the future. Right now, we have a plan in motion."

"And exactly what is our plan, Kent?" Lynn put her hands on her hips.

"I don't want to jinx it by saying it out loud."

"Seriously? Just say you can't tell me. I'd like you to be honest."

"Yeah, well, I do work for your grandpa, and he'd prefer it if I kept his theories private, sorry." Kent gave her a weak smile.

"Yeah, because I'm so untrustworthy." Lynn turned away.

"You aren't, but…well, we can't be sure who's listening, ya know? I mean, what if they haven't caught everyone?"

"He thinks…" Lynn stopped.

Alfred thought there was a spy among them? How? She didn't think it was likely that someone had been listening to them in the forest. What if that cute bodyguard Stacy couldn't get enough of wasn't what he seemed?

"He does," Kent confirmed. "Might be someone already in place before all of this happened. You see how calm Warren is…well, you know."

Lynn studied their driver, who was watching the white truck. He didn't appear to be paying attention to their conversation, but who knew? Yes, it could be one of the drivers. This was hurting her head. Well, Alfred had to be cautious. "I can see if someone was already in place and they could be here with us; that would make sense and why Warren is, well, so full of himself. I'm glad Warren is with Alfred now. All I want to do is go home and get some sleep."

"What are you two lovebirds talking about?" Stacy asked, coming up behind them.

"Oh, you're done flirting?" Lynn arched her eyebrow.

"Me? Flirt? You know me better than that. I was getting to know a hero is all. He even got my phone number so we can get to know each other better when this is over." Stacy smiled.

"Cool."

"Yeah! Well, I think it's time to get going. Been a hell of a long day, and you know, I'm like, starved. What do you say we get a bite to eat and then get some sleep?" Kent scanned the tree line.

"Sounds good. They gonna take us to your car? It's still there, right?" Stacy asked.

"Um, I think so. I should check in with Alfred before we go," Kent replied, watching Alfred load Warren into his truck. "I'll be right back."

"No, you're not leaving us here alone." Lynn grabbed Stacy's hand and followed.

As soon as they got to the other car, Kent whispered into Alfred's ear. Alfred looked at Warren and nodded. *More secrets, great.*

Alfred said out loud, "We should get on the road. From what we can tell, it's all clear. And I have old Warren here handled." Warren pretended he didn't hear. He was being surprisingly quiet. *What a show he's putting on, unless it isn't a show.* "Lynn, I hope you will consider allowing me to be in your life once you hear all I have to tell you." Alfred rubbed his shoulder.

Lynn felt chills run through her. *There's more?* "Yeah, we can sit down and chat once this is all over. Then we'll see where we go from there, I guess."

Alfred frowned for a moment but covered it with a smile. "I'll do it however you choose. Thank you, Lynn. I'm glad to meet you, Stacy, and to see you in person, Kent. This job is done. I hope to see you all again. Kent, I will have many jobs for you in the future, although I hope you'll consider a career in law. This can pay your way until then, but it's up to you." Alfred winked, adding, "I hope you don't mind if I have someone watching over your apartment, girls; and your place, Kent, until this is fully resolved to my satisfaction. I'll let you know when your parents are back home too."

"Thanks." She noticed Warren's grimace. *That was strange.*

"I'll consider it. Thank you," Kent said.

"Glad to hear it. Well, I need to get my beauties to a safe place and get Mr. Stone taken care of. Oh, and Stacy: that young fella you are interested in? He's a good one." Alfred offered a thumbs up before he climbed into his truck.

"Yeah, thanks. I was glad to meet you, and I hope we see you again," Stacy said.

Alfred waved as Kent and Stacy climbed into their truck. A peacock feather caught Lynn's eye. *What's going on with feathers today?* She bent to pick it up and noticed a large, yellow-tinted puddle under the black pickup.

"Um, Kent, what's this?" she pointed.

Kent hopped out and bent down next to Lynn, "What? Oh!" He pulled her and Stacy away from the vehicle.

"What's going on?" Stacy asked.

"It looks fresh, and I think it's brake fluid. I want you to keep your distance until we figure out what it is."

Kent yelled out to the other truck as it was driving away. The husky redheaded driver jumped out, glanced under the truck, and shook his head. Kent ran down the road, waving his arms and yelling "Hey!" until the other truck stopped.

A chill shot through Lynn. What if she hadn't seen the feather? Would their brakes have gone out, and would they have crashed? Was it a faulty line, or did someone cut it? She was leaning more toward the second explanation, but who could have done it? They'd never let Warren out of their sight, but maybe that was something one of the people who escaped had done. Alfred and his lanky driver were out in a second and looking under their truck. Had someone done something to that white truck too? Lynn watched them look under both vehicles and under the hoods. She glanced at Warren. His smug look indicated he knew about this, but who was his spy? She still wasn't safe. They weren't as in control as they'd thought.

"Yup, Mr. Justice. It's brake fluid. The main line is cut. Depending on how fast we were going, it could have been bad." The redheaded man wiped his hands on his pants.

Alfred nodded grimly. "I know your driver, Bobby; but our driver… Who are you, young man? I thought Rick was on call."

"I'm Andy, Mr. Justice. Rick had family issues. A death, I think. He called me to replace him. He said it would be okay with you."

"Well, Andy, I'm glad Rick had a replacement. Been with me for years, so I completely trust him. The brakes can't be fixed here, can they?" Alfred shot a glance to Kent.

"No, they can't," Kent said.

"If I had the right tools and a bit of time, I could do it, Mr. Justice. Do we have extra time?" Andy glanced over at the white truck.

"That's a great question, Andy, but I think you know the answer to that. No, we do not."

"Then should we all ride together?" Andy asked.

Mr. Justice exchanged a look with Bobby. *This is what Warren wanted,* Lynn realized. To have them in one truck. *Why?*

"I only need one driver, so Bobby will drive us, if you don't mind staying with the pickup, Andy, until someone can get here to help you fix it all up?" Alfred asked.

"I was thinking I should come with you. If someone is doing things like this, you might need all the help you can get, Mr. Justice," Andy replied.

"I think we'll be fine. We already have two bodyguards, plus Bobby and all my guests. Thank you so much for offering, though. I will make sure you're given a nice bonus for all you've done. Be careful, Andy," Alfred warned.

"Well, yeah, okay, Mr. Justice. Thanks."

"You're very welcome."

"We should get out of here. They can't be far behind," Kent said.

"Very true. Come on, girls, let's get out of here." Alfred took hold of them and almost pushed them in the direction of the white truck.

Lynn glanced at Kent, who was frowning at her. "Him?" she mouthed. Kent nodded.

"Really? How do we know someone didn't do something to the other truck too?" Stacy asked quietly.

"I'm sure," Alfred said. In a low tone they almost couldn't hear, he added, "He only wanted to drive our truck, not yours. He would have probably driven us into a trap after your truck crashed or got us all into one vehicle. Not sure how his evil mind thinks. Plus, I don't have a driver named Rick." Alfred glanced back at Andy and waved. He had lit up a cigarette, and he waved back with a big smile on his face. Alfred sighed and climbed into the white truck.

"Yeah, that could have been grim." Kent rolled his shoulders and massaged his neck.

Lynn didn't think Andy knew they suspected him. She saw he had a gun, and she realized how well Alfred had played that off. Stacy climbed in and immediately sat next to her bodyguard. That left two seats for her and Kent. She wanted to sit where she didn't have to look at her stepbrother, but that didn't seem possible. Her plan to never see him again had failed. She whispered to Kent, "Warren has a guy working for Mr. Justice? How?"

"My guess is he was able to take out the other driver once he heard about the rescue. Probably never really know. Let's hope there aren't more."

"Yeah." She got in and sat next to Stacy without looking at Warren. She watched Kent look under the truck and then under the hood again. He gave a thumbs-up and got in next to her.

"I had hoped this was over for us," Lynn whispered to Stacy.

"Me too." Stacy frowned.

"Hey, Warren, how did you decide which car you wanted to ride in?" Kent asked.

"I prefer white cars, Kent."

Kent and Alfred locked eyes for a moment.

"Yes, he did pick this vehicle. Sorry, Lynn. I should've known," Alfred said.

Warren gave them a lopsided smile. "Known what? Not my fault your truck broke down. Might want to take better care of your things, Mr. Justice."

"I hear a helicopter again." Lynn craned her neck to look out the window.

"Guess you have more than one of those, huh, Warren? Let's get out of here, Bobby."

"Done."

* * *

ZELINA SMILED. "Nice touch with the feather."

"Thank you. That Andy fellow is taking off."

"Yes. He knows his cover is blown."

"He could have killed Lynn. He needs to be held accountable for that," Thomas said with his hands on his hips.

Zelina nodded. "That will happen. It always does."

"I know. I wish we were inside that truck with them and that evildwel instead of just following along," Thomas said, his wings spread and gliding.

"Too crowded in there now. We will drop in soon and let the evildwel know it has not won, do not worry."

"Good. I saw Warren's face, though, when they mentioned the apartment." His smile faded.

"Yes, Alfred was clever enough to notice too. The best part of this is Warren's men will soon learn what happened to Warren's uncle. The boat was recovered, along with the crew. It won't take long to figure out the family wasn't on it. Warren is the only suspect. There is someone who was groomed to step in for the uncle, and Warren had not gotten around to taking him out, thankfully. In the meantime they are still safe until the ambush. We are finally at the part where we find out if Lynn and the parents live. These next few minutes are important, and much depends on what Lynn sees."

"That evildwel is getting bold," Thomas grumbled.

"I think that creature will be moving on soon. It is running out of ways to protect Warren. Soon it will let him die."

"I hope so. Then he becomes our problem to fix since that evildwel never keeps the souls. What is he looking at out his window?"

Zelina pointed. "Those reflections in the forest. Mr. Justice's team let many get away. A trap. Another reason we are out here instead of in there."

"No feathers to guide them? Or a beam of light?" Thomas suggested.

"Oh, well, maybe." Zelina smiled.

"I see it. The light is reflecting off their guns. They do not see it."

"Now we go inside and get Lynn's attention."

Both angels were soon next to the humans crammed into the truck. Thomas saw the expression on Lynn's face. "She sees it!"

"Yes. That is one unhappy evildwel. Now we observe what becomes of it."

CHAPTER 20

$\mathcal{L}$ynn squinted, trying to figure out what she was seeing. "Look!" she shouted, pointing into the trees. "We aren't alone!"

"Turn around, Bobby. This is a trap," said Alfred grimly.

Warren sneered. "You think they would leave me behind?"

"No, I was prepared for that, but not for sabotaging one of my vehicles. You won't catch me off guard again, I promise." Alfred studied the gun in his hand.

"Don't make promises you can't keep, old man. I did warn you they would regroup. Just in time too," Warren said as a gunshot just missed the skidding truck.

"Warren, with age comes wisdom. I assure you, I don't speak unless I have something to back it up. Trying to kill my granddaughter—you can imagine how I feel about that."

"I'm the only thing between you and your demise. I'd watch how you speak to me." Warren sat up straighter while everyone else was being thrown around.

"You are a punk, Warren. You've earned no respect from me or your men. That'll backfire on you. Don't you think someone is wondering about your uncle and his family suddenly taking a vacation? And making no contact? I wonder what would happen if they found out that someone hurt their boss. After all, there was someone who was being groomed to take over the business, and it wasn't you."

"I'm not sure what you're insinuating, old man. Or is there another name I should be calling you, like grandpa?" Warren smirked, but his eyes were darting back and forth like a trapped animal's.

"For you, I think I prefer Mr. Justice, since you so kindly asked. Just know it has been noted that your uncle's absence is unusual. I have been able to, well, get some information out."

"You know nothing. There is nothing you can do to hurt me, old man."

The truck was racing away from the trap, and Alfred shifted to match Warren's arrogant posture. "Did you know your uncle didn't trust you?"

"My uncle and I were very close. I'd check your sources again."

Lynn glanced behind them to check that they weren't being followed. Three men came out of the forest. No one else took a shot at them, but one of them was talking into a radio. *Uh-oh.*

"You weren't his second-in-command. From my personal sources, I've heard the real second-in-command is confused as to your uncle's last instructions about leaving you in charge. I'm sure you had planned to take him out, but wouldn't that seem a little suspicious? I don't think the man will just walk away from this. He was so loyal to your uncle. But I'm sure you have a plan in place, right, Warren?"

"I have no idea what you're talking about. I was just playing around with my stepsister. Like I have said, and will keep saying, my uncle and his family are on their boat heading to a tropical paradise. A long-overdue vacation for such a hardworking man. Of course he would trust his nephew to keep an eye on things. Who wouldn't believe that? I'm sure I can straighten it all out with him. I'm not worried, but you should be. Do you really think you will get away?" Warren shifted around to smile at Lynn.

She held his gaze. She wasn't going to be intimidated by him. *Karma is going to be a bitch for you,* she thought.

"Yes, I do think we're going to get away. We're going to let the authorities, the ones who aren't on your payroll, know that your parents are in Lynn's apartment."

Warren's face paled. He flinched and quickly covered it up, but not before they all saw it. "I was playing with her before."

"Thanks for confirming what I already knew: They are at the apartment. Now, the strange part is that key. You don't know what it's for or what to do with it. The funny thing is your uncle had no idea what it was for. It was something that belonged to his dad, who claimed it opened a great treasure, but he died before he could explain any more. One brother got it, and the other wanted it. That simple. An old Roman key, and no one knows what it opens. Kind of funny, if you really think about it."

"The key was found. And that apartment—it's burning down as we speak, sorry to say," Warren replied.

"What! We have to warn someone. We need to stop it!" Lynn cried.

"Too late. They burned alive, and you'll be blamed. And the best part is none of you will live to contradict that story." Warren was still smiling, but Lynn detected uncertainty.

"I don't like to work with criminals," Alfred said. "But I was able to reach out to the second-in-command. Mr. Jones is his name, right, Kent?"

Kent nodded and Alfred continued. "I admit you have some loyal men working for you, or that car wouldn't have been disabled. You'll find that last driver, Andy, ran off along with your shooters. Of course, you can be happy that you almost won. You will not have a warm welcome among your uncle's employees. I honestly feel like you would stand more of a chance of surviving in jail. So I offer you a choice: Shall I drop you off at your uncle's house or the police station?"

"I found you hiding in a tree, and now you want me to believe you've rallied all my men against me since then? You're bluffing." Warren's strong posture was marred by the fear in his eyes.

"Your car had a radio. We used it, as you well know. You planned on that, but you didn't plan on me contacting Mr. Jones. But believe what you want. I'm only giving you an option, since I'm not a cruel man. I don't want to be responsible for what is done to you, even if you deserve it after trying to kill us many times over. I assure you, my message was received. Mr. Jones knows who Mr. Hill is. He took what was said very seriously."

"So they'll listen to a man who pretended to be dead and then turned on their boss? Horror movies aren't even this stupid. Come on. You are just messing with my mind, but it's too late. There is no one to save my parents, and they will never find my uncle's body. My men will get me back from you. It's that simple," Warren said, but sweat shone on his face and darkened his shirt under the arms.

Lynn looked at Stacy, who shrugged. This was getting crazier by the moment. Warren had just said "uncle's body" in front of everyone.

"You get that, Bobby?"

"Yes, sir. It's recorded."

"Please pass it along."

"You're bluffing, old man."

"Or not. You'll see. The issue is being resolved as we speak," Alfred said.

"Losing it, old man. But I believe you're too late. That apartment building is burning down."

"They may have been bad parents, but you are pure evil," Lynn said.

"Evil is a good word to describe you, Warren. You're a shallow, selfish man driven to cause as much pain as you can, and you've been enjoying it all. Right?" Alfred asked.

"What you call evil, I call successful." Warren glanced back out the car window.

"No one is coming for you, Warren. What did you do with the bodies, burn them?" Alfred asked. All eyes were on Warren.

He gulped. "I don't know what you're talking about."

"You killed him and probably the entire family. I bet you killed them first and made him watch."

Warren shrugged. "Why would I do that?"

Alfred shook his head. "You enjoy killing, don't you, Warren?"

"You think you're going to get me to admit to killing my uncle and his family? Wrong."

"You spoke of your uncle's body, so you already admitted it. The boat and the crew's bodies have been found. I had another detective focused on that house, until he was found dead. Sorry, Kent, I only found out after Lynn escaped. Otherwise, we'd have known where she was."

Kent didn't respond, but he squeezed Lynn's hand.

"If you free me, I will set our parents free. Deal?" Warren asked, giving Lynn his best Hollywood smile.

"Aren't you burning down the apartment?" Lynn couldn't believe he could lie so easily. One untruth on top of another. *Did he believe what he said?*

"Of course not. I'm not an animal, just a guy trying to get on with his life. It was my bluff. This is how it works. I was never going to hurt you, Lynn. You go on with your life, and I go on with mine. Deal, sis? After all we've been through…"

"I vote we set him free at the police station. I will be the first to press charges for kidnapping and murder," Stacy narrowed her eyes.

Warren glared at her and shook his head. "Stacy, I would never have killed you. That guy you saw killed was a very bad drug dealer. He was going to kill you. I was saving you and letting you sleep off the drugs he gave you—honestly. And that guy you woke up next to, Lynn? His roommate killed him over drugs. You see how this can all be explained."

Lynn couldn't believe what she was hearing. She was about to speak when she saw Warren's eyes turn red. Either she needed some sleep, or she was seated across from a monster. *Or both.*

"Lying all the way to the very end. You should do well in court, but it's doubtful anyone will believe your stories but you." Alfred massaged his brow.

"We'll see," Warren responded.

"Yes, we will. Bobby, are they waiting for us?"

"Yes, sir."

"Good."

* * *

THE EVILDWEL LOOKED across the truck at Lynn. She was pleased the girl had finally seen her. She enjoyed scaring them. She'd been so sure the girl wouldn't survive. *Unfortunate.* She had encouraged her host to cut the rope around his hands yet again with that pocketknife she'd had him get before he abandoned the last truck. Luckily, these people weren't as clever as they thought they were, or they would have tied him up better or thrown him in the back dead. He was almost free. The gun was within his reach. Dian had to make a quick call on who should die first. The old man or Lynn? It would cause more sadness if the girl went first, she concluded. Then she'd finish this mess off with her host killing himself. Too many people knew what he'd done. His killing days were over. *A shame, really.* Her host had lost. His men had been stopped.

Dian had done her part in encouraging the damage to the other vehicle. She had learned a few tricks over the centuries and could have done this herself, but her host obliged her. Getting them all together again in this truck hadn't been in her host's favor. Alfred's operatives had communicated with the police, and arrests were already being made. The deal was with the real second-in-command. He would come out of this untouched and fully funded. *The idiots don't realize he will be worse than those that came before.* Mr. Jones wasn't her type of host, though. He loved his family too much for her taste.

She was aware, even if her host wasn't, that the parents had been rescued from Lynn's apartment unhurt. That fearful Gus didn't make it out alive. Too bad he went so easy—heart attack. The authorities would find the burned remains in the safe room and enough evidence to either put her host away for life or give him the death penalty. She almost considered sticking around in case of the latter, but that took years, and she didn't want to go back to prison with him. Besides, after all the fun he'd given her, she could at least give him an easy way out, no matter how stupid he was acting now.

Dian hoped that seeing her would haunt Lynn for years to come. Staying around these pesky angels was certainly killing all her beautiful negative vibes. This scenario had gotten too crowded, but it had been a good run. She would be out of there the moment the gun went off.

* * *

LYNN SAW a flash of light behind Warren. She realized that his hands were free and his eyes were on the unattended gun in Alfred's lap. Alfred and Kent were talking and didn't notice. Stacy was too busy staring at Dominic. That left her alone. She lunged for the gun and got it right before Warren could. She saw his look of surprise when she pointed it at him, but he still reached to take it from her at the same time that Kent and Dominic went into action. Everything got confusing for a split second—until she pulled the trigger. She watched Warren fall forward.

"Oh, my God!" Stacy screamed.

"Are you okay, Lynn?" Alfred shouted.

"Yes." She watched Warren take his last breath. She was positive she saw a dark mist leave his body. The same red eyes she'd seen before looked out at her from that darkness. Then it was gone as the truck skidded to a stop.

"Did anyone see that?" Lynn asked.

"It was horrible. I'll never forget seeing him get shot." Stacy covered her mouth with her trembling hand.

"I'm sorry, Lynn. I should've had better control of my gun. I'm not sure how you knew what he was going to do, but I'm glad you did what you did." Alfred awkwardly patted her shoulder.

"I saw his hands were untied," Lynn mumbled as the cats yowled in their carrier. Alfred reached in and scooped them out. They sat contently in his lap.

"I tried to stop him," Kent added. "You're okay—that's all that matters."

"I've never killed anyone."

"It'll be okay." Kent took the gun away from her quavering hand and pulling her into a hug.

242

A feeling of calm flowed over Lynn. "It was all I could do."

"It was," Alfred agreed.

"Yeah, you were kind of badass." Stacy leaned into Dominic who protectively comforted her.

"Whatever, but didn't you see that thing?" Lynn asked.

"What thing?" Stacy looked puzzled.

"The black mist thing with the red eyes above Warren after I shot him."

"Probably his black soul leaving," Stacy said.

Kent squeezed Lynn closer to him. "Must have been a reflection or something, Lynn. But I have to agree—you're a badass."

"Yeah, whatever." Lynn shrugged. Shouldn't she feel bad that she'd killed someone? She didn't. It was more like she had protected the people she loved from evil. She was positive it was pure evil that she'd seen.

"Whatever yourself, Lynn. That was a brave thing you did. Are you okay?" Alfred asked, looking concerned and checking Warren's pulse.

"I am, actually. What about my parents?" Lynn asked. "The fire?"

"Bobby called it in. Authorities are on their way to your apartment and your parents' home, and I'm hopeful my men got there in time. We will be updated soon, thanks to your uncle working from his hospital bed, Kent."

"No problem. I think there will be some cleaning up in that department too." Kent squeezed Lynn into him tightly.

"That has been in the works for a while. No more good cops will be shot anymore," Alfred said.

"You sure he's dead?" Stacy smoothed down her hair.

"Very." Alfred leaned forward.

"Could we cover him or something?"

"Yes, sorry. I should have thought of that." Dominic removed his Golden State Warriors jacket and covered Warren. As Dominic shifted his body, something fell to the floor.

Alfred picked it up. "'F*ck off & die?' Why would he carry a button like that on him?"

"It's mine." Lynn held out her hand. Alfred shrugged and handed it over.

"Talk about a literal meaning," Stacy shuffled her feet closed to Dominic.

Bobby interrupted the awkward moment. "Sir, the parents are safe and on their way to the hospital, and the fire was prevented. A man's body was found at the apartment, identified only as Gus, I'm told."

"Thank you. That's a shame. He was an ex-cop who mentored Warren. Backfired on him," Alfred sighed loudly.

"But my parents are okay?" Lynn asked.

"Yes. Do you want to see them?" Alfred signaled Bobby.

"No, but I am glad they're okay," Lynn said, and she meant it.

"Maybe another time?" Alfred gave a shake of his head to the driver.

"Maybe." The truck fell back into a comfortable silence.

Stacy fell asleep against Dominic, her bodyguard, as Lynn snuggled with Kent. When they arrived at the police station, they left Warren's body behind.

Lynn grabbed Kent's and Stacy's hands. She realized she'd finally answered all the questions from her list. She would check them all off, if she ever found it. She smiled up at Kent, and he smiled back. Lynn knew it was going to be a long day, but with him and Stacy by her side, she could survive anything.

EPILOGUE

CHRISTMAS 1984

*L*ynn pulled the sugar cookies out of the oven. It was her first attempt at baking, and they looked like they were supposed to. All she had to do was add the frosting and decorations, and her first Christmas cookies would be ready for consumption. Stacy was stirring the tortellini soup that she had just taught Lynn to make. Water, three packages of chicken soup, and a large package of cheese-stuffed tortellini—easy enough. Stacy got the parmesan cheese from the fridge. It was their first Christmas Eve meal, and all that was missing were their guests: Stacy's parents, Dominic, Kent, Lynn's mother, and her grandfather. There had been no communication between her and her grandfather for the past year, but that same time had been a healing one for Lynn and her mother.

Being kidnapped had had a positive effect on her mother. Carrie went to rehab and still attended therapy twice a week. She offered apologies, while her husband kept drinking to blot out what his son had done. On such different paths, they parted ways within two months, and none too amicably on his part, either.

Lynn arranged the freshly baked cookies on a kitchen towel to cool off. Stacy was so involved with the final touches to their meal that she wasn't hovering over Lynn and her less-than-stellar cooking skills. Lynn knew she needed to wait a bit for the cookies to cool before frosting them. She remembered from watching her mom bake on holidays.

Lynn smiled. She couldn't remember ever seeing her mother happy and kind, like she was now. She was wary about this new woman her mother had become and hoped she didn't find another abusive man. Lynn was hopeful and cautious at the same time. One huge surprise was that her mother adopted Lynn's new healthy life-style; they even took a yoga class together. Being sober had woken her mother up. Lynn hoped they never again had to see the man who had created one of the most evil people she had ever met—her stepbrother.

She hadn't gone to Warren's funeral. She was surprised he'd even had one, but her stepfather insisted on paying for it, as well as the coffin and the plot. Her mother had confided that he was the only one there, and he went to make sure his son knew how much he hated him. Warren was now resting eternally in a grave marked only by his name and dates. There was no message of love on his headstone. Lynn knew he would answer for all he did, but that thought didn't give her the satisfaction she'd imagined it would.

Impatient, Lynn blew on the tree-shaped cookies to cool them and then began to spread the canned white frosting. She probably should have waited longer, but she wanted to keep busy until her guests arrived. Her biggest worry about cookies was how they would taste. If their smell was any indication, they would be good. She snuck a bite. *Yup, not bad,* she thought. She heard the oven door shut. Stacy was humming along with "White Christmas" on the radio. Lynn caught the aroma of garlic bread mingled with the vanilla of the sugar cookies and the cheesy chicken tortellini soup. The aroma kindled her festive side and pushed away all her bad thoughts. She began to quietly sing along. "May your days be merry and bright." Stacy joined in.

Two songs later, her past crept back in. At least the flashbacks weren't coming at her all the time anymore, like that black aura thing that left Warren right after she shot him. She wished she could forget it completely, at least during the holidays, but as each day passed, the moments were less frequent and less intense. She was okay with the outcome because she'd had no choice. And after all she'd found out about Warren, she felt she had done the world a favor.

The police closed the case. The few bad seeds were gone, and Kent's uncle was the new police chief. The investigation had been thorough. Not only had they found the proof that Warren had killed his uncle and his entire family, but they found a string of other murders that had nothing to do with the crime family. He'd been a serial killer. It gave closure to the family of that cheerleader who'd gone missing after one of Warren's swim meets. The key Warren had been looking for was never recovered, and Lynn had no idea if her stepfather knew where it was. She really didn't care.

She was way too busy focusing on her college courses in marine biology. Kent was studying criminal justice and now leaning more toward law. He was still doing detective work full-time, and she was helping him. They made a good team, and she didn't miss doing hair. In fact, sometimes she thought she wanted to do detective work full-time with Kent and forgo marine biology. Maybe she would add a second degree in criminal justice, just in case. She was particularly proud that she had talked Stacy into college too. Stacy was focusing on photography when she wasn't all over Dominic, who was just as much into her. He was helpful with her photography, especially when it was for some of their cases. He wasn't rich like her previous boyfriends, but he seemed to be the right one for her. *Time will tell.*

Lynn was excited about hosting her first holiday meal and getting past what her stepbrother had done. She was going to spend the day with all her loved ones. The one exception was her grandfather. She hadn't seen him since their talk two weeks after Warren's death. That conversation had changed everything between them.

"Lynn, I told you I used to drink."

"Yes." Lynn wasn't sure where the conversation was going.

"I just got you into my life. I've never been happier," Alfred said with a weak smile as he wiped his hands on his black jeans. He had dark circles under his eyes. She wondered if he was going to tell her he was sick.

"Yeah, I'm glad you're a part of my life too." Lynn's heart was racing.

"I …I was responsible for the car accident that killed your friend Tammy and her family." He had tears in his eyes as he looked away.

"You what?" Lynn stood up in disbelief.

"It was me, Lynn. I had no idea at the time that it was your best friend, but it doesn't matter who they were—I'm the reason they're dead. It was late at night, and I fell asleep after a long day of drinking. I woke up to the sound of brakes and rubber squealing. I was able to stop safely, but they went over the embankment. I immediately checked on them, but none of them were wearing their seat belts, and…well…there was nothing I could do."

"You fell asleep? From drinking?" Lynn spat the words out.

"Yes, I did. And I should have stayed there at the accident, but I was supposed to be dead. So I did something stupid. I left. It's something I live with every day, and it's important to me that you know everything."

"She was my best friend, and you killed her!"

"I am sorry, Lynn. I quit drinking the very next day. Since then, I've done all I can to help people. I know it doesn't make up for it."

"Nothing will make up for it. I don't ever want to see you again!" Her image of him as she stormed out was of an old, crumpled man crying, and it haunted her. What he had said rocketed around in her brain with no place to go for an entire year.

Lynn gave her grandfather credit for turning himself in to the police the very next day. Justice moved fast, and soon one of his aliases, Alfred Trimble, was serving a three-year sentence for drunk driving and leaving the scene of a crime. He got an early release at Thanksgiving for good behavior and honored her wish for no contact.

She wasn't sure why she had picked up the phone last week and invited him to Christmas Eve dinner. Maybe it was the spirit of Christmas and forgiveness. Although she wasn't ready to fully forgive him, she was ready to move forward and include him in her life. He had paid for what he had done, although it would never bring her best friend and her family back. She dreamed about Tammy sometimes now; she was always smiling, forever twelve years old. She always said the same thing. "I'm okay. Be happy now, Lynn, and forgive." It was just a dream, but it also factored into her wanting to see her grandfather.

She knew through Kent that Mr. Justice was back in business. Mr. Jones and Mr. Justice reached a mutual agreement to leave each other alone, whatever that meant. Lynn sighed. It was going to be weird seeing her grandfather for the first time, but it was long overdue. Was he the same person after being in jail? *Guess I'll find out.* Stacy glanced over with a worried look as she chopped onions for the salad. Lynn forced a smile. Stacy knew her too well.

Lynn shook red and green sprinkles over the cookies before arranging them on a platter. She grabbed a black pen and crossed off "Bake cookies" from her Christmas Eve dinner list. There were still "Set the table" and "Light the candles," but the food part was done. She was about to show off her cookie masterpiece to Stacy when there was a knock at the front door.

"I got it!" Lynn rushed to the door.

"Too early for Dominic—must be Kent."

Stacy was right. Kent quickly kissed her and then pulled her toward her bedroom with a grin.

"We have company coming, you two," Stacy called from the kitchen.

"We know," Kent replied. He shut the bedroom door, locking out Princess Leia, who protested with a loud meow.

"Yeah, she's right," Lynn said.

"Don't worry, I have an early Christmas present to give you." Kent was sweating like he had just worked out. He wiped his hands on his jeans and then shrugged.

"I thought we agreed to open our present on Christmas morning," Lynn protested, shaking her head. *What does he have in mind?* she wondered.

"We did. You okay, Lynn? I mean, with your grandfather coming." Kent studied her face.

"Yes, I think I am. It's time to see him."

"I'm glad to hear that."

"I'm glad you're glad," Lynn teased, but he didn't respond. In fact, he looked very serious.

"Okay, now, back to my early gift. I have a good reason for it being now instead of later."

"Does it have something to do with dinner?" Lynn asked, confused.

"We came, we saw, we kicked its ass." he got down on one knee.

"Why are you quoting *Ghostbusters*, and why are you on your knee?" Lynn demanded. She felt her face turn a bright shade of red that she was sure matched Kent's.

"If I offended you, then I am sorry," Kent said with a small grin. He swallowed hard.

"Now you're quoting Indiana Jones. Are you trying to say something, maybe?"

"You know how you affect me. When I get nervous, I start quoting movies. The reason I am down here is to ask the woman I love to marry me and live happily ever after." Kent began to beam as he pulled a small black velvet box out of his pocket. He held it up to Lynn as he locked eyes with her. She shivered as she took it.

Her heart started racing as she opened it. It was a gold band with a small, sparkling diamond set in the middle.

"You are kidding me, right? Is this for real?" Lynn said as Kent stood up.

"Very real. I know it isn't the biggest diamond, but we could improve on it someday."

"I don't care about the size of the diamond. In fact, I don't even need a diamond," Lynn protested.

"I know, but I always want you to have the very best because I love you, Lynn Hill, and want to spend the rest of my life with you."

"I...ummm...I wasn't. Well...yeah, you are the best, even if you are a pain sometimes and quote movies at weird times. Well, I wouldn't want to spend my life with anyone else, so, well, yeah...sure."

"I will take your rambling as a yes?" he asked.

Lynn nodded with a huge smile as he put the ring on her finger and kissed her hand. "Oh, just one more thing." He pulled out a white button that said, in black cursive, "Happily Ever After."

"A button?"

"Yes. I think it's time to replace that F*ck Off & Die button that you insisted on keeping after…well, you know."

"Well, I wanted to remember my past, but it *is* time to pack it away with all my memories. This one will go on my purse—on the outside. To let people know what I'm doing."

"I can agree to that. So, wanna plan a wedding?"

"I do," Lynn replied.

Kent pulled her into his embrace as she began to compose a wedding list in her head, but she was soon distracted. They weren't going to be there to greet their guests, although Stacy wouldn't mind handling that for a bit, especially when she heard the news.

* * *

THOMAS WAS SMILING. "She gets a happy ending?"

"She does, although there will be a few bumps along the way. They will be very happy." Zelina wore an even bigger smile.

"I feel like the child who saves all the people is here. Am I right?"

"Yes, she is pregnant with him. They will move up their wedding date. As we saw, he is destined to be a hero. He saves all those people in that horrible terrorist attack. After that, he might be this country's best hope for a safe future and an escape from the dark road it is heading toward and taking most of the world with it. You have seen what a mess he tackles. Such a kind heart. Of course, his sister will be a handful. It is possible she will need our help someday. The twins, though—such a zest for life they will have. They will teach the next generation. This marriage will be a blessing for so many."

"I only saw what the oldest kid does. I cannot see the rest."

"With practice comes clarity. Of course, free will does mess it up sometimes, but plans are always in place to help as much as possible. As you know, I am almost always correct in my predictions."

"I suppose you are." Thomas grinned and pushed his hair out of his eyes. "I do not see Carrie going back to drinking."

"Correct. She is to become the mother Lynn always deserved. They will end up being best friends later. She is on course to finding a good man to love her, finally. He owns a health food store. But right now, she is healing and moving forward. She has some stuff to work out, of course. It will take Lynn a while to completely trust her. You know, if all things go as they should."

"Good. Lynn deserves that. The stepfather?"

"I see him drinking himself to death within a year or two—alone, much like Kent's mother. Too bad she never reaches out to Kent after his stepfather leaves. She goes from an overdose of pills and alcohol. Kent's dad never tries to contact him. Very sad."

"We cannot help the stepdad or mother or encourage his dad to, well, be a dad?"

"I wish we could, but we cannot. They have their own things to settle, and it does not include Lynn or Kent. Unfortunately, Kent will always feel some guilt about his mother. Humans have a way of undoing all the good they are given in their lives. Maybe one of them will get an angel to help them, but it's unlikely as things stand now. I know I would be willing if I did not have other places to be."

"Alfred? Will she ever really forgive him?"

"Yes, eventually. The problem is with Alfred forgiving himself for driving drunk and falling asleep. His swerving into the other lane caused Tammy's father to lose control of his car. The authorities had ruled it an accident, so it was brave of Alfred to come forward and insist he be charged for it. In prison he found some peace, oddly enough."

"Such a horrible thing."

"It is. Tammy and her family forgive him, though. Someday he will know that."

"Well, it is not like he took a gun and shot them, but drinking and taking painkillers and then driving…"

Zelina twined her hair into a braid. "Right, I know. We will see what happens. At least Tammy seems to be getting through to Lynn in her dreams. But there is no escaping what you do here on Earth."

"That is very true, Zelina. Hopefully, dinner will go well between them. I think the news will make a difference."

"Yes, and that new baby changes people."

"There is one more question that I have been thinking about. If Lynn had left the bar when you first told her to, could that whole thing have been avoided?"

"If by 'thing' you mean waking up next to Todd after he had been shot and killed, yes, that could have been avoided. She had already met Kent, so that was in play, but the rest of it, no. Stacy still would have been kidnapped, and Warren would have approached Lynn. He would have found a way to scare her into staying with him. If Lynn had avoided Warren completely, her friend might not have survived, or he would have kidnapped her too. Did I answer your question?"

"Yes. I get that certain things have to happen for the best conclusions, but not all the bad stuff needs to happen along with that. And sometimes bad stuff happens because of their choices; other times, because of other people's choices. It is all very complicated, but I have seen a lot, working with you these last few years. There is a part of me that wonders, 'What if?'"

"It is best not to wonder so much. Instead, focus on what is happening. That is much more important, but if I am to be completely honest with you, I wonder myself, sometimes." Zelina gently smiled at him.

"Glad I am not the only one."

"You are not."

"I am relieved to hear that. Thank you." Thomas bowed his head.

"You are welcome. But remember, with their free will, good might not always be the outcome, no matter how much we want it for them." Zelina paused and spread her wings. They sparkled like emeralds. "And you need to stay here with Lynn and her family. This has always been where you are supposed to be."

"I am getting another chance?"

"Of course. I have taught you everything I know. Now I have my own assignment that I need to get to. I will be there if you need me—just call out. I will hear you, and I will check in on you too."

"Thanks, Zelina."

"You are welcome."

"I love that Lynn got her happily ever after with Kent."

"Me too, Thomas, me too." And then Zelina was gone.

POEM

UNWELCOME GUEST

I feel it when I'm uncomfortable.
    It is always there, hiding, waiting.
    That shallow breath,
    that tight grip—that feeling.

It draws my attention
    back to where it came from.
    A time—
    a time when I wasn't so strong.

I was helpless.
    I was young.
    I'm none of those things now.
    Yet it stays.

It's an unwanted guest
    that lurks in my body,
    that has overstayed

its welcome.

It seems unaware
    that it isn't wanted anymore.
    So I carefully guide it to the door,
    fumbling with the lock.

It clings to the doorway,
    hanging on to my past.
    Smiling, I gently push it out.
    We are both free as I release it.

AUTHOR'S NOTE

AUTHOR'S NOTE

I want to thank you for reading *The Button This Final Chance*. If you enjoyed what you just read, please leave a review. It's the best gift an author can receive, with much gratitude!

This book was a work of fiction. A couple of things that I wrote about happened to me, but not like they did in this story. And for those who were there—this was for you!

I only touched on the subject of child abuse. The poem *The Unwelcomed Guest,* that I included here, is my personal experience. If you are able, please support your local non-profit charities that help abused children and their broken families.

First, I must thank my wonderfully supportive and loving husband, along with my family, as I continue my writing journey. Many thanks to my beta readers: Danielle, Gwen, and John! Their input was invaluable to me! A huge thanks for the person who makes my work readable: Denise at *Artful Editor.*

The most important thank you is sent to *you,* the readers who take this journey with me! Embrace that inner child.

ABOUT THE AUTHOR

D. L. Finn is an independent California local who encourages everyone to embrace their inner child. She was born and raised in the foggy Bay Area, but in 1990 she relocated with her husband, kids, dogs, and cats to Nevada City, in the Sierra foothills. She immersed herself in reading all types of books but especially loved romance, horror, and fantasy. She always treasured creating her own reality on paper. Finally, surrounded by towering pines, oaks, and cedars, her creativity was nurtured until it bloomed. Her creations include children's books, adult fiction, a unique autobiography, and poetry. She continues on her adventure with an open invitation to all readers to join her. You can learn more about Ms. Finn at her website www.dlfinnauthor.com or email her at d.l.finn.author@gmail.com.

EXCERPT FROM THIS LAST CHANCE

Chapter 1

"My name is Nester. I've been around a long time, way before humans invented their first stone tool. My kind migrated from a distant planet that couldn't sustain us anymore, in case you've been wondering where we came from. Although I doubt you winged ones—that's what we call you angels—give evildwel history much thought. Your attention goes to the humans, including this young woman, Amber. You hardly leave her side. It's an unsettling thought, but I can almost understand your devotion. I feel something from Amber that used to repel me, but now it draws me to her, much like you. Not sure what it is, though.

"I'm attempting to communicate with you, like winged ones do, by thoughts. I can't take the chance of speaking out loud and being overheard by another evildwel. Anyway, it's my hope you can hear me because my life is literally spinning out of control."

Nester paused and studied the beautiful winged one. Zelina didn't indicate she wanted him to stop, so he continued to push his thoughts to her.

"There was this planet before Earth where we ran out of food. We had no entities like winged ones to stop us, so the planet's inhabitants destroyed each other. We feasted well on their fear and suffering, something we've done since time began. I've heard some voice the opinion that it was even before that, since we only know we are here, not how we came into existence. I've never pondered much on the philosophical part of our presence but considered what we did like culling the weak from the herd, until now.

"Humankind was still new when we arrived, but they supplied us with a feast, much like the banquets spread out for kings and queens. I don't like to admit it to you, but I've dined on the hatred and misery with each blow inflicted through slavery, genocide, torture, burning witches, wars, serial killers, or a man simply abusing his wife or child. Human hatred and fear were delicious food for me."

Nester paused again, making sure Zelina wouldn't lash out at him for saying that. Her face was serene, gazing down at her human. It was as if he didn't exist. His discomfort sharing himself was painful, like a festering open wound, but what other choice did he have?

"Of course, you winged ones haven't made it easy for us evildwels, which is why some of my kind has already moved on to new planets. I've heard winged ones or goodness doesn't interfere with their feeding there, but it's only a rumor. I tend to believe good is as widespread as we are, and that last planet we landed on with only evil there was a fluke. Those blue-tinted, one-eyed beings made us feel like we'd won the lottery, much like these humans are always trying to do. It was great for many decades—until it wasn't. Then we were left with hardly anything to feed on after they used their lethal weapons on each other. It'll be toxic for years for those scant few that survived.

"Earth was different, and the population has increased immensely. This has left us the luxury of choosing our hosts. In these so-called modern times, there's been plenty of opportunity for joint feedings, like World War II, when the bombs dropped on Pearl Harbor or Hiroshima and all the pain and fear inflicted by the Nazis. We've gathered in New York, Iran, Iraq, London, Spain, India, Nigeria, and so many other places as large-scale terrorist acts occurred. I was on Air India Flight 182, where over three hundred died. Rape, murder, and massacres have been met with opposition from you winged ones, but you've barely made a dent in the larger-scale events lately, which causes me some concern for this planet's prospects, until recently, that is."

Nester sighed. He didn't know what to do with these new feelings he had, and he wanted answers. He wished Zelina would at least acknowledge he was in the room with her. He knew she saw him.

"But none of this has bothered me until now, and the consequence is I'm rooting for this girl while trying to get my thoughts across to you. My attempted communication with you is taboo and would be my death sentence if another evildwel knew. They would believe I'd gone insane. Maybe I have—I honestly have no idea. All I know is there's nothing I can do about what's happening to me.

"Do you understand how strange it is for an evildwel to observe this golden-haired human without the slightest intention of feeding on her fear? I watch simply because I feel like she's important in the scheme of earthly things. It's an evildwel thing to feel out the bad, and there's plenty of it around her right now, but to know she's important to humans is a completely new thing to me. To see that she's…well, good."

Nester hesitated to say more as Zelina hovered over Amber. He frowned. His dark mist swirled tightly around him as it did normally, but nothing else in his life was normal anymore. All he could do was try to get through to the winged one by staying close and watch.

Chapter 2

The gloomy gray afternoon was framed in the small office window like a dismal black and white photograph. Amber's world reflected this monochromatic existence as her fingers furiously tapped away on the keyboard. Even the rare shimmer of a positive political piece couldn't instill illumination into the murkiness labeled as grief. But how could she feel otherwise after what had happened? The fulfillment her job used to offer wasn't important in her new reality, including this piece about the new presidential candidate, Myles Stroud. The man her sister, Iris, used to work for... before.

Amber choked back the sadness that still threatened to consume her whenever she thought about her twin sister. If she let those tears escape the heavy barrier she'd built up over the last six months, she knew her coworkers would be at her side. They cared, and she couldn't fault them for trying, but their advice was meant for someone who had closure.

"You need to move on, Amber."

That line had assaulted her ears like an eager beginner's drum solo. She was surprised that her eardrums hadn't burst with good intentions. Amber shook her head and stretched out her legs and arms in her small white cubicle. Heavily buttered popcorn whiffed its way out of the lunchroom, but it didn't trigger hunger; instead, it promoted an uneasy queasiness. Amber slowly sipped water from her crystal-infused water bottle, forcing the kaleidoscope of emotions back down into that familiar numbness. Finally, working robot Amber took charge and was able to focus on double-checking facts and punctuation. Her reputation rested on truth. No slanting a story for either side, even for this candidate. Independent Senator Stroud made her job easier, though.

"I think he's the one who will finally fix things," Iris had declared brightly over breakfast one morning. Amber had believed her then, but now?

She sighed and muttered quietly to herself, "He's not magical or capable of bringing people back from the dead."

She pushed back the wavy blond hairs that had escaped from her ponytail. Her current condition could be summed up in that hairstyle: parts kept escaping from her tightly guarded emotions.

She continued to work on her article until she was satisfied there were no mistakes and sent it to her editor. She scanned her emails and responded in meaningless words when necessary. Peeking hopefully over her glowing screen at the clock, she shook her head as disappointment surged through her. Another hour to go. Would this day ever end?

Sighing loudly, she started another article for next week about a boy who was doing good in this world, saving homeless animals. She had a recorded clip from the event.

"Although they need our financial support, they also need hands-on support, which is why I am here to help in any way I can," Senator Stroud had declared to great applause.

Then the candidate that filled Amber with disgust every time she saw his smug face, Bo Wright, successful businessman, spoke up. "Here's an issue we can agree on, Senator."

The two men shook hands and smiled for the camera. She inserted that picture into the article.

Even doing something good, Bo Wright still managed to irritate her. He always had. The man was the worst of humanity—arrogant, pretentious, and something else she couldn't quite place. It might have been his friendship with her less-than-stellar stepfather, Jeb Cadwell. It showed Bo's lack of judgment, like trusting a curled-up rattlesnake not to strike if you got too close.

"Idiot," Amber mumbled between clenched teeth as she hit save.

Another glance at the clock finally granted her the reprieve she'd been waiting for. Without a single goodbye, she grabbed her coat and heavy black leather purse and bolted to the elevator. She knew if she even so much as waved at her coworkers, she'd end up at the club with them again, as she'd been doing for the last few months.

Tonight she had the elevator to herself. With no distractions her palms began to sweat, and her breath came out in short bursts as the claustrophobic vessel thumped to a stop. The silver doors slowly creaked open, offering her an escape into the parking structure that her newspaper shared with a popular casino. Surrounded only by waiting vehicles, she felt the loneliness surface. It was a familiar feeling since her sister's murder. She couldn't stop the anticipated quiver from surging through her with the image of Iris's body tossed away like trash next to the garbage bin. It hit her every time with the same punch as the first time she'd seen the picture. Nothing that happened that night made any sense to Amber. Iris shouldn't have been in that part of town in a dark alley. She was supposed to be at work. The very last conversation Amber had with her sister replayed in her head.

"Hi," came Iris's breathless voice over her cell phone.

"Are we still on for the movies later?"

"Um, not sure if I can get there on time. I have so much to do. If I'm not there, you go without me. I'll get there as soon as I can, okay?"

"We can go later," Amber protested.

"No. You've wanted to see it. I don't mind, honest. Well, sis, I'd better go and finish up here. When I see you, I have something to share."

"What's wrong?"

"Nothing, silly. You worry too much. My news is good—no, great. Gotta go. Love ya."

"Wait! Tell me now," Amber said, but Iris had already disconnected.

Amber hadn't even been able to tell her sister she loved her back one last time—and she'd never learned what the good news was. Since that horrible night, Amber had waited patiently for the police to find the murderer and supply some answers. Six months later, they had done neither. She thought they'd finally caught the killer three months ago.

Britney, a coworker who had taken it upon herself to be her grief counselor, took her to the police station. She attempted to console her afterward. "Just some crazy old man who didn't even know where she'd been shot. Sorry. It was the same thing with my aunt. Never did catch the killer."

Britney's words had rebounded off her that night and now. All Amber had left to think about were the terror and pain Iris must have felt with each blow she endured. What had been her final thought as the bullet penetrated her skull, destroying her existence? Amber clenched her hands tightly as if she could punch away those images as she slipped sideways between two parked cars. Her red nails drew a couple of drops of blood to match, but she didn't feel it.

Her phone buzzed, startling her out of the grim memories. It was Britney, who didn't realize that Amber wasn't as into their friendship as she was. Yes, Amber's best friend was dead, and maybe she did need someone in her life, but she wouldn't choose this needy woman as a replacement. Amber sighed and clicked on the message:

You must be so upset today with it being the six-month anniversary of Iris's death. I can't imagine the pain you are dealing with...well, that's not really true. Since my sweet auntie who raised me was murdered in her house four Halloweens ago, each year on that very day, it's been horrible. No one was there for me, even my ex, Steven. He was only all-in when we were in the bedroom, like I've said before. Anyways, I'm here for you always. So, I thought it would be best to follow me to my house later and drive me over to your house. I know you are kind, not making me drive all that way to your house in the boonies. Even Kyle backs my plans—for once. So, meet me at the usual spot and we'll go from there. Love ya, B.

Amber shook her head, knowing the best thing to do was pretend she'd never seen it. Although it did sound like Kyle might already be on the way out if she was reading between the lines correctly. She didn't like him. He had what her aunt used to call a wandering eye.

"Oh, Britney," she murmured, stopping to pick up a coffee cup someone had dropped.

The first time Britney told her story, Amber had felt for her. It was a lot for anyone to handle.

"It was only me when my adoptive parents died in a car accident. Like you, I went to live with my auntie at twelve years old. Then—it's still hard to say this—she was murdered right after I moved out. While I was grieving my auntie's death, my boyfriend cheated on me. Then I was really alone. Later I realized it was time to start over, and I ended up here." Britney wiped away a tear and shrugged.

After hearing the story over and over, Amber started to realize Britney needed the attention it brought her. If Amber were Britney, she'd ask that therapist she had been seeing for the last two years for her money back—it hadn't worked. A bottomless pit of need no one would be able to fill until Britney filled it herself. That was Amber's diagnosis.

A strong gust of wind cut through Amber's navy wool coat, sending a chill through her. She pulled the coat tightly around her as she suddenly felt she was being watched. She didn't see anyone in the garage, but that didn't mean they weren't there. She was frozen in her fear. Maybe leaving alone wasn't such a great idea, but if she had left with her coworkers on a Friday, she'd have gone out with them to eat and dance and ended up with a houseguest.

She shook her head and frowned. It was just her imagination. Besides, she had to honor the promise she made to her sister right before she scattered her ashes into Iris's favorite place, Lake Tahoe.

"I will live for both of us now. I might even break a rule or two, just for you."

She could imagine her sister smiling down on her at that moment as she released her ashes into the Nevada side of the lake. Amber couldn't bring herself to break the law and do it on the California side. Iris had been the risk taker. As she watched the cremains float away, she could have sworn that she saw her sister's face form in the white ash on the surface of the deep blue water.

"Iris?" she called out, with no reply other than the boat captain's inquiring look. "I will live life fully, as you did. I won't let this...you know...make me bitter or afraid, sis, and I won't add to the world's existing problems, either."

There were many times Amber couldn't prevent the rage or fear from creeping up and threatening to consume her, and she'd remember Iris's words, "Don't add to it."

Amber had almost broken her promise immediately when she considered joining her sister in death, but the need for justice and her sister's words deterred her. Her sister had been her only real family—Amber had to call their mother about the arrangements.

"I'm jusst tooo upset," her mother had responded, slightly slurring her words. "The doctor doesn't think your stepdad and I should travel to the West Coast now. We should take care of ourselves. Maybe take a local cruise or spend some time on the golfff course. There's a highly sought-after golf pro at our club that everyone is talking about, Neil Ramseyyy. Would you believe I can't get a lesson in with him for a year? Anyways, you know how golfing has always relaxed me, and well, that's what the doctor says I need after such a shock. So, ummm...I know you understand why we can't be there. I'll send you a check to cover the costs for the cremation and boat to disperse her ashes on the lake, like you were talking about. Okay? Well, someone's calling. I'd better check. You take caaare now. Love youuu."

Her mother always managed to talk about nothing when she was drunk. Amber hadn't spoken to her since that call. A check did show up. Sure, it made her mom feel better and only cost her $5,000—just an excuse to avoid pain. Her mother had been skillful at that since she lost her first husband, Amber's beloved father. She collected a huge life insurance policy and a payout for the car accident. Amber remembered her aunt talking about her mom winning in court. Her mother had been able to take care of her investments but not her daughters.

Amber shook her head to bring herself out of her stupor. She continued through the parking garage and found an overfull trash can that she topped off with the coffee cup she had acquired. Her thoughts had become like that mound of garbage, and they were overflowing. She cut through a row to her neatly parked car, threw her shoulders back, and took a deep, soothing breath. Time to dump all that trash. Her black ankle boots echoed against the concrete, but it was the silence within that sound that filled her with foreboding. The darkening clouds peeked through the sides of the parking structure, indicating an oncoming storm and adding to her heavy mood.

Amber struggled to rein in her spiraling thoughts. "Sorry, Iris." The only other person capable of pulling her out of a funk had been Aunt Kathy. Breast cancer had taken her two years ago. She rolled her eyes and sighed. "Okay, pity party over."

A sudden light flashed, blinding her for a split second. Her boot landed on a long, round object, causing her to lose balance and slip. She was able to plant her other foot firmly down while her arms flailed about like long hair in a windstorm, but she kept upright. She carefully glanced around, hoping no one had seen her ungainly display. Was she getting a migraine from that flash of light? Fortunately, no other flashes followed, and her vision was clear—none of the blurry, floating colors that preceded a migraine. Maybe a reflection from somewhere? She shivered and massaged her temples. Something caught her eye. A white feather.

"What..."

Her sister had believed that feathers were messages from angels, although Amber wasn't so sure she believed in all of that. Still, she was compelled to pick it up. A small part of her hoped it was from her sister, but her logical side insisted it came from a bird sheltering from the storm in the parking garage. Conflicted, she bent down to grasp the delicate, silky feather when she heard a slight whoosh above her back and hoped it was from the bird whose feather she held. Then there was a slight *thunk* off to her right, but it was the object right in front of her that made her mouth go dry. What she had tripped on was a yellow rope.

"It can't be..." was all she could get out as she straightened back up.

Not today. A short length of yellow rope—the very thing that had been found next to her sister's body. She trembled and stuffed the feather into her pocket as her eyes scanned the parking structure. She didn't see anyone but still felt like she was being watched. Unnerved, she bolted the rest of the way to her vehicle, leaving the yellow rope behind.

She unlocked her slightly used 4x4 silver Blazer with a beep, jumped in, and locked the doors with a sigh of relief. She heard a thump and crash coming from where she'd just been. She spun around but didn't see anything. Was someone hurt? Should she check? Then a car started, and she slowly let her breath out, unaware she'd been holding it. There *had* been someone else in the lot. Sometimes it paid to think like Amber instead of Iris.

An older white SUV, a common sight in Lake Tahoe, slowly pulled out of a tight parking space. The noise had probably been the owner trying to get into the truck. Amber shook her head, feeling a little silly, and turned the ignition. Cranking up the heater and shutting off the radio, she thrust in an old CD so she didn't have to hear any unwelcome news on the radio. A little Tom Petty was what the moment required. As soon as "Free Falling" started to play, Amber engaged her seatbelt with a loud click and put her truck into reverse.

The white SUV had stopped directly behind her, blocking her in.

Amber tapped her brake to let the driver know other people were driving too. It didn't work, so she pressed the horn.

"Hey, could you check your phone somewhere else, please?"

The white truck didn't move. She peered through her rear window, hoping to make eye contact. Maybe it was someone she knew. Or a casino guest who'd found his way into employee parking.

"Too many free drinks?"

Amber was about to lay on the horn when the driver opened their door and the interior light came on, but all she saw was a black coat and beanie. Flat tire or…

"Great," Amber couldn't get the *or* out of her mind after seeing the yellow rope.

Amber grabbed her cell phone to call…well, the woman she was avoiding.

The driver stepped out of the truck. Amber got Britney's voice mail and hung up. She quickly texted *Call me* and threw her phone down on the passenger seat as a roar of thunder echoed outside. She turned down the music and watched in her rearview mirror to see what the person's intentions were. The edge of a black coat was peeking around the back of the truck right when her coworkers burst out of the elevator laughing. The person in black retreated back into the SUV. Right before the door shut, she got a glimpse of a face covered by a full black ski mask and red eyes looking back at her. With a nod and a small wave of a black-gloved hand, the driver was consumed in darkness. The white SUV sped off with a loud squeal and disappeared around the corner.

Amber gulped loudly. She suddenly felt like she couldn't breathe. She forced the air in and out as Iris had always advised. *Think of the ocean gently hitting the shore and then pulling back. In and out…*the rope and the mask, though. She gasped and turned down her heater with a shaking hand. She could rationalize the red eyes being a reflection, but the intent of the person driving the SUV wasn't lost on her. She quickly checked her phone as she cranked up her music again. Finally, the awaited buzz of a reply. They would meet at the club.